MAELSTROM

The Stranger Trilogy: Book Two

SONIA ORIN LYRIS

Knotted Road Press

Maelstrom
The Stranger Trilogy: Book Two
Sonia Orin Lyris
Copyright © 2020 Sonia Orin Lyris
Published by Knotted Road Press
www.KnottedRoadPress.com

ISBN: 978-1-64470-161-4

Cover art:
Mark Ferrari - http://www.markferrari.com/
Interior design copyright © 2020 Knotted Road Press

Want all the maps?
https://lyris.org/seer-saga-maps/unmoored

Want the entire trilogy? Get your copies here:
Unmoored
Maelstrom
Landfall

It's True. Reviews Help.

If you liked this book, please consider giving a rating and a review. Even a short "Can't wait for the next one!" will do nicely, and help the author to make more books for you.

A note from Sonia:

Thank you for being part of my creative process. I have regular chats for subscribers, on my Patreon account, here:

https://www.patreon.com/lyris

Never miss a release!

I announce new projects on my Facebook feed:

https://www.facebook.com/authorlyris

You can also sign up for my newsletter:

https://lyris.org/subscribe/

Also by Sonia Orin Lyris

The Stranger Trilogy

The Seer

Touchstone

Mirror Test

It Might be Sunlight

The Angel's Share

Blades

Chapter One

"I REQUIRE A BODY."

Natun admitted to himself that his cousin Bolah's lack of reaction was impressive. He had timed his words to see if she might waver even the slightest. Mid-pour, she had been, the pink stream of tea forming a surface froth in his porcelain cup.

Her motion continued smooth and deliberate as she returned the tea cylinder to its place on the side table, then seated herself across from him.

"What sort of body, cousin?" she asked.

A body that could be viewed by thousands, yet still not truly be known. But how to say that, without revealing too much?

It was a terribly delicate matter.

Natun had been summoned to the queen's chambers, a tenday after Innel sev Cern esse Arunkel had been taken to a tower cell, accused of high crimes against his monarch.

Across the palace, anything that had relied upon the duties of the Lord Commander and Royal Consort was in upheaval and disarray. To make matters worse, Innel's

1

steward was missing, gone since that moment in the hallway when Innel had tossed the man on his ass.

Natun had half expected him to attempt to flee, and had plans to stop him, but he was gone, like a clever mouse into the cracks. At a guess, the man had gone downcity, from where he had come.

So when Natun had been called to the queen, he assumed that her majesty wanted to give him instructions as to the reapportionment of the Consort and Lord Commander's wide-ranging duties.

But no, the queen had wanted something very different.

She had put her hands on Natun's shoulders—that, shock enough—then looked into his eyes.

"Are you loyal to me?"

"With all my breath, Your Majesty," he had answered, despite—or perhaps because of—the unnerving touch, the riveting stare.

No monarch had ever laid hands on him so gently.

"I am gladdened to know it," the queen had said. "Because I need you to do something for me. Something extremely important. And it must be an absolute secret."

From the side of the room, the heir to the throne wriggled and whined in Sachare's arms. She set the baby onto the floor where the unnamed child grabbed an amardide block and attempted to put the entire thing into her mouth.

"Your Grace," Sachare said. "Someone will need to know. As capable as he is, he can hardly be expected to produce it from thin air."

The queen had not taken her gaze from Natun. He felt the intensity of her stare like a hot sun. She was the great Restarn's daughter, all right, and truly the Grandmother Queen's powerful blood ran through her veins.

Natun had always believed that the spirit of the Anandynars took the finest attributes from every House. In this moment, Cern seemed to be a living scepter, as though a line of fire ran down a fine rod that had been forged in seawater. Foolish imaginings, perhaps. But staring into her green eyes, Natun felt it in his very bones.

"Seneschal," the queen had said, "across generations, you have defended my family's most crucial confidences. You have held them secure, to your very great honor. I regret that I must ask you to hold another."

"It is my privilege and my duty, Your Excellent Majesty," he said in objection. He would have bowed then, deeply, but in her focused regard, he felt that he could barely move.

"As for my chamberlain's sensible advice, Seneschal, yes: rely on who you must."

And so it was that Natun had again come to Bolah.

He took a breath. "I require a body. One that is…" How to say it? "still alive."

"Ah?" Bolah held her cup between two hands. White steam drifted upward to the magenta-red draped ceiling. "As it happens, that describes a good many of them, so you may be in luck. Is that all?"

"No," Natun said shortly. "Cousin, this is quite serious."

"Of course it is." She gave him a long look. "Let me risk a guess: you want a body that resembles the man locked in the tower."

The Royal Consort and Lord Commander, accused of treason.

The look Natun gave her now should have frightened her; it certainly had brought a good many aristos and royals and even some high-ranking foreign dignitaries who had taken a step too far, and crossed a line, back to where they ought to be standing.

But no—her return look was starkly sober, steady. Not a hint of fear.

Had he already said too much? He pressed his lips

together. No one could know, not ever, what he was doing here.

"Calm yourself, cousin," she said. "Only a guess, and a risked one at that. It is my business to notice coincidences. It happens that I have such a body to dispose of. It would be very much in my interests to have both ends of my problem well satisfied. I could provide you with this body—"

"Alive."

"Alive," she confirmed, "but I require that it be kept quiet until such a time as it might no longer have the opportunity to speak. If it must be tongueless to achieve this, that can be arranged."

Tongueless. She knew. Damn it, she knew.

Without realizing it, he was moving his lips up and down over his teeth. He forced himself to stop, to think.

She would know the whole of the matter by the time it was over, anyway. And Sachare was right: someone would have to know; Natun could not produce a suitable body out of nothing.

Rely on who you must.

"Did you say you had wine?" he found himself asking. "Something strong, perhaps?"

Bolah's eyebrows shot up. "I do, indeed. A second pressing from Arapur-Bruent. But let us first conclude our business, cousin. If I can provide you with what you need, can you assure me of the silence I require?"

Easily. The right combination of kanna, duca, and kreathro would keep anyone from making sense, and a light gag would do the rest. It was hardly the first time the monarch's seneschal had needed to keep someone from speaking intelligibly while easing their way through a public performance in Execution Square.

He exhaled, then sniffed.

"Yes," he said.

There, it was done. He had said what he must and had revealed what he had to, in order to serve his queen and his country.

He heaved a heavy, shuddering sigh. Bolah put her hands on his on the table.

"They are fortunate to have you, Natun. They cannot possibly know how fortunate."

He made a grunting sound that, he hoped, would tell her nothing about how unsettled he really felt. But she was Bolah, so she probably already knew.

She patted his hands and stood, giving him a warm smile.

"Now, the wine. Wait until you taste this, cousin. I think you'll find it quite wonderful."

It was the queen's seneschal's duty to call the Ministerial Council to a meeting.

Usually, having gathered all of the ministers into the council chamber—also called the Amardide Room, though no one but Natun used the formal title any more—with its high ceilings, desks, and rounded table in the center, Natun would wait outside for the monarch, then open the door himself and step aside to allow the monarch to enter first. He would follow, then reverse course, exiting with his finest and lowest bow, to station himself outside the room to make sure the meeting was appropriately undisturbed.

This time, however, at the moment when the monarch might enter, he himself stepped into the room. The doors closed behind him.

This was so unusual that he immediately had the weighty regard of the full Council, their assistants, and secretaries.

Natun knew from his lifetime of service to the monarchy

that for the seneschal to take the center of attention was an exceptional occurrence.

The seneschal did not find it entirely comfortable. He cleared his throat, then did it again.

"Her Excellent Majesty," Natun said in his most officious voice, "will preside over the execution, to occur five days hence. The traitor—his name never to be spoken again, by royal decree—will be gagged, to protect the queen's ears from his falsehoods, and hooded to protect the heir from the wretchedness of the traitor's visage."

Putar, the assistant Minister of Justice, stood. "Seneschal, our execution plans are nearly complete. I need a tenday, at minimum, to arrange all the materials so that I may begin construction of the—"

"There is nothing to arrange," Natun said, cutting him off in his best the-matter-is-done tone. "And nothing to construct. It is to be a simple hanging, followed by the traditional chopping off of the hands and feet, and the burning of the body to purify the dirty betrayals of his actions against the entirety of the empire."

"A simple…what? No!" Putar turned a shocked look on his superior, the Minister of Justice, still seated.

"Seneschal," the Minister of Justice said, his gaze firmly on Natun as he motioned Putar to sit down. "This is unusually mild for a crime of this magnitude."

Natun took a moment to appear to consider the minister's opinion, then affected a slight change to his expression as if to partly concede the point. "It may well be unusual. I would need to consult the entirety of the histories of the empire to be certain, Minister." It galled Natun, this implication that he had not already done so, which of course he had, but to smooth the way, he must pretend otherwise. "However, the queen, in her great and abiding wisdom, has decided the matter is best resolved simply and quickly."

"An extended hanging, then," Putar said, only lowering himself to half-sitting, as if he might need to stand again at any moment. "Give me a day to arrange the details, Seneschal. A water drip, connected to the traitor's—"

"A simple hanging, *Assistant* Minister," Natun said.

A small grunt of dismay emerged from Putar's throat. He sat, his expression one of agony.

The First Minister spoke up. "A traitor. Surely this is far too much mercy to show such a disgusting creature."

Natun had known the First Minister since the man was a boy, serving as boot-man to the fourth assistant of the Minister of Accounts. Natun gave him a raised eyebrow that the boy would have recognized as disappointment.

"Perhaps the queen does not wish to glorify his person any more than the vulgar wretch deserves," Natun replied.

"But he is Cohort," said the ruddy-faced Minister of Accounts, who had never been.

Cohort, which meant something, even to those who were not.

Natun made a flat sound, one that he hoped spoke of his own polite forbearance. "Should a rabid mutt be dressed like a pheasant for the table, Ministers? Better to end the misery we all share than waste more time in pageantry."

Putar looked shocked, and mouthed the word: *Pageantry.*

The First Minister, demonstrating the flexibility of his convictions, nodded adamantly. "A commoner, too. Haven't we squandered enough coin on him already?"

Around the table heads nodded, all but the Minister of Justice and his assistant. Putar's face was more full of emotion and passion now than Natun could ever remember, even when the boy had been Cohort, enduring bullying because of his strange ways. Natun wondered if he kept a mental list.

Putar urgently whispered in the ear of the Minister of Justice, who shook his head tightly, waving him to silence.

"But why," asked the Minister of Accounts, "is Her Royal Majesty not here to tell us this herself?"

Natun drew himself up as tall as he could, ignoring the sharp complaints this produced from his lower back, and gave the Minister a look that he hoped would carry meaning beyond words. He looked at the rest of them, recalling how young each of them had been when they first came to serve at the palace.

"Her Excellent Majesty," he answered coolly, "has entrusted me to convey her commands to you, which I have done in most profoundly grateful obedience, a privilege that I trust I share with each of you. Have I been clear, Ministers, or do you require further explanation of the queen's instructions?"

"No, Seneschal," said the Minister of Justice, his hand now gripping Putar's shoulder tight enough to wrinkle the young man's fine garments, keeping Putar from rising out of his chair again. "We understand. A simple hanging it is."

Chapter Two

CERN SAT ON THE FLOOR, lockbox to one side, baby to the other.

She'd much rather look at the baby.

In her sleeping child's face she could see herself, her brow, her nose. But the child's chin was another matter, as was her grip, when she would simply not let go. Cern exhaled, dismissing these thoughts and the man who would always lie behind them.

The lockbox, Cern had found, held far more than letters. Lists. Scrawled maps. Cryptic notes of which she could not yet make sense.

Indeed, so packed was the box by her father's various writings, that it was unclear to her exactly where her own papers might someday fit. She would need to remove some of these papers that her father had decided were most precious. Remove and probably destroy. But which ones?

Just like her father to make more work for her.

She was tempted to burn it all unread. She wondered how her various ancestors had dealt with this same problem, and whether or not, at the bottom of the box, she might find a layer of ash.

Well, time to make a start on it. She must read it all, just as she must read the various letters that had come from the Cohort boys and all the other aristo men who were so sure that they now had a chance at the queen's bed.

That thought elicited a deep sigh. She fished down to the middle of the crammed box, drawing out a paper at random, and unfolded it.

Of all the boys, you encourage the mutts? This morning I see you strolling the garden, trailing one to each side, like a hen with two roosters. If this show is to annoy the Houses and unnerve the other boys, well done.

She stared distantly for a moment, clearly recalling that very morning. She had been fifteen. She had felt so mature, the handsome mutt-boys by her side, and had hoped that her father was watching.

He had been.

The letter continued: Pick one. Or pick someone else. The bitch makes the match.

Curious, how that phrase no longer pricked quite so sharply. As a child, she had learned to bear the humiliation of constantly being compared to his dogs.

Then, one day—was she eleven? Twelve?—she made a closer examination of how her father treated his dogs, only to discover that he showered them with touch and kind words. The hard truth, she realized bitterly, was that he treated his dogs better than he treated his daughter.

Envy was a greater humiliation.

And now?

In a sense, he had been right: she had made the match. Wisdom or foolishness, encouraging the mutts to court her, then choosing one, had been entirely her decision.

She read on.

If you ask my advice—and I know that you never will—I would lay out for you their respective virtues. Pohut can be charming and diplomatic, and that is a benefit not to be underestimated. But Innel is clever and there is steel within his impetuousness. In truth, the mutts show more ambition and wit than any of the rest of the Cohort boys.

That assessment surprised her. It matched her own.

Wed the younger. His edges can be smoothed, his abrasiveness reined to good use. I would choose the elder but for his sloppy sliver of tenderness, like a boy who cannot bring himself to toss a bag of kittens into the river.

She snorted, amused. Her father had hated cats.

Unless—do you encourage them only to annoy me? If so, your cut is wide of the mark. Rather, I would be pleased to see the mutts win over the rest of the lazy Cohort brats.

She laughed a little in spite of herself, and her thoughts turned to how cleverly the mutt boys had shaped their courtship of her. Why, she remembered the one time that Innel—

No.

Innel must be as dead to her as Pohut was. She must believe that she had seen him hanged, the traitor whom she had condemned.

She could not and would not imagine him alive. It was essential to arrange her thoughts, and not let them arrange her.

And this letter—it could never be seen. Never. She crumpled it into a tight wad.

"Sacha," she called. The other woman came quickly to her side. "A plate and flame."

Sachare glanced at the open box, then back at Cern. "Is that wise, your grace?"

"I doubt it."

A guard's knock at the door, and Sachare went to confer.

She turned back to Cern. "Mulack is walking the halls, properly dressed this time, and asking, rather insistently, to see you."

The moment Cern had sent the traitor to the tower, the letters from the Houses and Cohort had begun. They begged meetings and the chance to make their case. Why favor Mulack?

Because he had come to her delivering hard news that no one else had. He had worn servant's livery to do it. Annoying, yes, but Mulack had risked pride as well as reputation.

"Find out what he wants," she said grudgingly.

Sacha stepped outside, leaving the door cracked open. Cern got to her feet, after checking that the baby was still asleep, and stepped closer to eavesdrop as Sachare directed the guards to let the eparch-heir into the antechamber.

"One visit emboldens you to this intrusion?" Sachare asked chidingly. "This is not an audience chamber, Mulack."

"She needs someone by her side during this challenging time, Cohort sister."

"The ashes still cool in Execution Square, and you come to court? Have you no sense of propriety?"

"Again, I sacrifice my honor for the queen's benefit. There is no time to waste."

Sachare scoffed. "You exceed yourself, Mulack."

"Who else shall I exceed? Sacha, I am Cohort and eparch-heir of a Great House. Not least, not hard to look on."

Sachare scoffed.

"I simply want to present my petition, Cohort sister. I'll be blunt: the queen must have more children, and soon, to secure House and royal support. Of course we are all delighted to our depths and heights at the as-yet-unnamed princess, but perhaps a child by a father who is both alive and…"

"Mulack," Sachare said warningly.

"Pah. When a fine warhorse mates with an ass, who expects greatness? No one."

"Did you just insult the heir to the empire's throne? Has your sense entirely fled? You tread near the line, Eparch-heir."

"And not afraid to. Isn't that what she needs in a consort? I have proven both my courage and my loyalty. I am an exceptional candidate. Let me talk to her."

"When the queen is ready for such conversations, she will make her will known."

"You would have me stand in a crowd? Surely Her Royal Majesty understands that he who attends earliest attends best. My opinion only, Cohort sister, offered to her grace as a small increment to her vaster wisdom."

"I will inform her of that you came by. Uninvited and impertinently. Next time, consider a note and a gift."

"A trifle, for the queen of the Arunkel empire?" He barked a laugh loud enough to assure Cern that this was all performance, and that he knew she was listening. "When I have a Great House and a man of standing to offer her?"

An exasperated sigh from Sachare. "Good day, House Murice."

"Good day, Sachare sev Cern esse Arunkel esau Niala esse Arunkel."

Thoughtful flattery, that, Cern thought, using a formal name for Sachare that mentioned Cern, yet skipped her father Restarn entirely, linking her instead to her famous great-grandmother. It showed a certain amount of respect.

When Mulack was gone, Sachare came back inside, shutting the door behind. Cern motioned them both to the lockbox and the baby. Sachare brought a lamp and plate, then took the baby in her arms. The child reached out toward the flame, and whined when her desire was thwarted.

Cern set the paper ball that was her father's letter on the plate, then lit it. The three of them watched it as it flared and then contracted, going from coal-red to gray ash.

A fitting end, Cern reflected, to the experiment of marrying one of the mutt brothers.

Sachare was speaking to the child—who really needed a name—and offering her a ball to play with instead of the ash-filled plate, which Cern put up on a table that she could not yet reach.

Cern looked about the toy-strewn room, and considered with weary dread the many gifts now pouring in since the execution, the volume beginning to rival what was already in inventory for the heir's birth.

So many things.

The mutt brothers had understood gifts. In a box somewhere, Cern still had the rock that they had given her one Solstice long ago. A sweet memory, though perhaps tarnished by the years that had followed.

Her search for a new Consort would require delicate balance. Every House would send at least one candidate, and Cern would need to select even the order in which she received them with great care so as to not offend.

It had always been a lot of work to keep the Houses in balance. Favors, praise, and promises were never quite enough. This was why Cern had studied the empire's history so deeply, to know what had been done before, what it had meant, and what it might mean now.

The balance must be preserved, as must the conflicts. If the eight Great Houses ever stopped fighting among themselves, they might think to challenge Anandynar rule, and the monarchy couldn't stand against them.

Not even all eight. The most potent four would do.

Fortunately, that set changed every decade or so, and rarely did more than two Houses get along well enough to make trouble.

It hadn't happened yet, but it still could.

The current set of four included House Murice, wealthy from textiles and dye, and Mulack was uncontested eparch-heir. That would make him an interesting choice, since he couldn't possibly keep both positions.

How would Helata and Kincel respond to such a choice? Not well, Cern was certain; they considered themselves far superior to Murice.

And what about Etallan?

The crown had to make up with Etallan. Marrying them into the royal line would do it, but Helata and Kincel—and Murice—would object strenuously.

Mulack in particular would be offended, now that he had put himself forward so valiantly. So vulnerably.

She wondered if Etallan could be bought off again with the honor of two places in the heir's Royal Cohort, as it had been bought in her Cohort. Or if Etallan might finally have grown tired of chances.

She heaved a sigh. This was one of the many reasons Cern had been happy to take one of the mutt brothers. They had no House, so everyone could be equally annoyed at her choice. The balance was maintained.

That easy answer was gone.

"He is rather annoying, isn't he," Sachare said, drawing the baby's attention with a stuffed dog. The baby took it from her, and put one entire leg into her mouth, drooling around it.

Cern reviewed Mulack's words, spoken to Sachare but clearly meant for her.

"He is that," Cern said, "but he's not wrong."

"That doesn't make him right," muttered Sachare.

"We are ready, your grace." Sachare stood from her final inspection of baby, carriage, and the trusted quin of guards that surrounded them.

Cern gave a last look into the mirror, at her pomegranate and gold sleeves, a fuchsia vesture heavy with black brocade depicting the Anandynar crest, and the thick ribbon of gold weave across her shoulders that stood in for an unwieldy crown.

It all felt heavy. They had spent hours dressing this morning, to achieve what was elegant, formal, and—by royal standards—austere.

Only the weakest rely upon finery to make them appear royal. Dress well, daughter, but never expect fabric and metal to carry authority for you.

Cern stared at herself a moment longer, reflecting on these words and what she was about to do.

As they left antechamber, another quin of queensguards joined them. In the hallway, a third fell into place around them. Circles and circles, every step as choreographed as a royal Star Dance.

Another twenty paces, and Nalas and his own men joined her retinue. Cern exchanged a look with him and gave him a nod which he returned as a short bow.

Nalas had been a difficult decision.

"The royal guard and the army trust him," said General Lismar, Cern's father's sister. "Continuity of command is more than important—it's essential—especially in unsettled times. But he was Innel's man, Your Grace, and there's no getting around that."

When she showed Nalas the evidence against his former commander, he seemed truly shocked. Then angry. At himself. At Innel. He offered to resign.

Cern examined him for long moments. She considered the years gone by, and the many upon whom she must rely each moment for her very life.

Was Nalas wondering, as he bore her silent regard, if he would be lucky to keep his? Probably so. Yet there he stood, waiting for her judgment.

At last she spoke. "Can I trust you, Nalas?"

"Absolutely, Your Majesty."

"Will you re-swear your oath to me?"

"Without hesitation."

A balance of risks. Always. Cern made Nalas her new Lord Commander.

As her huge procession walked the hall, Nalas and his men nearby, palace denizens stood at the walls and bowed.

Her aunt had also mentioned Cern's uncle, Lismar's brother. "Your father's Lord Commander, Lason sev Restarn."

Lason, replaced by Innel, had resisted that change in status most adamantly. He had been furious and had taken his household to some far province, supposedly without leaving any notice, but anyone who really wanted to know where he was knew that he was in Palapa.

"You recommend him as Lord Commander?" Cern asked Lismar.

"Hardly," Lismar said wryly. "But he is Anandynar blood, and there are many among the royals who would be very pleased to have him back."

One of their own. *Bound in word and blood*, said the motto. Many royals seemed to think the blood part more important.

"We shall have him back, then. Would send for him, and see if he can be convinced?"

"Of course, Your Grace."

Cern and her retinue arrived at the great doors. She paused a moment to collect her thoughts.

Her limbs felt heavy, her eyes wanted to close, and she knew from the mirror that her pallor was not yet restored to normal. Yet she must convince the ministers that she was fully restored.

Show no weakness, her father had written. Step with assuredness.

She gave a sharp nod. The seneschal opened the doors for her, and stood back. Cern entered the Amardide Room, with Sachare and carriage and all the guards.

❧

A bell's time had come and gone, and the council had not yet moved from the first topic. Cern felt her focus fraying and the chair under her felt exceedingly hard. Her mind kept turning to how good her bed would feel when she made it back to her room.

Words pushed into silence become louder. You already know what you think; find out what they do.

She had let them go on for some time now, curious to see what they would do with her attention, gone for so long.

The First Minister leaned back in his chair, "Perhaps improvement might be achieved with regards to, hmm. The fourth, fifth, and sixth positions? Your aunt at the ninth— the problem there—" he poked at the air, as if it somehow that would make his point clearer, "Since she was favored by your great grandmother, only second to your father the great king, it may well be a stronger succession list if she were higher. Also—"

The Ministers will try to convince you that they know better than you do. Don't rely on it being true.

Cern held up a hand. The First Minister continued for many words before he came to a stop.

A small thing, a toe over the line, but Cern noticed it.

"Other than my daughter in position one," Cern said, "and two other names swapped, Minister, what I have presented here is little different from my father's list, which you must surely recall."

"Naturally. But times change, Your Majesty."

Enough for each of the Ministers to have been richly rewarded by royals with agendas, no doubt. But she would not say that, and they would never admit it if she did.

Just as they would not confess to being discomfited by her unnamed child, the one fathered by a traitor, at the top of that list.

"Ministers, I have heard your advice and perspectives on this matter of such essence to the prosperity and security of our empire. The list remains as I have given it."

"But—"

"I am no longer seeking your advice, ministers. I am directing you to carry out my will."

The ministers exchanged looks, along with small raises of eyebrows. There were even hints of smiles.

Cern clamped down on the flash of anger she felt. They would not have dared, had her father been sitting here instead. But she must pretend that she hadn't noticed. For now.

"Of course, Your Majesty," said the First Minister, a bit late.

She looked around. Dips of heads.

"And the regent?" asked the Minister of Justice.

"I have named the heir's regent," Cern said, bringing forth a piece of paper, sliding it to the First Minister. As the paper made the rounds to each minister, she watched their faces.

Cern was pleased to see shocked expressions. She had told only her most trusted scribe, who had clearly kept the secret.

The paper came back around the table to Cern. She put a hand flat atop it.

"Is my will on this matter evident to everyone?"

"Yes, Your Majesty. Most certainly," said the First Minister, unhappily. "Though it might well be sensible for you to consider the many other qualified persons, with far more experience in governance than—"

"All of whom have an agenda which is perhaps not in concert with mine. The name stands."

Opening mouths and inhales took her attention. One by one, she gave those ministers and the rest her attention, until each nodded or offered a seated lean that served as a bow. Cern took her time, gathering from each approval, or at least grudging acquiescence.

It would have to do.

As Cern looked over her shoulder, the ministers looked where she was looking.

She did, she had to admit, feel a pinprick's worth of guilt. But it was a necessary test.

To be regent, a Cohort education, fine and exacting, was a good start. But such a person must also be able to sustain grace and composure under quickly changing circumstances and sudden scrutiny.

Sachare looked up from the child, now fussing in the carriage, suddenly aware that the room had gone silent and all were staring at her.

Cern spoke. "Do you accept my appointment as regent, Sachare sev Cern esse Arunkel?"

One expressionless blink and a slight swallow were the only signs that Sachare didn't know in advance. Sachare stood from where she had been sitting by the carriage and gave deep bow to Cern.

"Humbly and obediently, Your Excellent Majesty."

Cern gave a sharp nod. Done and settled.

Now, surely, she could go back to bed.

"Does the heir have a name yet, Your Majesty, by which we might address her and her regent?" The First Minister asked.

"She does," Cern replied mildly, getting to her feet.

The room was so still that she could hear the creak of a leather seat as the Minister of Accounts shifted his ample backside.

Never forget that the ministers are your servants. Never let them forget, either.

"And what is that name, Your Majesty?"

Cern looked around the room. It did not seem to her that anyone else was breathing. Even Sachare leaned forward eagerly to catch her next words.

"When I am ready to tell you, you will know."

～

R*enounce me. Protect my queen and child.*
Nalas walked the hall, his men around him, the words echoing in his mind along with stark, gray images of the execution. At the last, the hooded body swung, nothing more than a man-shaped bundle of meat.

But were those the words of a traitor?

The question haunted him. Not that he had had much time to consider it, or much else, since then, now that he was now Lord Commander. He'd interviewed every queensguard himself, and he'd barely slept. He began to think he understood Innel's instability better than he wanted to.

Nalas had not been in Innel's office that final day—that shocking day. He had come running from the garrison the moment he had heard, to see Innel marched from the room, to have one last whispered conversation.

Protect my queen and child.

He had not been in that room, but what had been said made its way to Nalas's ears, so he knew something about what Innel suspected. He'd sent the guard Radelan to a lesser unit, far from the queen and child. "Until things settle out," Nalas had told him.

If they ever did.

Nalas turned a corner, increasing his speed to a fast stride. His men took double-steps to pace.

That there were threats against the queen and child, Nalas didn't doubt. Their source, though, he had no idea. So he tried to watch everyone, in every direction.

It simply wasn't possible.

If he'd been allowed to speak to Innel between imprisonment and execution, who knew what he might have found out. Maybe, as had been suggested, Innel was no longer to be trusted. None of his words. Perhaps not even his sanity.

And Srel had vanished, and that a true tragedy, with all that he knew about the Lord Commander.

Though, Nalas admitted, it might have been a tragedy for Srel if he had stayed, too. Nalas, in Srel's position, might have done the very same.

Nearly had, when the opportunity to slip out of the palace had presented itself. But he had stayed.

Why?

Well, Dirina and Pas, of course. Nalas would have needed to arrange to take them with him, and that would have been tricky. But there was more to it than that. It was those last words, Innel's last command. Using different words, they were the very oath Nalas had taken to the queen, an oath he would not betray.

Nalas was now striding the halls as fast as he could without looking like he was desperate for time, which he of course was. He had put off this very task now too many days in a row and would put it off no longer.

Innel had said one more thing to him in that whispered moment. *Watch your back.*

Queensguards and soldiers saluted, quick and sharp, as he walked past. The new title. Or maybe his new glower. He used to be friendly with them. Amiable.

He used to have a commander.

He passed an open door—a darkened room. Nalas scowled and one of his men peeled away to investigate. Little things added up to big things. Now Nalas thought about the palace and the queen's defense in a way he never had before.

It wasn't the same, having been deputy Lord Commander. It was simply impossible to do it all, to oversee both the army and the queen's security, until you stood right there and had to do it.

He wasn't even sure, were another Nalas presented to him now, if he would take him on as deputy. His past self of only a month ago seemed inconceivably ignorant.

These days his mind was stretched in directions he didn't even know possible, as he tried to cover all the vulnerabilities he could imagine, roaming a mental map of rooms, doors, windows, hallways.

Tunnels. And Fates knew how many of those there were.

His purposeful strides brought him to the apartment. The guards opened the door so quickly that Nalas didn't need to slow. Inside, he shut it behind him with a bang.

"Good, you're both here." Pas stood from his chair and drew himself tall, as if at attention. Dirina's eyes went wide at Nalas's expression. "Pack. You leave in an hour. You're going to the house."

"What? No! We're to be married in two months, Nalas."

Nalas blinked. He had entirely forgotten that part. Too busy with all the other parts.

"Not a good time for a wedding, Diri." Especially if Dirina weren't here, which is where she would be very soon, but he could not phrase it quite so bluntly. "It's only a delay. Until winterfair. Give Amarta time to join us."

Give circumstances a chance to settle.

There was not yet a letter from Amarta to confirm that she was coming to Yarpin for the wedding at all, which, to Nalas's mind, implied that she was not. But that was best left unsaid, even if it were obvious that Dirina quietly ached from the same conclusion.

Nalas took her hands, drew her close, resisting the temptation to kiss her. "You are my world, Diri. Without you, I am lost. With all that has happened, my honor may be injured, but you both are well, thank the Fates, and I will see to it that you stay that way."

Dirina made a sound, the beginnings of objection. Nalas kissed her, quickly, then pulled back.

"Diri, I will ask you, and I hope you say yes. But then, if you say no, I will not ask."

She pulled her hands from his. "Nalas, you can't mean what I think you—"

"Mama." Pas took her hand, gripped it. "Mama, I think we should do what he says."

Nalas put a hand on the boy's head gratefully.

Dirina shook her head, opened her mouth to speak. Nalas knew what she was about to say, could sketch the argument easily enough, but he didn't have time to take his part of the script. Too much else waited on him, and he could not focus on it if the most vulnerable parts of himself —Dirina and Pas—were in the same palace as the queen he was oath-and duty-bound to protect, along with whatever threats were coming.

"Pack," he said, cutting her off rather more sharply than he intended. "Please," he added, hoping to soften it.

He sighed at the hurt in her eyes, groping for a hardening heart so that he could do what he must to protect them both.

He looked them over, trying to see them as others might. Dirina's hair could hide easily in a scullery's headwrap. A maid's outfit wouldn't be hard to come by. A child's— perhaps less so.

"Pas, do you still have those clothes you wore before, when you were playing? When you were hiding?"

"Yes, da."

"Good lad. Get them on. I'm sorry, Dirina. I will see you soon."

Whenever that was. He left, shutting the door behind. To the senior guard in the hallway, he said, "Best of your numbers here. Get a maid's outfit on her. Then get them both out to where we discussed, but tell no one else. You have one bell."

"Yes, Lord Commander."

It was still a shock to be addressed with Innel's title.

Where do I look for these plots, that you knew about? Damn you, where?

As Nalas strode to his next urgent meeting, he passed hallway windows that revealed a glimpse of execution square, where still scattered across the gritty stones were the ashes of a hung, handless, and footless man.

Nalas's gaze returned to his own feet as they landed hard on the tile floor.

Was he himself blameless in all this? What had been wrong with him, these last few years, that he had been so complacent? How many chances had he been presented with to ask Innel questions, when his commander hinted at a secret, or gave a mysterious command?

Hundreds and hundreds. Nalas could have asked. Could have demanded to know. But he hadn't.

Why not?

Because Innel had been confident and easy to defer to. He was clever. Fast. He was Cohort.

Or maybe the truth was that Nalas hadn't wanted to take the risks that Innel was so willing to take, that a vein of cowardice ran through him.

Protect my queen and child at all costs.

"I will," Nalas promised.

As he trotted down the stairs that led outside to the garrison, memory again served up the hooded, tied Innel in his last moments, being led across the square toward the simple gallows that would end his life.

Nalas shook his head. Even then, he had looked wretched. Slumped and stumbling and not much at all like the man Nalas had known.

Chapter Three

INNEL LAY UNMOVING on the floor of the ship's cabin.

His lungs burned from inhaling riverwater, and there were rippling aches across his back and legs from the impact with the water after being snapped out of the rug into the air.

Now his mouth tasted of blood where Taba had hit him. Sharp pains were making themselves known where her boots had landed.

Taba had counted aloud, each hard kick. It was only when she had stopped, at seven, that he worked out what she had been enumerating. The years since Pohut had been alive.

For a time, Innel simply lay on the rocking wood floor of the ship, grateful to be unmolested by fist, foot, or river.

He was alive, and that was no small achievement. The usual outcome for a condemned traitor was execution. Instead he'd been smuggled out of the palace. Told not to come back.

Cern had spared him. He could draw no other conclusion.

Unless Cern had, rather, intended to deliver him into Taba's murderous hands.

But no, that did not hold. Sachare's tone with him in the boat had not been vindictive. Reluctant to help him, yes. Pitying, certainly. But there was no reason to think that Cern had intended her to send him to Taba, to die, rather than into exile.

A poor political move, in any case, though, releasing a traitor. It had no precedent in Anandynar history. It was a political mistake that would do Cern's rule no favors. It would, rather, embolden those moving against her.

Had Innel been able to advise her, he would have told her that a turncoat Royal Consort must die, and extravagantly, and that she could not be seen to be uncertain about it.

Despite the pain, his mind turned to the palace. What was happening to his daughter? To his queen? And would he ever find a way back?

Not if Taba killed him.

Taba.

He remembered that dark night. Just above freezing. He and Pohut fought wordlessly, brutally, in the frigid mud of a crooked lane in a small town.

Taba must have been crafting her vengeance every moment of the years since, but Innel had seen no sign of it, not in all those years.

Well, Taba was Cohort.

Innel gingerly rolled over onto his side and brought his tied wrists to his mouth, working the sodden, swollen knots with his teeth, at last managing to liberate his arms. He rubbed his wrists to restore feeling, then laboriously levered himself up, and climbed onto the bunk. He wrapped the blanket around his aching body and curled tight.

A familiar position, this. He and his brother had been beaten many times in the Cohort, before the mutt brothers had figured out how to make it stop.

Before the palace, the two boys had lived in a rural river valley of gentle people and playful children. Cohort life had been a shock.

He remembered lying as he was now, his brother on the bunk behind him, speaking softly and reassuringly until Innel's sobs subsided. Then they would discuss what had happened, ask questions, and reason together about what to do. Make plans.

Innel began to doze. He could almost hear Pohut's voice from behind him.

Vengeance is sought only by those who feel wronged, brother. What is her wrong?

"Something to do with you," Innel muttered.

As the light of dawn came through a brine-encrusted boarded-over window, Innel lost even that thought, falling into an uneasy slumber.

The door to the cabin opened. On the single chair, a sailor set a bowl of porridge and a jug of water.

Innel did not wait. The porridge was nearly tasteless, but he was hungry. Not having been offered anything else, he ate with his fingers, eyeing the sailor, who petted his scraggly beard, watching Innel in return.

When Innel had finished every morsel that finger and tongue could find, and drunk every drop of water, the sailor took the bowl and jug and went to the door.

"Wait," croaked Innel after him.

"Na," the man said, leaving. From the other side of the closed door, Innel heard a bolt drop.

The next time the sailor came, he brought two pieces of hardtack pressed together with a thin layer of suet. An unappealing meal, even by the standards of tower food to which Innel had recently become familiar.

He ate it all.

"Ya got the captain's attention real good," the sailor said, his tone both amused and curious. He chewed something, using his tongue to move it against his gums. Twunta. Maybe duca gum. "So who are ya?"

Innel blinked, inhaled, considered. It was not a question he was used to. For most of his life, he had been well-known, if not well-liked.

As for his clothes, they were nondescript. He rubbed his chin. He was shaggy with beard, the hair on his head crusted with days of lack of water and soap.

He certainly didn't look like he belonged in the palace. Who was he now?

A convicted traitor. An exile.

A man who had failed the most important task a man could hold: to keep his monarch, mate, and child safe from danger.

"I am no one," he answered softly.

The man grunted indifferently, then pulled from his pocket a length of jute rope.

"Hands."

Innel weighed his options. Healthy, he could take this sailor easily. In his current weakened and beaten state, the contest was much closer to even.

But even if he bested the sailor, this was Taba's ship, and it was on the ocean. Where was escape?

Nowhere.

After a long moment, Innel held out his hands.

Taba sat in front of him as he sat on the bunk. She smiled, her thick arms resting on the back of her reversed chair.

"Remember that one time," she said, fingers rising slightly, "when you and Pohut took out five of the Cohort boys right there in the hallway?" She chuckled. "You broke fingers. They whined for days. That's when I knew you'd both make it. Brother mutts, pretty as stallions, we used to say in the Girls' Quarters. We'd argue about who was prettier." She laughed, then clapped her hands to her thighs.

"I do remember that," Innel said, doing his best to summon an easy, jovial Cohort camaraderie, despite his hands tied tight behind his back. "We hid, waiting for them for hours, those five." He judged it a good moment to give credit. "But really, it was Pohut's idea. He—"

Her expression went blank. She had reach enough to hit him across the face with the back of her broad fist, without leaving the chair. Once, twice, three times.

Blood dripped from his nose into his lap. For a moment the only sound was his breathing.

"Who do you think you are?" she hissed. "I'll tell you who: you're a monster, that a far better man protected, a man you murdered."

Innel could not think of a good—let alone safe—answer to that.

Taba stood, kicked the chair aside, yanked him off the bunk by his hair, then slammed a fist into his gut. Innel doubled, gritting his teeth, stomach spasming.

"Come on, Taba," he choked out. "Hitting a tied man is easy. Untie me. Give me a fair chance."

For a moment, her expression turned ugly and he thought he'd said exactly the wrong thing. She pulled a knife, chuckling softly, then cut through the rope binding his wrists.

The ropes parted in one stroke. Easily.

He'd made a mistake, he realized, as she again hauled him upright. With him untied, she would feel even less restraint. But she still had a very sharp knife.

He had sparred with Taba across the years. She had always been big for a girl, and ready to get physical. So he knew her strengths and weaknesses, and recognized the flicker of her gaze across his body to various targets.

She was going to kill him.

"If I bleed out today, sister," he said urgently, "you'll miss me tomorrow."

Face tight with anger, she returned her knife to her belt, then gave him a familiar, amused look.

He let himself breathe.

She moved.

Years of Cohort training gave him the reflexes to twist as she came, her blow merely bruising. In moments they were both on the floor, struggling for holds. She gained a glancing hit to his sternum, then landed one on his still-spasming stomach.

Innel saw an opening. Her face. Her throat.

He hesitated. A disabling hit would buy him—what? More fury? This was still her ship.

The hesitation cost him; she kneed him dead-on in the groin.

Thought, reason, and the ability to respond fled. She followed the knee with a choke-hold. Innel struggled, but his body had been taxed too far, and he could not dislodge her.

A roaring in his ears, vision went dark.

When he returned to consciousness, Taba was gone.

She could have killed him right then, easily, but she had not. She wanted him alive. Why?

Taba visited him daily, and Innel gave up asking her why she beat him, because it only made the blows harder.

He was no longer kept bound all the time, but he grew weaker from the lack of sun, the paucity of food, and her daily and violent attention.

He sat there and took it. Again he considered fighting back, but it became increasingly difficult to find reasons to. Even if he broke free, there was nowhere to go, and nowhere to go back to.

After countless days, it became clear to him that she was pulling her punches. Aiming with more consideration. She didn't want to break him entirely. Saving him for something.

What?

Each day the sailor came to feed him, bringing warm water, poultices, bandages.

Beatings and healing overlapped. As the days went by, Innel lived covered in bruises, scabs, aches. Something always seeping.

One day, she almost told him why. He could see it in her eyes, feel it in the way she held herself, how she uncharacteristically hesitated before speaking. On her face, a fast flash of pain that changed to fury.

Then she lifted him, hurled him at the wall, the bunk, the floor, stomping on whatever parts of him failed to get out of the way in time.

When she left, he could not move without searing pain. This time, bones were cracked. A toe and forearm swelled rapidly.

Innel slipped into a fevered daze.

His sailor came, gave him duca gum and a paste that tasted like bad twunta, but helped.

"Why?" Innel asked as the pain eased enough to speak.

"Eh, it's the cheap stuff. I can spare it. And seems to me, whatever ya did, you've paid a few times over now."

Innel, in his sick, befuddled state, found himself shaking his head.

"Na," the sailor agreed. "She doesn't look anywhere near done. Get some rest while you can."

Innel muttered grateful thanks. The sailor left.

"Think I've paid enough yet, brother?" he asked the air.

The air didn't answer.

Innel felt the ship's motion change, then slow, then stop, followed by the sounds of loading and unloading.

Heading south, he guessed, from the warming air that found its way into his dank cabin. South to Perripur, along the trade route.

Daily, his sailor brought him food and water. And duca and twunta.

Each time, Innel eagerly pasted the bitter, forest-floor-tasting stuff onto his tongue. It eased the body pains, but the greater relief was the dulling inside, where the memories of his daughter had once lived.

His daughter. To her, he would never have even existed.

Which would matter only if she had survived.

Innel's world narrowed to the woman who daily sat a few feet in front of him.

She would talk, recounting past events, smiling fondly at some memory. Sometimes she would laugh.

Then she would hit him again.

Innel puzzled so many times over the why of this that when he finally figured it out, he felt a fool for having taken so long.

But then, given the foolishness that he had shown lately, why should he be surprised? Only a fool thought he wasn't one.

Innel was certain that he now knew why Taba sought vengeance against him for Pohut's death.

"Not death," he corrected himself aloud, annoyed. "It wasn't some accident or mishap. I killed you." He considered his words, wondering if they were as right as he could make them. "I have to say, though, she doesn't seem your type, brother."

He could imagine Pohut's laugh.

She wasn't quite this upset when I was around.

Innel chuckled, too. Pohut had been well-liked. Charming, when he set his mind to it.

"I imagine not."

Innel rolled over on the bunk, his mind going to his sailor, wondering whether the man might have anything stronger.

Innel's life fell into a routine.

In the mornings, his sailor would watch him eat porridge. If Innel were lucky, the bowl would include bits of gristly meat, or fish. Maybe scraps of cheese. Leftovers for the mutt.

Once the bowl was clean, the jug empty, Innel would wait. Quiet. Pleading.

"Eh, there. I got it for ya," his sailor might say, reaching into his pocket and bringing out the duca and twunta that had become the luxury of Innel's existence.

Innel found his eyes stinging at this gesture. He gave thanks, sometimes effusively, sometimes long after the sailor had left, the door bolted, when the blessed numbness came to him.

Pain waxed and waned, cresting with Taba's visits. There was no point in flinching or trying to avoid her blows, so he didn't. What did it matter? These pains were such small things when set against what Putar would have given, these losses meager compared to what he had already lost.

Gone. All gone.

He stared at the boarded-up window of his cabin. Daylight leaked in through hairline cracks.

"You used to say that the ladder goes up one rung at a time, brother," he said.

I did say that.

"But the fall. That comes all at once."

As Innel wiggled a loose tooth with his tongue, he recalled the tower room. How comfortable it had been. He laughed at how he had worried about the humiliation of execution.

Every time Taba came, Innel looked into her eyes, and saw Pohut there.

Every time she knocked him off the bunk, the gummy wood planking caught him in its dependable—if rough—embrace.

The days flowed together in a washed-out gray.

"I've lost my colors, brother," he said to Pohut, then laughed, amused, then wheezed. A cacophony of pain followed. "I don't even know what my colors are now. What are they?"

Looks to me like you wear the color of bruise and blood.

～

Taba was his calendar and clock. When she was due to visit, Innel felt it all through his body and wrapped himself tight in the wool blanket, waiting.

If she came late, he felt anxious, disappointed. A dog left alone too long.

Then she would come and do what she did and he would feel right again.

One day it changed. She walked in, turned the chair around, put her arms across the back, and did not speak.

He stared back, slack-jawed.

At last she drew from her vest a leather flask, uncorked it, took a long swallow. With an appreciative sound, she held the flask out to Innel.

Innel felt a sudden, intense craving for whatever the flask held. He restrained himself.

"Go on," she urged.

He took it hesitantly, tipped it into his mouth, and—oh! by the Fates—it was a black wine, heavy and potent and rich.

For a moment, fragments of his past life flashed through him: fine clothes, a shaved face. Good meals, taken for granted.

He held the liquid in his mouth until he could bear it no longer, then swallowed.

It was, without question, the best wine he'd ever drunk.

He lifted it to his lips again and froze.

It was Taba's. He guiltily offered the flask back to her.

"You finish it."

He watched her over a short, furtive sip, fearful that she would change her mind. Then he took a longer one. Then another. Each mouthful was a joy.

More flashes of his past washed over him, and he urged them to pass by quickly. Memory was the song of what was lost; he did not want to hear it.

Sip by sip, he emptied the flask, at last inverting it overhead, suspending it for whatever drops might yet be induced to fall. Then, with a sigh, he handed it back to her.

She returned it to her vest and brought out another thing, unwrapping a fine cloth to show slices of translucent, dirty-white resin.

"Go on," she said.

White qualan. He blinked in surprise and took it, breaking the slice in two with his fingers, stuffing half inside each cheek.

A bitter, exotic taste filled his mouth.

The room brightened. He stared at Taba, his beloved Cohort sister. Yes, his foot still throbbed, along with many other parts, but she had her reasons—good ones. Innel respected her.

They were Cohort, the two of them. Siblings. Always.

He loved her, he realized. Beyond reason. The room, dank and dark, was a blessing. Given his past, the dark better than the light. It comforted, like the blanket around his shoulders.

He stared at her. She was lovely. How had he never noticed before?

"Why?" she asked him.

"Why?" he repeated dumbly.

His mind was a mess and a muck, thoughts fleeing as soon as he caught a glimpse of them. He didn't want to disappoint her, so he cast about to find the question so that he could answer.

Ah, of course: Pohut. She wanted to know why he had killed his brother.

The reasons seemed a world away, but she was due an explanation. A true one, if he could manage it. He struggled, rooting around inside himself.

"He betrayed me," he said at last. "Well, I thought he had. But he hadn't, not really."

"No."

"He should have told me," Innel said.

There wasn't exactly time, brother. That night, you moved fast. Faster than I expected.

Was that pride in Pohut's voice at his younger brother's ability? Innel gave a surprised laugh, but a moment later forgot why.

Taba was watching him closely, assessingly.

His thoughts flitted around like gnats. Hard to catch. Hard to hold. He blinked, trying to focus. What had they been talking about?

"We're days from port, Innel," she said. "My plan was to kill you now. Dump your body in the ocean for the fish. Put you to some good use at last."

He looked back, vaguely curious. More than anything, he wanted her happy. She had been good to him.

Even though she seemed to be wrestling with something, she was beautiful, his Cohort sister. He could see what Pohut had seen in her.

"I've imagined this day for years," Taba whispered. "How I would cut you. How you would beg. Scream. Bleed. Die."

It occurred to Innel as he parsed the meaning of her words that how he was feeling—this adoration that threatened to break with bliss—might be the result of the qualan. The thought passed, and he found himself simply watching her marvelous face.

"Your eyes are like the ocean," he said of the light green that blinked back at him. "Or not," he amended quickly, as those same eyes widened with shock.

"He said that to me."

Innel nodded. "He was like that."

Now her face was sad.

It came to Innel that something was ending, though he wasn't sure what. For a moment he, too, felt deeply, achingly sad.

"I'm sorry, Sacha," he said.

No, that wasn't quite right. He tried to focus on the woman before him. Who was she, again?

"Cern," he tried. "*Taba*."

Taba heaved a deep breath, let it out slow.

"You'll die, Innel. But not today. Not on my ship." Her gaze was distant. "Not because he wouldn't have wanted it. Because…" She focused on him again. "Because I don't want the stain of your blood in the fibers of the wood of my home." She shook her head slowly. "I'd never be rid of you, you see. And I do want to be rid of you."

Innel nodded soberly. It made perfect sense.

Chapter Four

AMARTA'S STOMACH seemed to heave with the motion of the ship. Up, down. Forward, back.

She pushed herself through the narrow, tilting passage up onto the open deck, where she lurched for the railing and gripped hard. She drew full breaths, focusing on the crisp blue line of the landless horizon, the only thing not moving.

She regretted leaving the cabin and the interesting conversation that was forming between Tayre and Olessio. She had stayed until the moment vision and her stomach told her that she was about to vomit on the floor between where the two men sat, possibly right on the dice Olessio had just set down.

"A simple game," Olessio had said, picking up the dice.

"Stakes?" asked Tayre.

"Let's play for…" Olessio rattled the dice in his palm. "Histories."

Tadesh lifted a head from where she was, curled on one of the three bunks lining the walls of the small room.

"Stories with a—how to say it?" Olessio asked. "A hard bite of truth to them. Your histories. Perhaps even mine."

Amarta could not wait. She lurched for the door. "Need some air," she managed.

Here on the deck, the boat in constant motion in all directions, she prayed to whatever spirits might care that this dizzy wretchedness pass quickly.

"Hoi!"

A thickly built woman with light brown skin stood on the deck, not holding onto anything, as easily as if she were on solid ground. She stepped toward Amarta, holding out a long, thin roll.

"No, thank you," Amarta said reflectively. Whatever it might be—jerked beef, hardtack, dried seaweed, some kind of intoxicant—her stomach roiled at the mere thought.

For a flash, she recalled another ship, another woman, another offering. Amarta felt the pang of loss of all those she had left behind. Maris. Dirina and Pas. So many others.

"Helps with the pain," the woman said over the wind, her accent a heavy Zaneke one.

Hope poked through Amarta's haze of agony and she scanned the myriad of moments going forward, selecting the trails in which she put the sticky wad into her mouth.

Relief.

"Yes, thank you." Amarta said quickly, reaching forward toward the woman without letting go of the railing.

The woman laughed a little, but not unkindly, and closed the distance to give Amarta the roll, then a mock salute as she turned and strolled off. Amarta watched her graceful retreat with a mix of envy and gratitude, as the spicy-sweet, gingery something filled her mouth and began to settle her stomach.

The nausea receded at last and she hastened back to the cabin. Olessio had been right: the horses would not have liked this at all.

Tadesh lifted her head as Amarta entered, then stretched,

showing off her underbelly of pale spots. She yawned and reclined again. Amarta sat next to her. She stroked her gently and was rewarded with a tiny, chuffing sound that she could feel through the furred chest.

Both men shook their own die, then clattered them across the floor. Tayre's was higher, and he tapped the floor softly.

"Why do you travel alone, Farliosan?" Tayre asked.

"Tadesh is easily made jealous."

"A bite of truth, you said."

Olessio tilted his head. "I find most people a tad annoying and generally avoid them. Present company excepted, of course."

Tayre smiled in a way that made it clear that he didn't believe him. They both rolled again.

Olessio tapped, grinning. "How did you learn to fight so well? Knives and clubs against you in that alleyway, but you barely broke a sweat."

Amarta learned forward, also curious.

"Diligent study," Tayre replied.

"What? You call that an answer?"

"Can three play?" Amarta asked.

Olessio looked at her sideways as he shook his die in a loose fist. "My dear, I think you may have an unfair edge."

"I wouldn't use it."

"Just so," Olessio responded, agreeing. "And yet. Surely you understand my hesitation?"

Amarta gave him an incredulous look, recalling the trouble she had taken to prove her ability to him, only to now earn a greater suspicion. Must she always choose between telling people what she was and having them trust her?

She was tempted to tell him how fickle dice were, how easily influenced by the twitch of a hand, or the rocking of the floor below, that to predict one here and now would be true work.

Would it do any good to explain that her stomach, sour as it was, made foreseeing the outcome of a rolling cube of bone the last thing she wanted to do?

She met Tayre's look. "And you?" she asked, struggling to keep bitterness from her tone. "Do you also hesitate?"

Tayre shook his head. "I have different priorities than he does."

The contract, he meant. Her contract. A sudden wash of gratitude toward him came over her. Whatever game he was playing, it was not as simple as dice and answers, and he was not afraid to say so.

Olessio looked between them, back and forth, like a dog sniffing a trail.

Well, she thought irritably, if the Farliosan wanted a truth that could bite as hard as the past that she and Tayre shared, let him track it himself. She gestured for them to continue.

Another roll. Olessio won, but only by a point.

"Ha!" Olessio cried, tapping the floor. He turned his mismatched eyes on each of them. "What's between you two?"

"Years and miles," Tayre said.

"'Years and miles?' What kind of answer is that?"

"All you'll get for that roll."

Olessio scowled lightly, rolled again. Tayre followed. Olessio tapped.

"Where were you before Senta?"

"Shentaret Mountains," Tayre answered, describing, in two words, a mountain range that was hundreds of miles long.

With such meager answers, Amarta thought, this could

be a long game. Well, they had little else to do during the crossing.

She considered the long night she'd spent at the Sun and Moon, earning the money that now sped them on their way. She thought of the cards, the coins, the people. The conversation.

Opulent outfits. Glittering jewels. Subtle and overt manipulations. Games within games.

Perhaps everything between people was like a deck of Rochi cards in a messy pile, all facing every direction—a collection of overlapping meanings. She wondered what Tayre, such a good judge of people, was reading in Olessio now.

And Olessio, traveling by himself but for the odd Tadesh —what was his story?

Tayre tapped, winning the roll by many points. "Same question, Farliosan, but I want three prior locations."

"Pah." Olessio glared at the dice, then sighed. "Erakat. Munasee. Kelerre."

Amarta envisioned the map. Major cities, those, and the ordering described a path of travel that led south.

"Why did you skip Garaya?" Tayre asked.

A short shrug. "A confused city. Can't seem to make up its mind if it wants independence from Arunkel, Perripur, or itself. Not worth my precious neck to find out."

Another roll. Tayre tapped. "How did you lose your pony?"

A flicker of surprise passed over Olessio's face, then vanished in a studied curiosity.

"What pony?"

"The one that previously pulled your cart."

Olessio cocked his head. "I pull it myself."

"You haven't always."

Olessio blinked. "Maybe it was a donkey. Or a mule. A llama."

"A pony."

"You can't know that." Then, at Tayre's implacable expression, "How can you know that?"

Tayre gave a small smile.

"He's like that," Amarta said, enjoying Olessio's discomfort.

Olessio scowled, then made an amenable, amused sound, and leaned back against the bunk.

"A tragic tale. More a farce. Some fifty miles short of Senta, my pony diligently attempted to drink a watering hole dry. His greedy little eye stuck on a tiny island at the center where a patch of seductive green grew. Making an attempt for it, he twisted his leg. I managed to pull him out of the muck, which took me long enough to curse his ancestors many generations back.

"We both limped to a nearby village. By then he'd managed to convince me he was quite lame, though I still think he was faking it, cunning little twit. Finding myself tight on funds, I had to make the hard choice between getting to Senta to stake my bit of show-dirt or waiting him out." Olessio gave a wry smile. "Sold him to a gentle drayer and half my possessions—at a stunning loss, I'm ashamed to say—to lighten the wagon, determining that it would polish my fine character to pull it myself."

"Did it?" Amarta asked curiously.

He looked at her, mock-surprised, and made a flourish at himself. "Well, yes. Obviously." Then, with a wide-eyed innocence mixed with self-effacing humor: "Do I not shine and sparkle?"

Amarta laughed in spite of herself.

They two men rolled again. Tayre tapped. "Where is home, Farliosan?"

Olessio threw his hands wide. "How is it that you keep winning?"

"My die shows higher numbers than yours," Tayre said with a straight face.

Olessio's eyes narrowed. "I think you're cheating."

"With *your* dice?" Tayre's eyebrows raised. "A good trick, that. Where?"

"Everywhere. Nowhere."

"The Lady's Bowl, perhaps?" Tayre asked.

"No," Olessio said quickly, then scowled, realizing that his answer revealed something. "Never heard of it."

"Where is that?" Amarta asked Tayre.

"East of the Rift," Tayre said. "And he's been there. You've come a long way to perform tricks for strangers you don't like, Vagras. Tell us about your family."

Vagras. Amarta looked at Olessio to see if he'd be offended at the rude term, but no—he only grinned. "Not for that roll, Guard-dog."

"There's an east to the Rift?" she asked.

"There certainly is," Olessio said, with a spark of pride.

Another roll. Olessio tapped. "Where are your people, Guard-dog?" he asked Tayre.

Tayre had people? Family? She stared at him, trying to see him as Olessio must, beyond the tiny streaks of white color he applied to his hair and beard, the subtle lines on his face that he touched up regularly to make himself look older.

"Dead," Tayre answered flatly.

"Not all of them, surely?" Olessio asked, his voice quiet.

Tayre didn't answer, but shook his dice. They both rolled. Olessio snorted in disbelief.

"Do you see that?" This to Amarta. "Gets his way rather a lot of the time, if I'm not mistaken, does he?"

"He does," Amarta agreed, amused, watching Tayre.

He turned a look on her. "Have you been keeping score?"

"What? No."

"Our wins are just about even, though he's implying that they're not. Why do you suppose he's doing that?"

Amarta turned her attention to Olessio.

"I'm losing," he said with affronted dignity. "Obviously."

"To make us more sympathetic to him?" Amarta suggested.

Tayre gave a short nod. "Perhaps. Perhaps to seem on your side in particular, against possible future need, gathering that I am not as easily swayed."

"I can hear you just fine, you know," Olessio said, looking uncomfortable. A moment of silence later, Olessio took a deep breath. "Yes, you're right. Habit, I'm afraid, my friends. I'm not used to such clever company."

"I forgive you," Amarta said.

"Gracious of you, my dear."

Amarta met Tayre's look. In that moment she realized that he had broken the game he was playing with Olessio. To show her another layer of the game? Or was there another layer to his game as well?

One thing was coming clear: it was seductive to become so engaged in one level of a game that you forgot to look for the others. Games within games.

Tayre held out his hand toward her, palm up, offering her his die. At this, Olessio raised a bushy eyebrow.

Amarta took the die.

"When you asked me what I was," she said to Olessio, "I didn't just answer you. I showed you, again and again, until you were convinced." Amarta looked at Tadesh, who yawned and made a small noise as she showed a pink tongue. Amarta met Olessio's gaze. "I think I have already given you a story with a bite of truth as sharp as any you could roll for this entire crossing. I asked nothing in return."

Olessio inhaled, his gold-green eye intently upon her. He

nodded slowly, his smile warm. "You are quite right, Amarta, and there is no need to roll further. What question may I answer for you?"

She blinked, surprised at his sudden and unexpected concession. Tadesh lifted her head enough to groom a paw.

"Tadesh. How is it that you come to travel with her?"

"Ah!" His eyes widened in delight. "A tale of danger and daring!" He smiled at Tadesh fondly and reached out to stroke her head. "I was traveling a stretch of badlands when I happened upon the remains of some unfortunate outpost. Ruins. Huge stones. Scrub and vines snaked through the rock, grass clawing from between cracks. As I began to pass, I heard a mewling."

Olessio traced the stripes on Tadesh's head. "The stones shifted under my feet as I searched. Despite my personal peril, I located the source of the sound: a small opening in the rocks. This one. When she heard my voice, she howled piteously. Try as I might, the great stones would not budge. Loath to abandon the mysterious creature, I dropped bits of food into the hole and dribbled in my own precious water."

He tugged Tadesh's ear gently. She pulled it free, the ear twitching.

"I realized that I must engage my ingenuity and charm before I ran out of provisions. I found a stick to use as a lever and moved the first stones to see within. She was trapped there, a paw caught under a rock deep below. A puzzle, how to free her. It would take three sticks in combination, to move all the rocks at once.

"So young! So small! She poked her tiny nose out, took a look at me and went back inside. Not, perhaps, our best moment. Fortunately, I was able to demonstrate that the food and water were not entirely distinct from my good self. She decided to give me a chance. I bandaged the hurt paw and have been feeding and watering her ever since."

Apparently unable to sleep through Olessio's renewed attention to her ears, Tadesh heaved a great sigh and stood, stretching from head to shuddering tail, then climbed down off the bunk to curl into Olessio's lap. His expression went quite tender.

He looked at Amarta. "Are you well-answered, now, sera?"

Amarta sniffled a little. "Yes."

Olessio gave them both a lopsided smile. "I've lost my appetite for this game, but I do believe we have some very serviceable wine, delivered to us just yesterday by the fine sailors tending to our comfort. You don't drink, do you, Guard-dog."

"I do not."

"More for me and you, my dear. Shall we? Ah…" He looked down at Tadesh in his lap, then back at Tayre with a helpless expression. "Would you mind fetching it for us?"

The port town of Mibrin rippled with color. Ships' flags and rooftops shimmered in brilliant purples, blues, and greens. Streamers flew from tall, thin spires whose tips glinted with prismatic tones of pure light.

The crew navigated the ship around two harbor rocks into which had been planted yellow flags, the fabric edges glinting with tiny yellow stones.

"Mibrin is famous for glass," Tayre answered when she asked. "Lenses, prisms, and more. This is not Arunkel, where Greater and Lesser Houses own production charters. In Perripur, anyone can make or sell anything they like."

"That sounds confusing," Amarta said.

Olessio laughed. "You should see how we Farliosan

bargain, how we exchange food, favors, and friends. Makes the Perripin method seem downright tidy by comparison."

"We'll need to be able to present ourselves convincingly," Tayre said. "A married couple visiting Taluk, now returning home."

At this, Amarta's delight at the colorful port city was abruptly doused.

Tayre tilted his head toward Olessio. "And you?"

Olessio smiled wryly. "House servant, sent by the Dominus, your father, to bring you home from your indulgent adventures in the decadent lands to the north. Needs your help with the family bookbinding business." He shook his head slowly, disapprovingly. "Time to abandon your adventuring and settle down, ser. The Dominus-your-father would like to see your lovely wife get busy with the important work of making babies."

"What?" Amarta craned her head around Tayre to give Olessio an outraged glare.

"Only for show, my dear," Olessio assured, pulling his head back to avoid her look. He gestured to the port city. "See that circular glass roof? The crew recommends it. Expensive, they say, but entirely in keeping with our story, Dominus's son, eh?"

"We'll arrange a spot in the stables for you," Tayre replied.

"Don't think the Dominus would like that. Always said I was nearly family."

"Not to me, he didn't."

Olessio grinned at the shore, his eyes shining. "I've always wanted to see southern Perripur. It's good to have guides."

Amarta slowly frowned. Olessio glanced at her, then at Tayre for a longer moment, then began to laugh, and laugh, finally pounding the railing in mirth before he paused for breath. "Truly? Not one of the three of us has been here before?"

A shrug from Tayre. "A second time requires a first."

As the ship neared the docks, sailors called back and forth, ropes held ready to toss to the crew.

"Ah, adventure," Olessio said, still chuckling. "It's a fine thing. I hope we have maps."

The inn was indeed expensive, if Amarta understood the numbers being rattled off in heavily accented Perripin by the woman who met them there.

Olessio stepped out in front of the two of them and began a complicated negotiation of rooms and meals. He picked up their bags, in one of which was Tadesh.

The dining hall's tables were brass-edged glass, small lamps at the center casting splinters of rainbow light across the walls. Afternoon sun came through slats in the high, circling walkways, cleverly angled into prisms that fanned out onto pale walls and the ceilings, casting shadow and light in the shape of plants, birds, feathers.

The hall was loud and full of well-dressed patrons chatting, laughing, drinking. A foursome of musicians played a tune, a handful of dancing couples putting it to motion. They drew together and apart, then traded partners, then turned and did it all again. Amarta watched, fascinated.

Olessio led servers from the kitchen who filled the table with glass dishes arrayed with rainbow shades of foods and bowls of colorful soups and breads. Olessio hovered, as if confirming the quality of each one, then nodded imperiously at the servers to go.

Tayre gestured him over. Olessio came close, his posture

and inclination painting him entirely to be an attentive, proud servant.

"Subtle," Tayre said quietly. A direction, Amarta realized, not a compliment.

"Subtle performances are wasted on unsubtle audiences," Olessio said, with a subservient smile and bow quite at odds with the tone of his words.

Then he turned away, standing ready, looking about the room with a snotty look on his face. A small drama for whoever might be watching. Amarta had to drag her gaze from him back to the food.

The music picked up speed. The dancers spun, clapped. More joined, seamlessly inserting themselves into the pattern.

As they ate, dishes were cleared, others brought. Tayre gestured again to Olessio.

"We're being watched by four men at the far end. Amarta, don't look."

"Watching her," Olessio suggested. "A strange woman, strangely attractive…"

"No. Trained fighters, with focus and intent. Settle our bill directly. Hire that mule wagoner we talked to earlier, and bring him around back. Amarta, look ahead and see if we'll have any trouble, if we leave soon, out the front door, without our bags."

It was specific enough. She looked down into her folded hands, ignoring the room. "We'll be fine," she said.

A few minutes after Olessio left, Tayre stood, pulled her to her feet, muttered loudly about wanting to test the sturdiness of the bed, and gave her a narrow-eyed grin that held far more intent than she'd seen in the faces of the men watching them, who, with great effort, she still wasn't looking at.

Unsettling, this pretense. Which no doubt suited the

drama, or he wouldn't have done it. Sometimes she felt a bit too much like a Rochi deck.

As they left, he leaned on her as if for balance, until they were back in their expensive room, whose bed, it seemed, she would not get a chance to try after all.

Tayre made fast work gathering their things and ferrying them out the back stairs, then returned to escort her out the front, visible to all. As they went, he launched into an odd, drunken-seeming rant in three languages, about the rainbow city and its specialty anknapas.

As Amarta had predicted, they exited safely. Before sunset they rode inside a canvas-covered wagon, jostling along the road and out of the port city.

"An expensive caution, this," Olessio complained when they were away, shifting himself around their bags and the rolls of hay that lined the inside of the wagon. "You could have taken those four, if it had come to that. You disposed of more than that in Senta and easily. Your devoted servant never even got to taste the soup."

"In Senta, I had no choice. Here I did."

"I didn't think," Amarta said, "that this far south, across the Mundaran, they would follow."

"No?" Tayre asked. "Coin easily overcomes distance."

Amarta sighed, looking out through a side flap in the canvas into the fading light. Would someone always be after her? Before vision managed even a flash of an answer, she changed the question:

What would it take to make them stop?

Black helmets shimmered in the sunlight, by the hundreds. By the thousands.

Olessio cleared his throat. The glimpse vanished.

"It occurs to me," he said, "that it might be safer, were I to travel independently."

Tayre gave him a sharp look. "Safer for whom?"

"Well—you. Of course! We Vagras…" A wave of his hand. "We can attract the wrong sort of, ah, admirers."

"Admirers? Who do you mean?" Amarta asked.

"Who can say?" Olessio responded.

"Did you steal something?" Tayre asked.

A short laugh, a shrug. "Who can say?"

"Well, *you* could, I would think," Amarta said, annoyed. "Don't you know if you've stolen something or you haven't?"

"Pah. What does it really mean, to own a thing?" Olessio asked, giving each of them an earnest look.

"Did it belong to you or did it not?" Amarta asked slowly, feeling as if she were speaking to a child.

"It's not stealing," Olessio insisted, "if it's not being used well. To leave a thing with people who don't understand and honor it is itself a sort of theft—a theft of the commons. Really, taking such a thing would be—" he waved a hand. "Returning it home. Tools should be used properly, and animals should be treated like family."

"How you got the pony," Tayre said.

"Possibly," Olessio admitted judiciously, looking out at the dark lands passing.

"Possibly?" Amarta asked.

"They were not caring for him properly. And besides, I had true need, where they did not. I share everything I have with those who require it and can appreciate it. Case in point…" He dug into his pack and pulled out something wrapped in wax paper. He unwrapped it to reveal a smooth flat of something dark. He broke off a small piece, offered it to Tayre, then another to Amarta.

Tayre put a quick hand on her arm. "What is it?"

"A gift from the kitchen staff," Olessio replied.

"Not stolen?"

"Certainly not! I'm charming."

Tayre brought his piece to his nose, rubbed it between

finger and thumb. "Nothing more than cacao and inert spices, Vagras? The kitchen staff might not be our friends, even if you are."

"Even *if…*?" Olessio snorted offense. "I've already eaten some and I'm fine." He frowned. "Wait, I don't seem odd, do I?"

"No more than usual," Tayre answered.

Amarta held her bit to her nose to smell it, as Tayre had. She wondered how it would taste.

Earthy, sweet, gritty, and spiced. It settled the discomfort in her stomach from the motion of the wagon. In a few hours, she would ask him if there was more. "Alas, no, my dear, we've eaten it all. Good, though, wasn't it?"

"Yes it was," she breathed, smiling.

"What?" Olessio asked.

"She's foreseeing," Tayre said.

"Quite good," she said to Olessio, answering a question that he had never asked, and, now, probably never would.

She was still smiling as she put the aromatic shard into her mouth.

Sometimes they rode, tucked into the back of a trade wagon, tight among boxes and sacks, Tadesh exploring the corners. More often, they walked. Either way, disguise and misdirection became their work.

On the road, they would cycle through hats and scarves. Outside a town, they might change bags, shoes, and tales. At one town, a series of midnight transactions left Amarta as utterly confused as she knew Tayre intended to make their potential pursuers. If someone were still on their trail after that, she decided, they were formidable trackers.

Road by road, village by village, the four of them

approached the foothills of the Xanmelkie Mountains. Every market they passed offered monkstones in various colors and styles. At every town, the price rose. Each time, Amarta reached into her pocket to be sure that hers was there.

This morning, Tadesh rode Olessio's shoulder, sniffing the predawn air.

"What is our tale today?" Olessio asked.

"On our way to the Tree of Revelation," Tayre said. "Humble suppliants, hoping for answers to whatever it is that troubles our lives."

Not far from the truth.

"I'll have plenty of questions, then," Olessio said brightly.

"You'll be disappointed," Tayre replied, "unless you have a monkstone."

"What, those expensive rocks? Always a catch. Pah, who needs answers, anyway?"

"You don't want answers," Amarta said.

"I don't?" asked Olessio.

She shook her head. "Answers make bigger problems. When I give them, anyway. No matter how I answer, the person who asked is more miserable, not less."

"Why?"

"Knowing what might yet be changes everything." She shook her head. "Just live. Let the future take care of itself."

"Ah," Olessio said. "Wise words. Is that what you do?"

"No," she said flatly. She'd tried to purge her vision once and had almost died as a consequence, her sister and nephew along with her.

Again, the stomach-dropping recollection that Tayre had then been the one coming after her.

Olessio, seeing her expression, launched gamely into another story, one about Farliosan elders consulting a lunatic, and how she led them to a hidden treasure.

By midday, they found themselves walking through a

meadow, thick with tall, long-petaled flowers of yellow that somehow put Amarta's mind on Dirina. The wedding. Guilt and affection chased each other around inside her.

Vision snapped a quick, sharp warning, and Amarta slowed her steps, letting Olessio stride by to take the lead. What had it been?

A moment later, Olessio swore and slapped at something on his leg, then dropped to a knee to examine it. A red welt was forming. He'd been stung.

"I'm sorry," Amarta said quickly.

Pulling a stinger from his shin, Olessio tossed it into the grass. "Bit of a poke, is all. Give it an hour, and I'll be right as sky." He grinned reassuringly as he limped forward.

A queasy feeling came over her. How many times would she let someone else take the sting meant for her?

Another day and another. In a small tavern at the foot of the rugged, rising hills, they sat around a table, Tayre fingering the remains of oily bread crumbs on a plate, as if casually fiddling.

For a moment Amarta was both charmed and amused. Then she reminded herself that he did nothing casually or without reason.

"We're here," Tayre said, pointing to a line he'd made in what she now realized was a crumb-sketch map of the area. "We'll take this road through the pass, and either this one or that one, depending on what Amarta foresees when we get there. They both lead to the Xanmelkie Valley."

"The Tree of Revelation." Amarta felt her excitement rise.

Olessio pursed his lips, looking unsettled.

"Do you object?" Tayre asked him.

Olessio's eyes flickered to each of them, then down to Tadesh in his lap. "We can go our own way from here. No offense would be taken by either of us. One last chance to be rid of me," he added with a smile and levity that didn't seem entirely sincere.

Tayre bent his head down slightly, tilting it to keep an eye on the few people scattered across the room.

"No one is chasing you across the Temani Gulf for a lame pony, Vagras," Tayre said, "and I don't believe you're simple enough to think so, though apparently you think we are. Do you want to tell us the real reason someone might be after you, or shall we all continue to pretend?"

Olessio's expression went fixed, and Amarta thought she saw fear behind his eyes.

Then it was gone, replaced by a too-wide grin. He gave a breathy laugh, leaned back, laced his hands behind his head.

"More than happy for the company, Guard-dog. On to the Tree of Revelation, I say. If you'll have me. Hmm? Amarta?"

Amarta felt into various futures, finding Olessio in most of them along with Tadesh's smooth coat under her fingers, the thrumming of a contented chuffing in the animal's chest.

"Come with us," she said.

Chapter Five

AMARTA, Tayre, and Olessio ascended the Xanmelkie mountains. The road went to rock and scrub grass, trees and vines tangling across the steep mountainside. They walked a wooden bridge spanning a steep, cascading waterfall, then resumed the slow, steep climb.

Olessio began a story, and Amarta was pleased; he was good at them, and the stories made the hard hike go by more easily.

"I was only a lad. Perhaps six years old," Olessio said. "Always asking questions, getting into trouble. Like you, I'd wager." Olessio raised an eyebrow at Tayre, who didn't respond. Olessio shrugged. "The old man's face was tan from the sun, and deep with crevasses, and you could see blue sky through his ancient straw hat, which surely was as old as he was. The old man tugged up a ragged pants leg to show me the truth of his words. There, where his leg should be, was a heavy club of red wood the color of dried blood."

"Amardide," Amarta said.

Olessio nodded. "Probably so. I gaped, my eyes wide as coins.

"'Shark took it straight off,' the old man said. He raised his right arm, which ended, not in a hand, but a wicked-sharp hook. 'But this, I lost to the pirates. We were traveling east, from Kelerre, to the Spine of the World. Deep of night they boarded. The first one lopped my hand off! Lucky cut, I'll tell you. But even in flight, my fingers were clever— they let go my sword, which I caught with my other hand. Then put that fine blade into the bastard's back, levering him overboard with my wooden leg. Fought off the rest of the ruffians and sent twelve of them to the deep.' The old man circled his hook in the air. It sparkled. 'Never rusts. Won't even scratch. Mage-made, it is.'"

"Was it?" Amarta asked.

"It glinted dark silver," Olessio said. "Metal to bone and no rot. Mage-made, most like."

"Or good cutting and clean healing," Tayre said. "But none of this holds. An off-hand defense of multiple attackers, while losing blood? But go on, Vagras."

Olessio gave Tayre a slightly annoyed look, then cleared his throat.

"'And your eye?' I asked, breathless with wonder. In color and hue, the old man's left eye matched his hook. Where a soft, living ball of white and iris and pupil should be, was instead a silver orb. Quite startling, and to my child's view, quite enchanting! His eyelids moved over it as if it were alive. Could he see through it, I wondered?

"I wove in front of him to see myself gaping in that curved mirror. At that moment, nothing in the world could be finer. I wanted an eye just like his."

The four of them passed a line of trees that gripped tight to the sloped mountainside, long-needled branches swaying in the high breeze.

Olessio continued. "'What happened to it?' I asked him eagerly. 'Ah,' says the old man. 'A seagull shat me in the eye.'"

Tayre exhaled, somewhere between a sigh and a snort.

Olessio glowered, followed by a bright smile at Amarta. "I stood on my tiptoes, staring into that curved mirror—most rudely, I'm sure! But I was six and could perhaps be excused. 'What?' I cried. 'Seagull crap turned your eye silver?'

"My mind was full of wonder. I had mighty plans to find the nearest port town, and look upward for as long as it took. A boy of six can dream large."

Amarta thought of Pas, nearly that age. Was he dreaming large? Who was he becoming in the Arunkel palace?

"You must know my excitement at this plan," Olessio said to them both, "to understand how disappointed I was at what he said next."

The silence stretched. "Which was?" she prompted.

"Ah! He laughed, he did. 'No bird dropping turned my eye silver, fool boy.' 'Then what?' I demanded." Olessio grinned, looking from Tayre to Amarta, to be sure that they both were paying attention. Then, in a victorious tone, Olessio said: "'Twas my first day with the hook, you see!'"

For a good number of steps, no one spoke.

At last, Amarta did. "Wait. Are you saying that he put his hook into his own eye to rub away the bird dropping?"

"Well," Olessio said, "yes."

"He ruined his eye himself?" Amarta felt horror, but at the same time, she understood; it was so easy to make such mistakes in life, terrible mistakes, ones that could never be repaired. "How awful. I feel terrible for the old man."

Olessio's mouth went slack. He stared at her a moment, then cocked his head at Tayre. "Doesn't have much of a sense of humor, does she?"

Tayre made a thoughtful sound. "Years of people trying to separate your head from your body can do that."

Amarta suddenly found it hard to breathe. She didn't

slow her pace up the steep road, but around her, the sounds of birds and crickets seemed muffled. Her eyes on her feet, she plodded forward.

"Her—head?" Olessio choked.

Now Amarta realized that her heart was speeding. Strange. She heard Tayre's voice as if from far away.

"Quite a bit of coin has been spent across the years to bring Amarta dua Seer into the hands of the Arunkel elites. When that failed, they offered money for her head. She has spent many years fearing for her life and the life of her family. It's put a damper on her ability to be amused."

Olessio's tone was distressed. "How dreadful. To lose one's ability to laugh—a sort of death itself, is it not?"

There were, Amarta noticed, thick tufts of grass growing alongside the dirt road. In one, a tiny white flower was blooming. It seemed so lonely. Did it wish for another?

"Amarta?" Olessio asked.

"I…" Amarta managed. Her voice sounded toneless. "That's over. I don't know why he keeps bringing it up."

From the corner of her eye, she saw Tayre's expression, which wordlessly communicated that she'd answered her own question.

"Stop that," she snapped, anger cutting through the strange fog.

"Yes, of course," said Olessio quickly, misunderstanding entirely. He slowed a little, dropping back to follow.

Amarta felt herself flush, her emotions tangled.

For a time, they hiked in heavy silence. When they paused for a break, Olessio knelt, pouring water into a cupped hand for Tadesh, who lapped it up thirstily, and Tayre stepped away, walking around to look out over the valley they had climbed up from.

Olessio's tone went uncharacteristically sober. "I am truly

sorry, Amarta. I didn't mean to make light of…of what is in your past."

"No," she said. "That's not…" What was it not? She could not fathom her own thoughts. She shook her head, unable to speak.

Olessio nodded as if he understood, and did not press for more.

There was simply no way to explain, not without saying more than she could bear. Every time she tried, the words got caught in her throat.

The path became steeper yet, and Amarta fueled her feet with her inner storm. Whatever Olessio guessed from the occasional looks he stole at her—then at Tayre—would remain his alone.

Dusk began to darken the land. They found a flat place to camp alongside the river, where Olessio prepared food, his tone subdued, his words solicitous. She saw him restrain himself from his usual humor. Amarta was touched by the gesture, but guilt lay hard across the kindness.

He was trying to make right what he had not made wrong. Tayre, of course, behaved as if nothing were amiss.

That night she put her bedroll on the far side of Olessio, away from Tayre, and buried her tangled feelings.

It didn't help to realize, as she struggled for the balm of unconsciousness, that her reactions today brought his touch no closer.

She curled around the ache until sleep finally took her.

The morning's hike was quiet, but by midday, Olessio had, without warning, begun telling stories again. They were nearly at the ridge, making their slow way up steep switchbacks.

"They retreated back and back into the tunnel," Olessio said. "Hand in hand, as the sound grew ever louder. Then, wide and bright as moons, came two eyes out of the darkness, surging toward them, It was the white wyrm itself."

They were at high elevation, trees spindly, groundcover straggly and tenacious. They topped the rise, breathing hard, and paused there to look at the valley through brush and trees. On the far side, farms and roads were outlined with dark green lines of trees, jagged lines of scrub. They continued along the ridge trail.

"Go on," Amarta urged.

Olessio grinned happily. "The impossibly huge creature came at them. The tunnel was small, the wyrm large. A rumbling through their feet. In their very bones! They would be crushed, if she could not find the small alcove she remembered. Where was it? She found it! They pressed themselves into it, like dough into a baking bowl. The great serpent reached them, its mouth open wide. And then…"

The trees on the valley side had cleared. Olessio paused, then drew breath. Amarta looked at him to see why he had stopped. His smile was gone.

"And then?" she asked.

"Ah! How does it go? Give me a moment. Too much sun! Once we're in the shade, I'll have it again. There." He pointed down the gently descending ridge trail, to where the trees resumed, shading the path. "Push on, shall we?" He quickened his pace. Amarta followed.

Behind her, Tayre spoke. "Don't do that."

"Do what?" Amarta asked, pausing to look, puzzled, at each of them in turn.

Olessio's smile went brittle. "I only meant to spare her. Given everything she's been through."

"She doesn't ask to be spared." Tayre looked at her. "Or do you?"

A chill came over her as she understood the warning of his question. What was she missing?

A distant, chilling scream. Smoke.

Amarta slowly turned, even as she found herself shaking her head. *I don't want to know.*

She sought across the valley for what Olessio had seen, and what Tayre had refused to protect her from.

There it was: a trickle of black smoke rose from a farmhouse on the far slope. Fields of yellow and tan spread out to either side. From this distance, Amarta could barely make out the small figures.

A large group of men. Horses. A woman running from a smoking house. A man close behind, a child in his arms.

The group grabbed the man, pulling the screaming child away.

She looked at Tayre. "What are they doing?"

"Taking what they can carry, burning the rest." He gave a short nod. "Look well, and we go. As visible as they are to us, we are to them."

Amarta looked back at the scene. "Can we not help?"

"I make twenty-five," Tayre said. "At least fifteen horses. Even with your ability, Seer, no. It's too many."

Olessio put a wide-eyed look on Amarta. "You can't mean…" He didn't wait for a reply. "No, no." he said, hands up as if to stop her. "They are—" he exhaled. "Beyond help. Lost, in fact. A horrible thing, but truth it is. We must take care of ourselves. He is entirely right. This way."

"But what will happen to them?" she asked, not moving.

"Don't you…" Olessio began, confused, then fell silent. *See the future?*

Yes, but that would mean taking her eyes off the now.

Another figure—a girl, Amarta thought—fled the farmhouse as orange flames flickered from the windows. She was met by a handful of the brigands, who knocked her to the ground and surrounded her, blocking Amarta's view. A simple, overwhelming brutality.

"Will no one help them? Neighbors? Authorities?" Amarta asked.

"Not in the moments that remain to them," Tayre answered.

"We can't help them," Olessio said to her, urgently motioning down the trail.

"If we can't help them, then—" What would she want, in their place? *If you can't help me,* she would have screamed across the valley, *don't look away and pretend you don't see!* "We must watch."

"Watch?" Olessio asked, incredulously. "Why?"

Amarta exhaled a half-sob. "Because otherwise, they're alone."

The family was no longer standing, hidden by the band of men, their cries terrified. Amarta made fists and blinked to clear her eyes.

"They have horses. We don't," Tayre said. "They will come for us faster than we can outrun them."

"You don't know that," she said in a low voice. "You can't know that."

Tayre glanced at the sky. "Then tell us, Seer: are these men in our future, if we stand here to give them the chance to see us as clearly as we see them?"

The brigands were looking across the valley, in their direction. One raised an arm. Pointing?

Amarta shifted her focus elsewhen, and gave the question to vision. Futures crowded together, vying for existence.

Olessio was limping, his arm dangling uselessly, face ashen, weeping for the loss of Tadesh. From atop a horse, someone laughed.

Amarta blinked back to the moment. The farmhouse was

engulfed in flame. Olessio, eyes on her, backed away, down the path, toward the cover of trees.

"I understand, my dear," he said. "I truly do. There are times to face down a wrong thing, because you can make it whole. But this is not one of them."

Across the valley, the sounds of the family's cries had ended.

"It's not right," she said, again and again, but she let Tayre lead her down the trail to where the foliage blocked the view.

"It is not," Olessio agreed soberly, from her side. "But of this I am certain: it is less right for us to be their next victims."

They walked the path. Trees, bushes, and then the mountain itself hid the far valley completely.

"What is this," she whispered to Tayre, rubbing tears from her eyes. "That we do? What is it?"

"What we must," Tayre answered.

Amarta still smelled smoke.

"I don't like it," she said.

He shook his head slowly. "You don't have to."

Days and mountain passes later, they stood atop the final rise and looked down across the Xanmelkie valley. Tadesh crawled from Olessio's pack to perch on his shoulder.

The town was far below the cliff on which they stood. A river wound through it, under bridges and past buildings, like a thick gray ribbon. Smaller shapes of people and wagons crawled along the road, like colorful insects.

"There," Tayre said, pointing to the north end of the valley, where a circular white area, like a drop of milk, was surrounded by tiny brown-tan structures. At the edge of the circle rose a tree that seemed out of proportion to the buildings, its branches visible even at this distance.

"The Tree of Revelation," Amarta breathed.

"That's not right," Olessio muttered darkly. He was looking elsewhere, to the far side of the wide valley, where a waterfall dropped straight down a huge cliff of green stone to a frothing lake that fed the valley's river.

"What isn't?" she asked, baffled.

"Those jade cliffs," Olessio said. "See how the water fans out evenly, wider at that shelf there, and then again?"

"It's a magi-khrastos," Tayre said. "So?"

Olessio snorted, waved a hand angrily. "What error did nature make here that must be thus corrected? Was the water too fickle in its fall? The rocks providing a mere jagged flow? Did the water's tendrils fail some obscure magi aesthetic?" His voice rose. "Vulgar, pretentious, self-aggrandizing…"

Bemused, Amarta turned to Tayre. "What is he talking about?"

"The magi," Tayre said, studying Olessio a moment, before turning his attention back to the great tree.

"Is the Tree of Revelation a magi-khrastos?" Amarta asked.

"I doubt it." Tayre said. "Probably just a big tree."

"If it were mage-made," Olessio said, clearly still agitated, "The bark would…" He waved his arms. "Glow. Every leaf would have the mage's name on it."

"Are they really so vain?" Amarta asked, thinking of the two mages she knew: Maris and her aetur, Keyretura.

Olessio scowled. "There's an old adage: a good mirror may be had from the clever Farliosan, but the finest must be mage-made, because in all the world, none are so pleased with themselves as the magi."

Amarta looked at the tree and the roads that led there,

only now realizing that the figures, carts, and carriages were all moving in the same direction.

"So many," she muttered. She put a hand in her pocket to check that her monkstone was still there. An urgency took her. "We must go."

Chapter Six

SO MANY PEOPLE.

"Lodestones." Olessio's tone was speculative as he held his pack to his chest, Tadesh inside, to keep her protected from the crowd tight around them. He pointed up with his free hand at the great tree towering overheard. "The lodestones move the chain and pendulum follows." He turned the hand palm down, circling a finger to illustrate.

Where he had pointed, an iron chain was attached to a high, thick branch overhanging an open area, barely visible through hundreds of people. The other end of the chain—the pendulum—was wrapped and tied against the huge trunk.

"No," Tayre replied. "To move that amount of metal, the lodestone would need to be substantial."

"How substantial?"

"A team of horses and a wagon to move it," Tayre answered. "Too slow."

Amarta saw a ladder set against the trunk from beyond the crowd. A monk in white linen and skullcap climbed it to examine the tied pendulum. Now the scale of the tree was clear. It seemed to Amarta that a horse, if not two, could easily hide behind the trunk.

The tree's branches spread overhead like grasping talons, green foliage against a blue and white sky. Who had been brave enough to climb so high a tree, to secure that heavy chain on the limb? A long time ago, it must have been; the branch had thickened, swallowing the chain where it was attached.

"I suppose so," Olessio said. He squinted upwards against intermittent flashes of sun through cloud and tree. "Don't see anyone up there, ready to yank on it and make it swing in the right direction, either."

Who were all these people? Judging by what they wore and carried, they came from everywhere. But the mood was far from what she'd seen in Senta at the Accord Festival. There were no smiles here, no celebratory air. Faces were tight, expressions full of fear, tinged with hope.

"Ah!" Olessio exhaled. "The monks have tamed the wind to move the branch and thus the chain to swing as they wish it to." His fingers waggled horizontally, as if a breeze fluttered through.

Tayre was scanning the crowd. "Unlikely, Vagras, given that even mages complain about the weather."

Olessio bounced in place a few times. "They stomp, then. All the monks together. Shakes the tree, moves the branch, and thus—"

Tadesh poked her head out of the bag he held against his chest, chittering at being jostled. Then she saw the crowd and pulled back inside.

"Or maybe," Amarta said crossly, "it's not a trick. Maybe the tree predicts the future."

"A tree?" Olessio frowned.

Amarta glowered at him. "We came to find out, not to guess."

"Attend!" shouted a monk from atop the highest of three scaffolds surrounding the tree. "The abbot of the order of the Monks of the Revelation speaks!"

Heads turned and necks craned, but voices did not much quiet. A gray-bearded man in a high, white headdress stood by the monk. In a deep, booming voice, he called out: "Is there a querant?"

People shouted back, waving hats and bright scarves.

"Me!" "Hoi!" "I've got a monkstone!" "Tell us true!"

"Never seen this many before," muttered an old woman.

On a lesser scaffold, two white-clad monks opened a huge book, arranging writing implements. On the third scaffold, a huge brass gong flashed in a brief moment of sunlight.

"Is there a querant?" called the abbot again.

Cries and screams surged to an astonishing volume. Olessio hugged his pack. Nearby, a slender Zaneke woman comforted a small boy, frightened at the din. "Now, now, little flower—soon we'll know about papa."

The abbot lifted both hands in the air, his sleeves draping like some odd bird, then lowered them abruptly.

A monk swung a club across the gong, once, twice, and again and again. The stunning, deafening sound drowned out all voices.

Amarta clapped her hands to her ears. Olessio's backpack shuddered.

As the ringing slowly began to subside, children wept and people muttered softly.

"Why ask a question," Amarta whispered to Tayre, "without waiting for an answer?"

"He doesn't want an answer," Tayre said. "He's training the crowd. Watch."

The abbot raised his hands again. The crowd instantly fell

silent. He paused for a long moment, looking across them. No one spoke.

"Once a year," the abbot said at last, "we Monks of Revelation offer the world our greatest gift. Those privileged to hold a mark of the order may step forward. The rest, step back, behind the outer line."

"Outer line?" someone asked quietly. Everyone began to look down. "Back here," said another. White chalk in the dirt."

"Mark of the order?" someone asked. "The pink monkstones," answered another. "Pink? No! Mine is gray!" "Mine is clear. Will they answer my question?" "This one cost me a la-sorin. They'd better." "We only need to know about the watershed. Can't we just ask?"

"Only those with marks!" bellowed another monk. "Step forward into line. Everyone else back away."

Churning, the crowd surged forward and backward at once.

Tayre's gaze flickered. "I don't like this," he said, taking Amarta's arm. "Let's step back."

"What? No. I have—" her voice dropped. "I have a mark." Her hand was in her pocket, clutching it tight.

He gave her a searching look. "What do you intend here, Amarta?"

"I must know."

The three of them stood in a fast-clearing area, some thirty paces between the outer crowd, and the line forming around the arc of the white sand circle.

Letting go her arm, he nodded sharply. "So be it. Use your ability, Amarta."

He and Olessio withdrew from her to join the thick outer crowd. Amarta hurried to join the queue forming around the fenced white sand circle.

Another ladder next to the first. Two monks climbed to

unwrap the pendulum, a huge pale rose gemstone. Like the stone in her pocket. A teardrop shape, gripped at the top by iron fingers that attached to the chain that stretched up and up and was swallowed by the tree's mottled orange-and-brown bark.

She'd seen chains like this before, on sea-going vessels, each link as big around as two of her fists.

"Move on!" she was poked in the back by the man standing behind her.

"Sorry," she muttered, closing the gap between herself and the next person, as the line moved toward the entrance of the paddock that surrounded the white sand circle.

The line shuffled forward to the monks, who examined each mark. Ten people before her. Then eight. Then four.

"You go in," said a monk. "Next."

A half growl. "This is not ours. You insult us!" One monk held high what looked like a bit of broken slate.

The man snarled at the monk and stepped in close—too close—his posture challenging. Three other monks drew near to the first, making four.

"Fie on you and your Revelation," spat the man, striding away.

The Zaneke woman was next, her two small children's hands gripped tightly in hers.

"Your monkstone, sera. Show us."

He held up the stone she gave him. In his fingers, it looked pink, just like Amarta's.

"Not ours." He tossed it toward the outer crowd. It landed on the dirt.

The Zaneke woman looked stricken. "No! I paid so much for it. My husband, please, I only need to know—"

"A forgery. Get back with the rest," the monk said, gesturing her away with one hand, and Amarta forward with the other.

"Quickly, now," the monk told her as the Zaneke woman hunched, fighting tears, backing away with her children.

Amarta opened her now quite-sweaty hand to show the stone. The monk took it, looked through it.

Her breath quickened. What if hers, also, were a forgery? She thought of the man who had sold it to her at the Accord festival. Another swindler? Or perhaps himself fooled?

Or was she the fool?

"I've come so far," she found herself blathering. "Please—"

"Yes. Go in."

She exhaled relief as she hurried inside the enclosure to stand alongside some twenty other querants. A waist-high dais faced the white sand circle, which was bright and flat as a pond.

One by one, the waiting line was sorted, emptied, a few more allowed inside, the rest turned away despite pleading, arguing, and declined bribes.

Then, from four corners around the white sand, monks lit briers. Thick smoke billowed, dispersing the scent of sage and cinnamon. Chanting began. At the ladders, the monks untied the ropes that kept the pendulum at the trunk.

Then the abbot gestured. The chanting stopped. The pendulum was released.

It swung toward the center, picking up speed, then, close enough to kiss the sand as it sailed by. At the far end of the arc, the huge stone had risen many feet above the fenceline. There, it seemed to pause before reversing direction.

No one spoke. It was mesmerizing, the massive stone's motion, the way the huge pale facet caught the light as it passed. Amarta counted to herself—one, two, three, four—as the rose-colored rock slowly swung down over the sands and rose up again on the other side, hung a moment, and reversed course.

"Attend, querants!" called the abbot. "The Tree answers only well-formed questions. Compose yours for a reply of motion or stagnation."

"Motion?" someone nearby asked. "Stagnation?"

"Straight for yes, curve for no," said one of the nearby monks, a tall, slender man.

"It only answers yes or no?" Amarta asked, surprised.

"Of course," replied the monk. "Any other answer would be confusing."

She had not expected this. Her own foresight rarely led to answers as simple as yes or no. Though there were times. A cow about to birth a calf, male or female. A coin landing on one side or the other.

And sometimes there was only one answer. Yes, tomorrow the sun would rise.

But for most questions, Amarta saw a fog of overlapping possibilities, of choices yet to be made, of shifting outcomes.

If the monks and their Tree could be so certain that they could give a yes or no answer—motion or stagnation, as they called it—what did that mean?

Had Amarta been answering ill-formed questions all these years? Was that why she foresaw so many possibilities, rather than a simple yes or no? Her mind spun. If that were so, then the monks knew something that she did not.

She watched the pendulum intently as fragile hope bloomed inside her.

The huge rose-quartz rock reached an apex, turning slightly as it fell. Was that a curve as it sailed back across the white sand? Or was it straight?

As the stone passed the center point, sunlight broke through the clouds and the lush canopy above. For the briefest of moments, the crystal flashed a deep rose-color.

"Oh," someone exhaled in wonder.

"Attend, querants!" The abbot pointed to the raised dais

in their paddock. "Step up there. Speak your name. The Tree will decide if you and your question are pure enough to answer. Who is first?"

Querants looked around, confused, motionless. A blink later, a handful of them surged to the platform, trying to scramble atop it since there was no other way up, grabbed at by those just behind them. They pushed and pulled as each tried to get the others off the platform.

Amarta and the rest of the querants backed away from the dais.

The victor was a large man, thick around the arms and chest, a farmer's hat with folded brim on his head. He kicked viciously at another man trying for possession of the dais. He was breathing hard, his attention torn between his challengers, the abbot, and the moving pendulum.

"Say your name," said the abbot.

"They call me Pula."

"It's a curve," someone near Amarta whispered. "No, it's not." "Hush. They'll say."

"The Tree will hear your query," the abbot said.

The man's face changed to hope. He tilted his head to look up at the tree. "Great Tree, our crops come up weak and small. We barely eat. Worse each year. Nothing left. Are we cursed? We can't afford a mage. Not even a half-mage." His voice dropped. "But some say, use the old ways: heal the land with blood." A pained look came to his face. "My boy said he would…do it. For us all. But is that—how can I—please…"

"Stop, stop," shouted the abbot, waving his hands. "Do you see how the pendulum wobbles? Your words are muddled. Yes or no. Reform the question."

Amarta saw no wobble, but perhaps the abbot's view from the highest scaffold was different.

The man's mouth opened and closed. In a hoarse voice: "Will my child's lifeblood bring back our crops?"

Amarta had been asked such questions before. Shall we sacrifice a goat? Seer! My baby's life for my husband's? If I cut off my third toes and bury them at the full moon, will the water well return?

They were horrible questions. Restore water, fertility, lost fortunes, a mate's affections. More wretched yet to foresee, as Amarta must, to answer them. Each time it was the same: blood or life taken, goat or child or one's own, did not repair soil, purse, body, or heart. Blood was just blood.

At the edge of the outer crowd, a young boy jittered in place, his gaze at the farmer on the dais fierce beyond his years. The man looked back, then to the Tree.

The man's son, Amarta guessed. Reluctantly she asked herself the farmer's question. Vision answered.

The farmer walked through a field of twisted, spindly trees, the boy's hand in his. In his other hand was a cleaver.

But would he do it? Would he really take his son's life? She didn't want to know, but she pushed herself to see, just a little further.

In many futures he would. But the crops would not return.

Atop the high platform, the abbot and two monks conferred. One pointed at the pendulum, another whispered into the abbot's ear. The abbot nodded, inhaled to speak.

The answer is no.

Amarta let out a sigh of relief.

"The answer is no."

At the huge book, another monk was writing.

"But no," the farmer said, his hat in his hand, his face a war of relief and agony. "If we do nothing, we starve. I've five children, Great Tree. My da. My sister, her children."

"Your question has been answered. Step down."

The man's face fell. Shaken, he stumbled as he left the dais. The monks escorted him from the paddock. As he began to cross the open space to the outer crowd, the boy broke free and ran to him, hugging him tightly. He hugged back.

"Next querant."

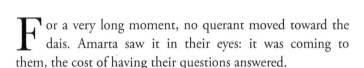

For a very long moment, no querant moved toward the dais. Amarta saw it in their eyes: it was coming to them, the cost of having their questions answered.

A well-dressed, graying man levered himself up onto the dais with no challenge. He drew himself tall.

"I am Melunant, from the great port city of Vilaros. The sailors say the Island Road is moving now to assemble. My Dominus wants to know, should he put his holdings into a sea ship? If the Island Road does not assemble at Turia—or the Island Pearls are not for sale—he is ruined. My question is…"

"No, no," the abbot shouted, hands waving at the man. "You must wait for the Tree to accept you."

Melunant stopped, mouth open, his gaze following the moving pendulum. The rock sailed through the center point and up, reversing.

Straight? Curving? Amarta couldn't tell.

The abbot spoke. "The Tree will not hear your question. Step down. Next."

"What? But why not? I did nothing wrong. I am pure —I am—"

"Do not question the Tree. Step down!"

Melunant's face tightened, as if he might resist. He looked at the monks and Tree, realizing, Amarta supposed, that he could not force an answer. Then he dropped off the dais and stamped out of the paddock, shouting about how much he'd paid for a worthless stone.

Now, on the dais was a small woman, her skin a dusky olive, watching the pendulum swing.

"The tree will hear your question," said the abbot.

"I am called Saifutal," she said. "Our life in Dulu, it is good. I do not miss the rains of Seute Enta, or how we must bury ourselves to survive the Eufalmo. But I do miss my parents. When I left them, they said the land was their breath. They believed they would be accepted into the Body of Seuan. I was so angry." Her chest heaved. "Thirteen years since I left. I send letters, but no reply. Are they dead? Have the Eufalmo turned them to dust and bones?"

The abbot gave an exasperated sigh. "One question only! Unmuddled. We have said this!"

The woman considered the swinging pendulum. "If I cross the ocean to go home, will my parents see me?"

The answer is no.

"What?" Amarta asked, shocked at her vision of the monk's reply to come. Amarta had read the woman's future and saw the woman and her parents. Holding hands. Tears of joy.

"The answer is no."

"That's not right," Amarta said. Other querants eyed her uneasily.

So the answer was right the first time, but wrong the second. Was the Tree wrong? The abbot mistaken in his reading of the pendulum?

Amarta turned to the monk who had spoken to her earlier. "Do querants ever return to tell you that your prediction was wrong?"

"Na, na," he answered. "Ears can hear wrong, but the Tree and abbot are always right."

Amarta puzzled over this. Perhaps the Tree could see farther than the tearful family reunion Amarta had glimpsed.

A monk helped Saifutal from the dais. Her expression was sad and resigned.

Amarta craned her neck, as if looking at the outer crowd to find someone. She took a step to the side and bumped into the small woman, as if by accident, then grabbed Saifutal's arm as if to steady herself, and muttered an apology.

Pride flickered through her; if he had seen it, Tayre would have been proud.

As Amarta touched Saifutal's arm, she dropped into foresight.

"Next querant," boomed the abbot from above.

"Your parents want to see you," Amarta whispered to Saifutal. "Go home. Now."

Saifutal's eyes widened in shock. She pulled back and hurried away.

Amarta turned to stare up at the Tree, the swinging pendulum, and the abbot. All answers came through the abbot.

Olessio was right, she decided. The motion of the pendulum meant nothing. An ancient tree and an impressive gemstone, but there was no foresight here.

A limping woman was being helped to climb the dais.

Why weren't there stairs? Even a small box to make the ascent a bit easier? Why put querants through such struggle? Even the raised platforms at the Sun and Moon gambling house had easy stairs for the players' convenience.

All at once she understood: it was like winning one's way to the gemstone Rochi tables, as she had: having worked so hard to get there, it mattered more. The monkstones, the deafening gong, the smoking briers—the dais that must be climbed to be achieved—by the time each querant arrived there, they would feel fortunate.

By then, none of them would want to doubt the answers.

Games within games.

"The Tree will not hear you," said the abbot.

The woman keened sharply. "But I must know. If I give him everything, will he stay silent?"

"Step back. Next querant!"

The woman crumpled to the dais in grief, was pulled off by monks, and, sobbing, was escorted out of the paddock.

Amarta searched the monks' faces, the one now writing in the huge book. Did they believe? Did they doubt? And the abbot? Did he know he was a fraud?

Did it matter?

No, it didn't. Whether deliberate pretense or foolish credulity, their predictions weren't true.

"I am Dakalet of the Temani Gulf and surrounds," spoke a large, heavily bearded Perripin man, legs wide atop the dais. He wore a tunic and headwrap that proclaimed him a wealthy Dulu merchant.

"The tree will hear you," said the Abbot.

"Storm of the century, they told me," Dakalet said. "The mast shredded by howling winds, the ship ripped in two on the Nelar Ocean." Dakalet's expression was grim. "My son was swept overboard. But." The man pounded his chest three times and Amarta heard the thumps. "I feel my son lives. I ask, Great Tree: will I see him alive again?"

Amarta looked. The man was right: his son lived.

"The Tree says no," answered the Abbot.

The man's inarticulate cry was sharp, choked off as quickly as it had begun, his expression turning stony. He jumped down off the dais.

Amarta reached out to him as he pushed past, but he did not slow. The bare touch of his arm showed her a winding future trail, distant but possible, in which Dakalet and his son were reunited. But it would never happen if the man did not know enough to search for him.

She had no more doubt: the Tree of Revelation and its monks were no more mystical than the rolling of dice.

"Next querant."

The tree will hear you.

The dwindling number of querants gave Amarta wide berth; her earlier words had made them uneasy. Well, that was nothing new.

Amarta clambered atop the dais and drew herself to standing, looking around at the crowd, the many looking back, desperate for answers. Desperate enough to come here, across hundreds of miles, across sea and ocean. They paid for monkstones to get answers that would change their lives.

Wrong answers.

"Say your name, querant, so the Tree may decide."

Amarta's breath caught in her throat. The question was nothing like simple to answer. Should she pretend to be the young heiress from inland Vilaros? A Borderland girl named Kiki?

The pendulum sailed by. There were other names yet. Which one to use? Would it matter?

In the wash of images that tried to answer the question, she sensed that something in her own future hung precariously on what she was about to say. Distant, barely there, like a whiff of wood smoke on the breeze.

She would want something that would take years to acquire. But it could be faster.

Drawing a deep breath, she looked around at hundreds staring back. She spoke, determined to be heard to the end of the outer circle.

"I am Amarta al Arunkel."

The seer.

No, she would not say that. Not yet.

The abbot watched the pendulum. "The Tree will hear you, querant. Ask your question."

At this, Amarta stifled a surprised laugh. A question hadn't even occurred to her. What should it be?

Her foresight swirled, trying to answer what her question would be, near-future images spraying out into a mist of all possible questions, a range that only multiplied as she began to examine it.

She yanked herself back abruptly lest she circle endlessly as she stood here. Sweeping the storm of half-answers away, she blinked back into the present. What to ask?

Do you know that your Tree's answers are based on nothing more than wind and the pull of the earth?

Are all of you liars, or do some of you believe?

No—it didn't matter.

Will I find someone who can foresee as I do?

That was the question most dear to her, but for that, they would have no answer.

She squinted up at the thick fringe of green. The sun intermittently cleared the clouds, casting flickering patches of light onto the white sands. The wind moved the tree's great branches which accounted for the pendulum's varying swing.

The wind also accounted for the clouds and the sunlight. Wind, a challenge even for mages, Tayre had said. Amarta understood; weather was one of the most difficult things she ever predicted. Easier to foresee a season of storms than the next hour's rainfall.

This close to the next moment, though—that was another matter. She could, almost…

Almost…

"Ask your question!"

Trees. Clouds. Sun. The swinging of a huge stone. This moment. The next. And…

There.

She raised her arms as the abbot had done, then lowered them abruptly, hands clasped together, her forefingers pointing at the pendulum. In that instant, the sun shone, burning a clear shaft of light into the pendulum. It glinted a vibrant magenta.

Murmurs of surprise. Cries of astonishment. She dropped her arms to her sides, looked at the crowd and monks with a feeling of elation at her timing.

There. That would convince them that she—

"She's a mage!" "The magi have come!" "Are they here to destroy us?"

"What? No!" she said, shocked. "I see the future, is what, unlike…" Her gaze sought the abbot's.

He bellowed, "querant, ask your question!"

"Your answers are false," she shouted. "This—" She waved her hands to take in the sand circle, the pendulum, the monks, the Tree—"This predicts nothing."

"You have no question. You are no querant. Step down. Next!"

Behind her, one monk asked another: "Why did the Tree choose her, if she has no question?"

"Do not challenge the Great Tree's wisdom, brother."

"Because," she snapped at them, "it's only a tree."

She ignored their outraged looks and gazed across the hundreds watching her, hungry for answers, trusting the wrong people to give them. The abbot was yelling at her to get down and the monks were collecting around the dais where she stood. She did not have long.

"Dakalet," she called, casting about for the large Perripin man. "Your son lives. His memories are broken, but you, he will know. Saifutal of Seute Enta—go home! Your parents will not live long. Farmer Pula—" she gasped for breath, shouting to get the words out as fast as she could, "your land is ill. No blood will fix it. Move north. Sera, with the limp. Your blackmailer will never be quiet. Instead, tell the truth to all. To the woman who—"

The gong sounded, hard and loud, again and again and again. Hands clasped to ears. Wide eyes and unheard screams.

The monks around the dais reached over, lunging to grab her feet, to pull her off.

Amarta danced through and around their hands, out of their grasps, their fingers brushing her, unable to gain hold. At last, they stood back, their faces full of shocked comprehension.

Such a familiar look. How many faces with those same expressions had she seen across the years?

The gong was still banging, deafeningly, unceasingly. Amarta briefly met the abbot's furious glare.

The outer crowd was surging forward to consume the open space around the paddock, more intrigued than repelled by the sound, and clearly no longer in a mood to obey the abbot's angry gestures to stay back.

Now what? She was silenced by the gong, but was she voiceless?

Again she raised her arms with clasped hands, abruptly lowering them to point to the great rose-colored teardrop, at the very moment it again sparked into sun-fed magenta brilliance.

The crowd gaped, touched each other, pointed. At the rock. At Amarta.

In the moment of focusing to find the timing of sun and wind and pendulum, she was distracted enough that the monks were on the dais, and it was too late—they held her arms tight.

Tayre would be watching. He would not be happy about this.

No matter; she was done here, ready to be quit of the entire thing. Her ears hurt from the ceaseless banging of the gong, and her chest from yelling. She allowed the grim-faced monks to march her to the edge of the dais, to lower her to other monks on the ground. They took a firm hold on her arms as they led her to the paddock and toward the gate.

So many people, reaching toward her over the fenceline. The monks stepped through the gate, but there, the crowd was surging to block them. The monks yelled at them wordlessly to get back.

For a moment, Amarta felt the tickle of alarm.

But no—foresight would protect her. Guide her. She must look.

Grabbed, pulled, the crowd was a confusing onslaught. She stumbled, lost her footing. A sharp agony as someone landed on top of her, and she was crushed, unable to breathe.

Amarta gasped back into the present. People called, waving to get her attention, their expressions hungry, but no sound rose above the banging gong.

She must act, and soon. But what to do?

At her side, the monks looked afraid, as if realizing that all that stood between the crowd and its desire was them.

Vision was humming a warning. Arms stretched over the fenceline toward her. A man climbed over the fence. Another followed.

What brazen notion had made it seem sensible to Amarta to name herself? To offer visions to hundreds of people?

Foolish, that. As the crowds thickened around them, it came to her just how foolish.

Vision was now howling at her that the futures in which she would walk free again were being cut like threads. She whirled, trying to find an opening. The crowd swarmed over the fence, surrounding her and the monks. Fingers brushed her, monks were jostled against her. She struggled to keep her feet.

Panic took hold. What now? What next?

A face. A familiar one.

"Here!" shouted a voice, nearly into her ear or she would never have heard it over the gong. It was the Perripin merchant Dakalet, at her side.

With a shout, he somehow cleared a space where they stood. He took her by the waist and hefted her over his head and onto his shoulders, as if she were a child.

"Make a path!" he bellowed, somehow making himself heard over the ceaseless gong. "Make a path for the seer!"

To her surprise, some did, pressing back against others to make a scant but passable route through the sea-like crowd.

Dakalet strode from the paddock and through the milling many, ruthlessly shoving aside those who did not move fast enough.

Faces stared up at her, full of need, gestures of entreaty, cries that could not be heard over the deafening gong.

Then, all at once, the sound stopped.

For a moment, the crowd stuttered to quiet, as Dakalet continued to press forward, pushing aside anyone who did not move willingly. Then the cries and yells began again.

Behind her, people were flooding into the sand circle. The great brass gong lay on the ground, along with bodies, prone, and clad in white.

Five men hefted the huge gong onto their shoulders. Another handful blocked their way in challenge.

Overhead, the chain and pendulum hung taut and unmoving. Two men had climbed atop the huge gemstone, each balancing with their feet on the iron claw, their hands gripping the chain. On the ground, others tried to mount up behind them, pulling, pushing.

A woman following in Dakalet's wake dragged two small children, holding their hands high to keep them from slipping underfoot. "Will their father return? Please, Seer!"

"The grain harvests of Plalal, Tsamasin, and Hrmala—Seer, will they exceed last year's? I'll pay you!"

"Should I buy the elixir to restore my baby?" A woman held a small, unmoving bundle high in the air.

"Amarta, look at me!" A young man, his face disfigured and blotched red. "From a fire. My mother…will she live?"

"What of the trade winds of Scamosinea? Before autumn? I have uma-sorins for you!"

"The rains! Before the harvest or after? Our family starves!"

"Does Chosolua come first in the Island Road, Amarta? Tukimpe? Just tell me this."

"Will Havoritrus the Elder keep his seat in the Congredia? Just say—only say!"

"Is my wife's son really mine?"

Rattled, shaken, Amarta could not seem to keep the questions from landing within her. Vision lurched from one half-formed answer to another.

"My village!"

"She suffers…!"

"Just one question…"

"If we only knew…"

"Amarta! Amarta!" Olessio's voice.

Her eyes snapped open. Olessio was trailing in her wake. She looked for Tayre, found him, then he was gone.

The woman towing the two children dropped their hands and reached toward Amarta imploringly. Amarta's breath caught. In this crowd, the small ones would soon be trampled.

A man grabbed up one of the children, bringing the boy to his shoulders. Another fetched up the girl in his arms. As swiftly as that, the children were out of harm's way. Not relatives, Amarta was sure. Strangers, caring enough to help.

It moved her. She reached her hand down toward the woman's, as Dakalet grabbed her legs to keep her from falling. The woman stretched up a hand. Their fingertips brushed.

Night, and he stood outside a small house, peering through a window. He turned and left and would not return.

"He lives," Amarta said, looking away, shame burning at this half-answer.

"Thank you, Seer! Blessings upon you!" cried the woman, falling behind.

"Why her, and not me?" shouted another, angrily.

"She paid you nothing! I have gold!"

Dakalet's determination had brought them to the edge of the monks' land, to the main road. Then, from behind, came a massive, thunder-like crack.

The crowd fell silent. Dakalet paused, turning to see.

For a moment Amarta didn't understand. Then the howls and screams began, and she did.

Impossible, she would have thought, to break so massive a branch. But with enough people pulling, it seemed, it could be done.

She looked up. Gone was the huge branch from which the pendulum had hung. Through the crowd she saw a group of people trying, in vain, to move the tree-sized branch off of those that it had crushed.

The blood drained from Amarta's face.

The highest scaffold was toppling. A bright flicker of flame licked up from the far side of the circle.

Under her, Dakalet resumed his motion forward, striding purposefully away from all the chaos, on the road to the Monks of Revelation.

Out of the corner of her blurring vision, Amarta saw Tayre join him, and the two men began to speak.

The crowd following began to thin, falling away as Dakalet's men surrounded them, providing protection.

It was only when Dakalet put his large hands atop hers,

on his head, and patted gently, that Amarta realized how tightly she was gripping the thick locks of his thick hair.

"It's all right, Seer," he called up, reassuringly.

But it wasn't.

Amarta looked back. There, on the white sands, no scaffolding remained upright, and no monk's white could be seen.

What had she done?

Chapter Seven

"REALLY QUITE TASTY," Olessio repeated, still holding out the flatbread to Amarta. Bits of pork speckled the glistening, flat baked disk.

Amarta shook her head.

"Just a bite, hmm? Tadesh loves it, so it must be—ow."

Tadesh cocked her head at Olessio.

"Careful with your teeth, darling," Olessio said, smiling, then scowling, but tentatively holding out another bite to her nonetheless. With exaggerated care, Tadesh took it gingerly between her teeth.

Was this exchange genuine, or an act they had rehearsed? Amarta found that she couldn't summon interest in the question.

While Olessio eyed Amarta with concern, Tayre was wrapping food for travel. Wherever they were going next.

Next. After the Monks of the Revelation. And their Tree.

They escaped from the Xanmelkie valley and crowds with the help of Dakalet, his men and his carriage, and a number of cleverly improvised diversions by Tayre and Olessio.

Amarta traveled in the carriage with Dakalet. It was

unsettling, how he deferred to her. A mature, wealthy merchant, with enterprises on both sides of the Temani Gulf, yet he trusted her over himself. By the end of the trip, she found herself watching every word she said.

But before they parted, Amarta told him everything she saw, in the future in which he might be reunited with his son.

"High bridges," she said. "Slender copper spires."

Dakalet's face lit. "I know it! I know the very place! I owe you a great debt, Seer. Wherever it is you journey next, allow me to help."

"Just a bite?" Olessio asked, pushing a plate of warm stew toward her.

Dakalet could, perhaps, go on the side of the scales that measured those people whom Amarta had helped with her visions. If only the other side wasn't already so heavy.

Tadesh chittered.

"I agree," Olessio stage-whispered to Tadesh. "It's quite good! But she's not listening to me. Maybe you should tell her?"

Tadesh sniffed at the stew as Amarta stared distantly. Again she saw the scene: no monks in white, the sand all ground into dirt.

"It shouldn't be so easy to fool people," she said quietly.

Olessio's smile fled. "It is. All too easy. Where's that Rochi deck? I'll show you a trick I learned in Erakat that will leave you believing I can read your mind."

"No," she answered more sharply than she'd intended. Olessio ducked his head, and guilt pricked at Amarta. As she was struggling to say something kind to soften it, Olessio bounded to his feet.

"The kitchen's putting out another stew about now," he said with just a bit too much levity. "Bay leaf. Cardamom!"

He waggled his eyebrows. "Besides, Tadesh needs a walk. Back in a bit."

At a sound, Tadesh leapt onto his shoulder from the table, and Olessio waved at them both, then left.

Tayre watched him go, took off his jacket, then sat in the chair, clearing a portion of the table. From a small bag he unpacked a familiar tin and a green-handled knife, one of many. He opened the tin and took out a sewing needle and thread.

"Are you angry at me?" Amarta asked, very softly. "At what I did?"

Tayre laid the jacket across his lap, taking the needle and thread to one of the many small pockets in the lining.

Moments passed. Even knowing that his silences were intentional, she discovered, didn't make them any easier to take.

Well, then—she'd look to an answer from the future: what would he say, when he finally spoke?

What does our contract say?

"Why would I be angry?" he asked.

She blinked at this unexpected reply.

"Because I…"

She recalled how it had felt to stand on the dais before hundreds and say her name. It had felt very, very good.

But the cost…

"Because I showed myself. Gave my name. I made them believe."

You did, and most convincingly.

"And? So?" he asked mildly, his eyes on his stitching.

Amarta frowned. Again, not the answer she had foreseen.

"And so," she said slowly, bemusedly, "won't it be harder now, to disguise ourselves, with all those who have seen me and who know what I can do?"

Far harder. You decide our course, Amarta. I've said that before.

But what he said was, "Why would I be angry?"

She opened her mouth, closed it again, as he meticulously knotted the thread and then cut it with the knife.

"Haven't I made your work harder?" she asked.

What is my work?

He looked up at her. "Do I seem angry?"

"Stop that," she snapped.

"Stop what?" he asked.

Her head swam at the gulf between what she foresaw and what was coming out of his mouth.

"You intend to say one thing, then you say something else. No one else does this." Until Tayre had come into her life, she had not even known it was possible.

He put his jacket down in his lap and leaned forward, his gaze on hers.

"I'll stop, Seer, if you will. None are so blind as those who already know what they will see. Listen to what I actually say, and not what I might."

She drew a ragged breath, upset and unsettled.

"You didn't answer my question," she insisted.

"Didn't I?"

Why couldn't he be just a little like the many who had called to her at the Tree of Revelation, who had offered her anything, hungry and hopeful for just a moment of her attention? He never looked at her that way.

And yet, those people—what had she given them, really? Thinking back on it, she realized that the few she had given visions to were the easy ones, that she had avoided the harder questions. But people didn't want the complicated answers of what was possible. They wanted…

Unambiguous answers. That's why so many people went

to the Tree of Revelation. It mattered far less if the answers were right than if they were clear.

And was that really such a terrible thing? As she had told Olessio, her answers never made people happy. Maybe it was better to give simple answers that let people get back to their lives, rather than give them reasons to live in hope for a future that might never be.

She had shown all those watching that the monks' predictions were false. Would they rebuild, someday? Tie a new chain to a new branch? Restring the pendulum? Offer simple answers again?

Hundreds of years in the forming, and Amarta had taken them down in minutes. She drew a breath. "Did I destroy the Monks of the Revelation?"

"Probably."

His answer landed like a blow.

"I didn't mean to," she said, feeling small.

"No," Tayre said gently. "I don't think you did."

She exhaled her relief that he understood.

"Tell me," he asked, "does your lack of intention to cause harm change the outcome?"

Soberly, she considered the question. Was she really so innocent?

"I wanted to prove them wrong," she admitted. "I wanted to break them."

"You succeeded." He opened a hand, fingers spread. "Thus, you learn."

At what cost? "But no one died, surely."

His dark eyes seemed to burn into hers. "Does that seem likely to you?"

She looked away. "You don't know. You can't know."

"Why ask me, then? Answer your own question."

"I don't foresee the past," she said shortly. "You know that."

He shrugged. "Then look for a future in which you go back to the Xanmelkie Valley to find out."

Either no one had died—which was surely possible, wasn't it?—or some did, and she was the cause. What good did it do now, to know either one?

She shook her head. "It doesn't matter."

"Or," he said, "I could go back and look around for you, then return and tell you what I saw."

Her breath quickened, hers shoulders tightening at the very thought of him leaving, even for only a few days.

The more she thought about it, the more certain she was that she had seen a flash of a white-clad figure moving through the crowd in that last glimpse of chaos. At least one. It had all been so fast. She couldn't be sure. A touch of white, anyway. The monks would be fine.

In any case, first she had to understand what she was. Only then could she understand what she had done.

"The past is over," she said decisively. "We must go forward."

Tayre inclined his head. Acceptance, if not agreement.

She waited for him to say something, anything.

"But where is forward?" she asked at last. "Where do we go next?"

Tayre repacked the needle and thread into the tin, slid the knife into its sheath, and put both into the small bag from which he had taken them.

Silence and more silence.

Despite having resolved not to, Amarta peered into the next moment, and the next, where still he said nothing. In both the now and the possible some-when, he was silent, making her memory of what he had almost said even louder:

You decide our course, Amarta.

❧

To the patterned knock at the door, Tayre let Olessio inside. Tadesh bounded off the smaller man's shoulder, ran across the room, and jumped into Amarta's lap.

Amarta laughed in surprise, running her hand along Tadesh's striped head, down the spotted back and long tail. Black nose quivering, Tadesh looked up at Amarta with large gold eyes. Even if Olessio had somehow instructed Tadesh to do this, Amarta took comfort in Tadesh's soft pelt, musky scent, and the contented thrum in the creature's chest.

Memories intruded. *Our mother...will she live?* So many in the crowd had only wanted to find or save those that they loved.

A jumble of Dirina-and-Pas-flavored future flashes began to thicken around Amarta like flies. She brushed them away.

Olessio set a large carafe of red wine on the table.

"If you won't eat, my dear..." With a determined smile, he poured two mugs, pushed one toward her. "Drink."

Amarta took a sip, then another and another. Something inside unwound just a little.

"Is it all tricks, then?" she asked, the wine raising the bitterness she felt to the surface. "Am I a fool to search for those who are like me?"

Olessio looked at Tayre. Then, when it became clear that Tayre wasn't going to answer, he sat.

"Since you're asking me," he said to Amarta, leaning back in his chair. "It's the dance of life, is it not? If you must know a thing, then you must. And if you must," He gave Amarta an unusually sober look, "then open every door in service of that need." He took a mouthful of wine, filling his cheeks, then pressed them flat and swallowed. "Now, me, I prefer to leave all the doors safely locked and barred on both sides. Never know what might be following. But then, I'm Vagras, so..." He shrugged, let out a long belch, and grinned wide.

"I can't be the only one," Amarta said, "There must be others who are true seers, even if they seem different. What do you know of any other such…doors?"

Olessio picked his teeth with a fingernail, looking thoughtful. "The Handless of Vilaros?" he asked. "They say it's stunning, what those people do with fire, though the man who told me about it didn't seem very satisfied with his answer."

"They never are," Amarta muttered.

"I have it on good authority that it's trickery," Tayre replied, "designed to funnel the skeptical to the university for study."

"Oh really?" Olessio raised his eyebrows. "That's clever. What about the Saripechi Wall?"

Tayre tilted his head. "I watched for three days. Inventive, the fish falls, but not predictive."

"Delicious, though," Olessio said, smacking his lips. "Fine chefs, the Saripechi. The Island Road?"

"Aristo wagers. Nothing more," Tayre replied. "No one even pretends prediction."

"Wagers? On what?" Amarta asked.

"The order in which the Islands will assemble," Tayre said.

"An astonishing sight, that," Olessio said wistfully. "They say the islands come from all over the world, link up, then days later, break apart for who-knows-how-many years. If you ever get to see them form, count yourself lucky."

"They make a road?" Amarta asked, bemused.

"A temporary peninsula, really," Tayre answered. "Anchored at the tip of the Spine of the World's northernmost island, Turia. It's said to be a place of fast-fertility, with plants and animals that reproduce only there and then."

Olessio downed the rest of his cup, then refilled it along

with Amarta's. "And the Island Pearls. Fortunes made and lost on those. I wonder what they are."

"Some sort of eggs, maybe," Tayre said.

"The islands are alive?" Amarta asked, bemused.

"Why, yes, of course," Olessio said. "Isn't everything?"

Amarta gave him a look of mild rebuke. "You know what I mean. Are they mage-made, then?"

"Mage-made? No, indeed!" Olessio jumped to his feet. "Pah! The world is full of astonishing things. Exotic lands, devastating loves—" At the center of the room, he whirled and caught Amarta's gaze in his own wide-eyes. Then he stretched his hand toward her in a sort of supplication and clear invitation. So compelling was his smile and gesture that she found she'd given him her hand without even thinking.

He drew her to her feet, took both her hands, and began to spin the two of them in place. He spoke with his story-voice, but also something more. It was almost a song.

"My dearest Amarta, I've seen mountaintops sketch the gods' voices in the sky. Snakes of bright light across the cold nights of Chaemendi. Did you know that at the bottom of the Mundaran sea are schools of iridescent fish? They dance, Amarta! They dance. Just as you and I are dancing. All life is magic, mages an entirely unnecessary accessory. Inhale!"

With that, he did, audibly. Unable to do anything else, Amarta took a breath as well.

"Now exhale!"

Amarta laughed with her breath.

Olessio raised an arm, twirled Amarta delicately under it, then again and into her seat. He gave her a final flourishing bow, and rejoined them at the table.

Amarta felt warm. From the spinning, from the wine, from Olessio's smile. He moved so differently than Tayre did. Where Tayre was all coiled power and edges, Olessio was sweet and bright, like a hummingbird.

She realized to her surprise that in this moment she could almost be happy, if she ignored the images still crowding her mind from the disaster at the Tree.

"The Heart of Seuan?" Olessio asked Tayre, continuing the conversation.

"The what?" Amarta asked.

"The Seuans call their leader the Heart," Tayre explained. "He is supposed to be able to protect them from storms and earthquakes by predicting them before they happen."

She sat straighter, attentive. "He predicts weather?"

"And those wretched insects that eat everything," Olessio said. "The Eufal…something."

"The Eufalmo," Tayre said.

"The what?" asked Amarta.

"You've got one," Olessio said.

"What?"

"Well, part of one, anyway. Where's that green scoop you sometimes eat with?"

Amarta went to her pack and struggled for a moment with the knot at the flap which had again become snarled. She dug out the shell Tayre had bought for her at the Accord Festival and handed it to Olessio.

He turned it over in his fingers, rubbing a thumb against the brilliant dark green, then the paler, concave side.

"It's not a seashell?" she asked.

Olessio shook his head. "A Eufalmo back. In all my travels, I've seen some truly spectacular beetles but…" He held up the shell, turning it so that it glinted against the light through the window, like a dark forest in bright sun. "Nothing like this. A small one, too, from what I've been told."

"Few know for certain," Tayre said. "Of those who witness the Eufalmo, few return to say more."

Amarta's mind was farther back in the conversation. "This leader. Are his predictions true?"

Tayre gave a slow shrug. "The city-state of Seuan survives rains, floods, earthquakes, and the Eufalmo swarms. They're doing something right. I doubt it's that, though."

Olessio added wistfully: "I had Seuan qualan once."

"Just once?" Tayre asked him.

Olessio sighed. "A gift. Expensive beyond my means." To Amarta's questioning look, he said, "Seuan exports the finest tinctures, medicina, and intoxicants in the world, qualan among them."

She considered. A breath of her future tasted of salt air.

"Where is Seuan?"

"Hoi! Just the question I've been waiting for." Olessio took Tayre's plate, which held a half-eaten circle of flatbread. With a fast, apologetic smile at the other man, he crumbled the bread, and began to trace on the plate. "Isdren port, here in Dulu. Nelar ocean there. Not to scale, mind. These dots? The island chain, called the Spine of the World." He glanced at Amarta with amusement. "Unlike the Island road, these ones don't move." He put the bread at the edge of the plate. "This is the start of the continent of Seute Enta. Seuan is north. Off the plate entirely, I think. Never been. And this —" He poked a finger into the small bit of plate—ocean— between the southern coast of the flatbread that was Seute Enta, and the northernmost Spine island. "This is where the Island Road is said to be forming up, right now. If we could afford to cross the ocean on a month's notice, now would be the time."

"Dakalet gave me a generous letter of credit," Amarta told him.

Olessio's eyes lit. "Did he? Well, well. We could go." His eyebrows waggled. "See the Island Road form up. A once-in-a-lifetime chance. From there, go north so you can have a look at this Heart fellow. Hmm? What do you say?"

Amarta didn't look at Tayre. She knew what the contract said.

She resolved to do as Olessio wanted, then felt forward into the fog of futures. Nearly level with clouds, they looked out across vast ocean. Dots of vibrant green were spread across the glittering blue.

Another flash: Scent of ocean, exotic flowers, strange spices. The strange chirruping of crickets.

And, finally: I've always wanted to see this.

"Yes," she answered. "I say yes."

Olessio smiled wide, his eyes sparkling.

She would do it, she decided. She would open the doors. Every one of them.

Chapter Eight

THE BABY CRAWLED DETERMINEDLY across the floor to the other side of the room. She took two red amardide blocks and, grinning, began to bang them together.

"You could tell them, your grace," Sachare said to Cern.

"You too, eh?" Cern replied softly, drawing herself up in the bed to watch her child move around on carpets of red and black geometric designs.

Every time Cern went to the ministerial council, the book of names crouched on a side table. A huge thing it was, bound in fine black leather, the royal crest in gold and silver, and thick with rubies.

The closed tomb sat upright in a polished amardide stand, facing her seat. The stand and book were in different places in the room, on different side tables, but always facing her. One time it was left open on its stand, as if some minister had needed to consult the history of the empire by Anandynar lineage, and forgotten to close it before the meeting.

The hints were not subtle.

The book itself was large enough that if Cern had had

twins instead, they could each have their own page to sleep on.

She looked back down at the singleton she had given birth to, who was trying to fit an amardide block into her mouth. Sachare dropped down and offered the child a wooden spoon to chew instead, which she took greedily and began to gum wetly.

"You could tell me," Sachare said. "Given that I am regent."

A dry tone, bordering on sincere, if mild, offense. Cern gave Sachare a moment's examination, wondering if the other woman was entirely happy about the appointment of regent or was feeling its weight. The latter, she suspected, from how sober Sachare had been in the months since Cern's proclamation.

Cern nodded, then drew herself as upright in bed as she could.

"Listen well, my regent," she said, using her best monarchical voice, "as I name your charge and the heir to the Arunkel throne."

In a blink, Sachare went from crouching down with the child, to standing rod straight, her eyes wide and mouth agape.

An entirely satisfying reaction. Good to know that even Sachare could be snapped to attention by Cern's training, even from bed.

The formal words rolled off Cern's tongue easily enough. That lifetime of training.

"I am," she said, "now and forever, Cern esse Arunkel, rightful and righteous Anandynar monarch of the Arunkel Empire. The heir on whom my eyes now light, this one, shall be named, and named in this moment, by my breath as law. The child's name is Estarna etau Restarn esse Arunkel."

Sachare opened her mouth, closed it again.

Estarna was the feminine version of Restarn. Not only had Cern named the girl after Cern's own father, but had laid out the child's title to refer to him instead of the child's biological father.

Not entirely unlike the actions of her great grandmother, Niala esse Arunkel, who passed over her own children in royal succession, instead bestowing the monarchy on Cern's father.

Curious how such things repeated.

Cern regretted the need to link her child so tightly to her own father, but it must be done. It would remind people that Cern hadn't fallen onto the throne by some happy accident of gravity, that she was the daughter of a great king, bred and raised to rule.

Her reign might be young, and the ministers pleased to remind her of that frequently, but it was no lucky breeze that had put a crown on her head.

"Do you approve, Sacha?" she asked.

"It is well done, your grace," Sacha said, with a slow, growing smile. She looked at Cern, then at Estarna, who she bent down to lift off the floor and into her arms. The child was still clutching the long wooden spoon. "Estarna," Sachare murmured into the child's ear. "We shall call you Esta, those of us who have been made regent, and regularly change your diapers." She turned to Cern. "When will you tell the others?"

"When the moment is right."

Cern took up the letter at her bedside table, and mused on her father's words again. Undated, but she knew the very day to which he referred, could even recall the weather. Most of all, how it had felt to have Pohut on one side of her, and Innel on the other. Handsome. Attentive. She had felt so alive. So mature.

Fates, but she had been so young.

You delay. You invite both the mutts to dine, to stroll, to chatter, making a performance of your bestowed favors. For shame, girl. Pick one, and let the other go. Or choose a House boy. Tokerae is weak of will, but has Etallan, and might yet mature. Fadrel is Helata to the core and would make a better Eparch than Consort, but at least he has Helata behind him. Mulack and Sutarnan? Shallow, vain creatures, more intrigued by the spectacle than the work.

But you must choose one of them and soon. You have no siblings. We must get you with child to secure our legacy and quickly. Emulate Niala, girl. Have many. Don't make my mistake.

A mistake. The implication that Cern was the mistake was hard to avoid.

Pick one of them, damn it, before I pick one for you.

She slid the letter aside, the last line echoing in her head.

She sighed. "Sacha, issue personal invitations. Every Cohort boy. Anyone else remotely suitable. Schedule them to meet with me. Separately, of course."

"All at once might be…untidy. I understand."

Humor from Sachare? That would be encouraging. Cern examined her chamberlain as Sachare bounced Estarna in her arms, her expression innocent as dawn.

Humor, then.

"Just one at a time, Sacha," Cern said, to see how far she could press before the other woman cracked.

Sachare turned away slightly, to hide her amusement.

"Who shall we start with, your grace?"

There was no choice, not really. "Mulack dele Murice. He did want to be first."

How to gain his support without marrying him? That would be the trick.

"He always does," Sacha said, now smiling humorlessly. "And next after him?"

Regardless of who Cern eventually chose as her new Consort, she must do careful work to set the stage. The balance must be just right among the rest so that no one felt slighted. It would take skill to keep each of them hoping without committing herself.

She sighed. "It must be House Etallan. I must somehow keep the conversation off marriage."

"Your father never married."

"And my Great Grandmother churned through consorts as if they were seasonal cloaks. Niala the Conqueror, after all," Cern gave a wry smile at the double meaning. "But it is not an option for me to forgo that bond. Not now."

Cern eyed the lockbox, wondering if her father had left anything in there about Cern's own mother. Not even a consort. More a broodmare and barely present in Cern's earliest memories. The old pain still ached. She pushed it away.

What, she wondered, would the histories call her? Cern pushed that thought aside, too, and held out her arms for Estarna, whom Sachare delivered. Cern held the child, rocking and nuzzling her close.

"If anything should ever separate us, Sacha," Cern whispered, "will you make sure that she knows about me?"

Sachare's mouth opened as if to object. She closed it again.

"Estarna will know her mother, Your Grace. My word on it."

C ern returned at last to her office. She was heartened by the orderly and tidy state of the desk. A few piles here and there, but nothing as overwhelming as she had been expecting.

Her seneschal bowed. "I am still attempting to sort out what we took from…" The slightest pause as he clearly sought just the right term. "The former Consort's papers."

"Only what is most pressing," she said, seating herself at the desk in a heavy wooden chair that had been a gift of House Nital, from her father's youth, the carved back inlaid with the emblem of the monarchy. Down the heavy legs were the sigils of the Great Eight Houses.

Symbolic. But what wasn't?

In the corner of the room, Sachare set Estarna on a blanket, and opened for her a box of small toys.

She reached for the first pile. "Let us address the most crucial, seneschal, and get it done."

"Yes, Your Majesty," he said gravely.

At this, her attention came back to him. She followed his unhappy gaze to the wall.

Not a wall. A wall of boxes, stacked one atop the other, nearly to the ceiling.

"They can't all be…" she trailed off.

"Urgent? Ah. Yes. I'm afraid so, Your Majesty."

"What was Innel doing?" she found herself asking aloud in an annoyed tone, then cursed inwardly, having broken her resolve never to say his name again.

"That I cannot say, Your Majesty, but there are an equal number of boxes in his office, full of papers already resolved. Correspondences, Accounts and Petitions responses, and more. But given the source…"

They would all have to be checked again.

She had been abed far, far too long. Letting out a slow stream of air, she considered.

"We will need help."

"Wise words, Your Majesty."

"Who do you trust to help us with this, Natun?"

At his name, the seneschal's normally composed expression flickered.

"Trust is in rather short supply these days, Your Majesty," he whispered.

"So it is."

She thought of the Cohort, some now eparchs and eparch-heirs, others—like Cern—having children and building a legacy. The whole point of the Cohort—of all Cohorts—was to strengthen the bond between the monarchy and the Houses. To provide the heir to the throne with companions whom she knew well.

And she knew them, all right. Well enough not to trust a single one. From guards to royals, everyone had an agenda that might well be counter to her own.

"And yet," she said, responding to her thoughts, "we must have help. Find people you can—if not trust—at least rely on."

"Yes, Your Majesty."

She snorted in soft frustration. There was nothing for it but to go forward.

"Let's begin."

～

"Does this please you?" Mulack asked softly from between her thighs.

It didn't, but she could not say that; politics was a powerful force, even in bed. Especially in bed.

The truth was that Mulack had always been somewhat clumsy. Cern knew that he harbored the fond belief that he was expert at such things, because he had been saying so in the Cohort for quite some years.

"Very much," she muttered, apparently convincingly, because he resumed for a few moments with more enthusiasm than skill, before—at last—drawing himself up to lie alongside her.

She forced a smile. The man didn't smell or act anything like Innel. She remembered Innel's eyes and how they would narrow slightly, calculatingly, just before he smiled. It had touched her, then, how hard he was willing to work to please her.

And he had.

Now her thoughts were traitors, too. She pushed them away.

"Does something trouble you, Your Grace?"

"The Houses," she said, ignoring this more familiar address. "They push, they plead. They demand."

Would he hear the not-so-subtle warning in her word and tone?

"Let me make those problems go away for you," he said.

She propped herself up on her elbow and gestured for him to continue. She knew exactly what Mulack was implying, what he was now clearly working himself up to say, but it was oddly satisfying to pretend that she did not.

The work of ruling is endless, daughter. Take your pleasure where you can.

Mulack propped himself up on an elbow, mirroring her, and put on a smile that she knew he thought was convincing.

"Marry me, Your Majesty. I will bring the power of House Murice to your feet, and the fuss from the other Houses will be ended."

"I doubt Etallan, Helata, Kincel—and the rest of the Eight— would be very satisfied with that. You think you can take them all?"

"Absolutely."

Ah, Mulack and his confidence. "Mmm," she said, with a tone both thoughtful and noncommittal. She lay back to stare at the ceiling.

Innel would have been two steps ahead of Mulack in this conversation, his confidence riding on top of a well-thought-out plan.

But he was dead, and she would not think his name again. Hanged in Execution Square. Everyone had seen it.

Her mind went readily to the other truth, that at the last she had found that she could not order the death of her child's father, that she could only order that the fates kill him instead.

Sachare, get him away. Alive. Tell him never to come back.

Mulack turned onto his stomach, propped up on his forearms, looking downward. He frowned.

Was he really examining the fabric of his pillow? He was. Probably assessing the dye.

Cern could too easily imagine Mulack as her Consort, facing a lifetime of critical review of palace textiles. Could she bear it, for empire and blood?

She gritted her teeth, and rolled out of the bed on the other side, putting on a robe, then opening the door to the attached room, where Sachare and Estarna were playing.

"Bath," she said shortly to them, then turned back to Mulack. Thankfully, this clue he took, and he was rolling out of the bed on the other side to dress.

"May I visit again, tonight, Your Grace?" he asked with a hopeful smile.

A most unappealing thought. But then, when had any of this been to do with her appetite?

"What a fine pleasure that would be," she replied, hoping the salting of regret in her tone was believable. "Alas, other issues require my urgent attention. But I will send for you again, when I have need of you. You may be certain of that."

He made a respectful reply, soft enough that she barely heard it, his expression fallen, nearly wounded.

A new strategy, this, for him to pretend to feel rejected.

She turned away to hide her amusement. The door closed as he left.

❧

"I t has been too long, Your Majesty," said Tokerae with an accusatory whine. "This is quite good."

To Cern, the surprise in his tone seemed genuine, which is what made it insulting. A twenty-year Arapur-Selsane brew, the best year in a decade. It was better than good.

Tokerae's small cup was silver, Cern's was gold, and both were rimmed with a rare black metal that sparkled in the light. Etallan's work, naturally, given to a young Grandmother Queen after one of her triumphant conquests.

Symbols were so important.

"I regret," Cern replied gently, "that my various obligations have kept me from your unparalleled company for too long, Tok."

She had changed her mind about the politics; it was a careful calculation, to put Etallan not second, not even third, but fourth in the list of Houses represented in her meetings. She had done it all very quietly, but Cern was counting on Tokerae to know.

He gave her a respectful, Cohort-style smirk. Good: he knew.

"You look marvelous, Your Grace. So good that I might credit a particular rumor."

She blinked. "Which one?"

His eyes dropped, slowly, pointedly, to her abdomen.

"Ah, that one." She was not yet showing, but she had made sure that the rumor was.

His gaze now met hers. "Is it true?"

Mulack had been the first meeting. Fadrel, eparch-heir of Helata, had been polite, gracious, and unassuming, which

Cern took as a hopeful sign that Helata was not going to soon cause her trouble. Next had been Putar, who had been downright mute the entire evening, apparently at a complete loss as to why he was having dinner with the queen.

"Not your business, Eparch-heir."

"I suppose not. Not yet, anyway. I'm certain Mulack offered you all the clothes you could ever wear, and Fadrel the finest ships Helata can build. No small thing, that. But I can't imagine what our Cohort brother Putar would offer you that you would want."

"A rock," Cern lied with a royal smile. "Simple basalt. Not even polished. Why, Tokerae, do you have something better to offer me?"

Tokerae snorted, and leaned his tall frame back in his chair. "House Etallan."

"The very house, Tokerae? Your mother eparch and many relatives might object."

"You do know what I mean."

"Do I? You are not yet eparch to make such offers."

His smile vanished suddenly. "I will be. You may rely on it."

She inclined her head. Acceptance of his words.

Both of them took another sip, followed by another tight silence.

"Cern" he said, breaking it at last, "we've known each other since we were children. Allow me to speak plainly."

She gestured for him to continue.

"He was a mistake. We all knew it. But all this… turbulence…" he circled a hand in the air, as if to include the drinks, this dining room, and perhaps the entire empire, down to Garaya, "…could be easily calmed. Marry a strong House. The strongest. Mine. Wed me, and do it soon."

And Cern had thought Mulack arrogant. Tokerae is no longer weak of will, father.

With effort, she set aside her annoyance, as was surely her duty, and considered his words. Such a union would put an end to one set of tensions, certainly, but give rise to a whole new set.

"I was married once," she said. "It didn't suit me."

"Truly, you are not to blame for that, your grace."

"Oh," she said dryly, "Thank you."

"What I mean is this: he was good to look on, and charming, yes. But he wasn't one of us. Neither of the mutts were. Commoners to their core. Not worthy of you, Cern. Not worthy to sit at your feet."

She stifled a sigh. The mutts had been outside the influence of the Houses, an advantage Cern missed keenly.

It was tempting to ask Tokerae if he thought himself worthy to sit at her feet, then let him demonstrate. But he might, and that would be more trouble yet.

"I think best we not discuss that."

He dipped his head. "As you say. But Etallan is entirely unlike any other House. I know what useless trifles the others have sent, demanding shelf-space in your vast rooms." Cern suppressed more annoyance. Was her palace staff nothing but spies? "Now I would send you something that requires no storage, yet amply demonstrates why you should marry me."

Was that a threat? Cern could easily imagine a metal horse so large it could not fit through the palace doors.

"The Anandynar royals," she said, choosing her words, "have always had a special relationship with House Etallan, one based on mutual devotion to our great empire."

He nodded. "Just so. Speaking of which, I'd like to mention a small matter to do with Phaltos."

Cern stood. "Alas, Tokerae dele Etallan, I have a good amount of other business to attend to." *Because that's what you are: business.*

For a long moment Tokerae did not move. Then he

stood, but slowly. An old game: how slowly could one comply with a royal command and still be obeying?

So childish.

"My esteem to your eparch," Cern added softly, irked at his sluggishness, to remind him of his position. Or lack of it.

His eyes narrowed slightly, replaced by an uncertain expression, as if he were searching for something else to say. Cern looked past him and gave her guards a sharp nod. They opened the doors smartly, and not quietly.

Tokerae, seeming deflated, bowed and backed out.

C ern was not at all surprised to have her presence requested by the Ministerial Council first thing this morning.

She didn't hurry, but she did comply. Now she settled into her plush chair in the large, high-ceilinged Ministerial Council chamber with a look to check Sachare and Estarna and the Princess's full Guard in the corner, and she turned to the ministers.

"Yes?"

She was becoming taciturn, she realized, more than a little like her father had been. The familiar loathing warred with the new insights that his letters—and her being the monarch—were providing daily. Perhaps he was not quite the man she had thought him to be. Some of his letters were actually proving useful. This moment reminded her of one.

Listen to the ministers' silences. You will hear in them more than in the rush of words that follow, too often at stupefying length.

The ministers were all looking at the First Minister, who cleared his throat, his eyes flickering around the room.

"With so many things changing, Your Majesty," he said,

"in this time of great upheaval…of wind-blown waves. The sands beneath our feet are shifting. We are like hawks in the storm. You have courageously endured so much, and yet—"

"The point, Minister," she said.

He dipped his head, eyes on her.

"We wish to inquire as to the nature of your evening visitors, Your Majesty."

Let them speak. You can hang them later.

With a hand, Cern made a circle in the air. "Say what is on your minds, ministers, so that I may understand you well."

For a moment, no one spoke. "Mulack dele Murice," said the Minister of Justice. "Fadrel dele Helata. Putar de Kincel. Tokerae dele Etallan."

Three eparch-heirs and the assistant Minister of Justice, Putar, who was not present.

"I'm pleased that you're keeping a list," Cern replied dryly. "Saves me the trouble. Though it's hardly complete. But, so? These men are my Cohort. I've had them to meals and beds across the years and no secret about it. What is your concern?"

"Do you intend another child?" the First Minister blurted.

"I haven't decided," Cern lied coolly.

She was almost certainly pregnant, but only she and Sachare knew this, and Cern intended it to stay that way for as long as possible, because rumor was more potent than fact.

"Another child would be prudent, of course," said the First Minister carefully. "But it would be best for you to be wed before the conception, so that there is no question as to the lineage."

"My father took countless women to his bed," Cern said tightly. "Niala had lovers by the tens, and her children traced lineages to no fewer than five Great Houses. Yet you question me?"

The ministers exchanged looks. The First Minister turned a pleading look on the Minister of Justice, who took a breath.

"You are not the Grandmother Queen, Your Majesty," said the Minister of Justice, "And you are not your father, either. Not quite."

Not quite.

"With the Consort at your side," said the First Minister, apparently regaining his courage, "the Houses were held in check. No opportunity for them to step in."

"I'm aware," Cern said shortly. "And now, to raise any one of them above the rest would swirl a storm. It may be best that I take my great-grandmother's example, and make children from various sires to keep the Houses in line until I can—"

"That would be disastrous, Your Majesty," said the First Minister. "Absolutely disastrous. Let me explain."

He continued to speak, but Cern was not listening, swallowing her anger at being cut off mid-sentence. Her father's fury at lesser slights had been legendary. Niala had once had a man thrown from a window, for whispering to someone else while she was talking.

Perhaps they were testing her.

No, they were condescending to her.

In the early days, your every command will be questioned— in the mind, if not on the tongue. You'll be blamed, not for what you do, but by comparison to some imagined ideal. Show no weakness.

For the first time, it occurred to Cern to wonder whether a young Niala esse Arunkel had ever faced a similar moment. But of course she must have. And Cern's father, ascending the throne in the great shadow of his grandmother? He must have, too.

Her grandmother Niala had enjoyed many men, but only after expanding the empire's borders. Her father had similarly excelled before indulging in the ornate horizontal adventures for which he would later become so famous.

So, she must concede, the ministers were partially right: Cern had yet to prove herself. But, also, they were wrong: they didn't have Cern's education, intensive training, or knowledge of the Cohort.

Or her father's letters.

Cern stood from her chair and pitched her voice to crack like a whip.

"Silence."

The First Minister stopped mid-sentence.

"Ministers," she said, "I have heard you well. Also, I now realize that in order to give me your best service, you must know my intentions, so allow me to make them clear to you."

She took a step toward the door. The queensguards moved to open it, but she held them with a gesture as she turned back to face the ministers, silently counting to ten to sharpen their attention.

Then, gathering their gazes in her own, she said, "I will fuck who I like, have babies as I see fit, and if any of my Cohort-siblings object, they can tell me so with their head between my thighs."

A palpable, shocked silence filled the room. Her belly shuddered once in suppressed amusement, alongside the as-yet secret child, but she held tight to her sober expression.

"You are entirely correct, Ministers: I am not Niala and I am not my father. I am Cern esse Arunkel, and their blood— and that of a thousand years of Anandynar monarchs—flows through me. I have already survived both traitors and assassins. I know who moves against me." A blatant lie, but from their expressions they weren't sure, and that would do.

"Those who support me, I will remember. Those who oppose me, I will destroy."

For a moment, she thought she saw an uneasy flicker on the faces of some of the ministers.

She would remember.

~

"And when is the food?"

Tokerae's eparch-mother seemed at a loss at the mage's oddly accented greeting.

Tokerae understood her reaction, rather too well. He could not have imagined any person looking less like a mage than the man that stood before them.

Undul Etris Tay dua Mage was short and thickset, his thinning, pale hair unkempt and slightly matted, locks of it pointing in different directions. Across his shoulders were the somewhat stained robes of a mid-city accountant.

He was expensive.

"High One," his mother said, smiling. Then, to Tokerae's shock, she bowed. Tokerae had never seen her bow to anyone but the empire's monarch. "You wish food?"

The mage looked at her, mouth hanging open slightly. "In truth. Why else would I have said yes?"

The yes to which the mage referred was the expensive contract that Tokerae had made with him, one that was quite nearly one-sided.

On House Etallan's end, there would be a great deal of coin provided to the mage, along with whatever he might like.

On the mage's side, well. He would help if he could.

Tokerae's mother turned on him a glare so fast and hot that he felt it like a needle into his gut. He tried to serve back a look of innocent outrage at the implication that he had not offered the mage food, which of course he had, but his mother had already snapped a finger at his sister Ella, who stood at the door.

This meeting was, of necessity, family only.

Ella was clearly not pleased to be treated as a servant, but at their mother's repeated snapped fingers, Ella glowered and left to fulfill the silent command.

"A meal will be sent immediately, High One," his mother said. "I apologize for my thoughtless children, not offering you refreshments immediately."

"There was food," the mage said. "Some of much. It wasn't…" he scratched the back of his neck, examined his fingers, sniffed them. "Wasn't the expected. You are a Great House, yes? You are eparch, yes?" He gave Tokerae's mother a curious look.

"Yes, I am Eparch of House Etallan," his mother said slowly, clearly trying to extract meaning from the mage's odd words. She gave Tokerae another brief but less certain glance. "It is my pleasure and honor to host you, High One. What might best please you?"

What might best please you? Tokerae had not known his mother capable of that phrase.

The mage grunted indifferently. "Maybe I should go to Elupene. They're the food House, right?"

His mother looked to be swallowing a good many words right now, and her smile looked uncomfortable.

"We are the House of metal, Great High One," she said adamantly. "That means that we have the finest of ovens and stoves and brilliant cooks to use them. Elupene is known best for their animal feed. I doubt their offerings would please you."

"Why I came here," responded Undul Etris Tay. "First among the Eight, yes?"

His mother nodded decisively.

"So you have the best food."

"We do. We most assuredly do." She gestured urgently at Tokerae.

He knew what she wanted: find his sister Ella, make sure that food was coming, and that it was absolutely splendid.

Tokerae sighed. As he backed out the door, the mage went to the mantel and shook his mother's silver bells. Her expression tightened as she pretended not to mind.

Tokerae and his mother watched as Ella set a tray of dishes before Undul Etris Tay dua Mage, at the table where he sat, in the suite of rooms they set aside for him.

"Lamb shanks," Ella said in a slow, seductive tone. "Braised with sweet wine and apricots, and finished with the zest of orange and rare Yebsodid spices."

Ella lifted the lid of a wide bowl, wafting the scent toward the mage. His eyes fluttered.

Tokerae felt his own mouth water at the meat, the tang of citrus, ginger, cinnamon, and mace.

Good work, sister.

The mage's gaze was riveted to the steaming plate before him. Next Ella set down a glinting silver plate with a large white wedge atop which were three candied raspberries. "Aged yak cheese, from the mountains of Pelapa."

She now held a crystal carafe of dark wine. "And this, the best of the blue, from Arapur-Bruent."

The mage showed teeth. Perhaps it was even a smile. He reached forward, then frowned. "Where is the basin and towel?"

"The what and the what, High One?" Ella asked.

He held up his hands, wiggling fingers. "To clean. I eat

with these." He looked with annoyance at the knife and prong set on the table.

"Of course," Tokerae said, snatching up the knife and prong and signaling his sister with a look. Her eyes narrowed in return, but she left, returning in moments with a silver bowl of warm water, a small towel over her arm. She set them on the table, then poured the blue wine from the carafe into a small crystal goblet.

"Not that," said the mage with a flick of his hand. "Stinks."

Tokerae and Ella took the carafe and goblet from the table.

The mage washed his hands in the water, wiped his fingers on the towel, and reached into the bowl for a piece of lamb and took a huge bite. The drippings found his beard, bobbing there while he chewed and made lip-smacking, sucking sounds.

For long moments, Tokerae, carafe in hand, his mother, and his sister, watched the mage eat.

He looked up at them, wiping his beard on the back of a sleeve.

"And what? Why do you watch?" He flicked greasy fingers at them. "Go away."

They fled the room.

Outside in the hallway, their mother took an arm from each—the ones not holding carafe and goblet—and pressed them forward along the etched tin tiles, passing walls of glinting metal landscapes and portraits. She thrust them into an empty alcove.

"Make him happy, whatever it takes," she muttered. "You —" this to Ella. "Hire the best chef in the city. He'll soon tire of lamb. You—" this to Tokerae. "Stand ready at his door to obtain for him anything he desires."

Ella gave Tokerae a quick, meaningful look.

He looked back flatly. Yes, sister, I will ask.

Ella left at a brisk walk, downing her goblet of extraordinarily rare blue wine as she went. Clever of her to take the goblet, while Tokerae took the carafe, from which he could hardly sip.

"What have you to report about the traitor's woman?" his mother hissed at him, increasing her grip on his arm.

"I have a tencount of trackers on her trail, mother. When I find something worthy of your time, I'll tell you." Implying that they had reported back, which of course they had not. None of them. Damn it. "Does it matter though, now that the traitor is gone?"

"You fool. What if she's actually a seer? Think of it." She leaned closer, and Tokerae bent down to hear her whisper. "The mutt shouldn't have won at Otevan. Maybe this is how he did. Find her."

"I've been a little busy, mother, I—"

"All this time, and you know nothing?"

"South. She went south. In the company of three others."

"South! How helpful that is," she said caustically. "Or it would be if I didn't know that already. Who are the others?"

Stories differed. Tokerae opened his mouth to say that, then closed it again.

"You have a picture of her, at least?"

"Yes, mother."

A vague sketch from an innkeeper's year-old memory, but it was something.

His mother released his arm, and stood back, giving him a look that he felt like a weight.

"One thing right, then, my boy. Send it around with coin and an offer of more, when information—or better yet, the woman herself—is brought to us. Or do I have to do all your thinking for you?"

Tokerae had done that already, but no sense in saying so.

She was simply taking out her frustration with the mage on him, and he knew better than to argue.

Besides, he must bring up the other thing.

"Mother, listen," he said quietly. "I think it's time."

Her anger turned to intensity. She pinned with a stare. "No it is not," she breathed.

Though no one could be seen in either direction, up or down the hall, the two of them were whispering.

"We have all the pieces, at last. We can fit them together and take action. Delay, and she may regain ground." The *she* to which he referred need not be named—he meant the queen. "Mother, we are ready."

"I have waited a lifetime for the right time, boy, as did my father before me. Your half-wit enthusiasm is far from sufficient. No. We wait until it is a certainty, not a hope."

"But, mother—"

"I will not wager our House on your childish, glory-seeking urges."

He gritted his teeth. "Then tell me what is lacking, my eparch, and I will make it whole."

"Must I say it a third time? No. When we are ready, I will say so, not you."

She glared at him another moment, then turned and strode off down the long hallway.

He found himself staring after her, even when she was no longer there. Staring, and staring, and wondering what it would take for him to become eparch, a carafe of expensive wine dangling from his hand.

At last, he raised the carafe of deep blue liquid and took a long swallow.

Chapter Nine

INNEL'S SAILOR had begun to bring him a better quality of food. Chunks of cheese swam in the gruel. Sometimes even slices of sausage. Innel ate ravenously.

The sailor's special gifts—kanna, twunta, maybe even a touch of duca—were now a pile of powder, dried leaves, and stems, dumped on top of the porridge in his bowl.

Taba no longer came to visit. Innel felt the lack like a gaping wound, an unfillable hunger. Emptiness echoed through him.

And yet, meal by meal, Innel felt life begin to return to his limbs, if not his spirit.

One day the ship docked. Innel's sailor entered with jute, wordlessly tied Innel's unresisting hands, looped a catch around his neck, dropped a hood over his head, and led Innel from the cabin.

Innel could see, but only dimly through the dark weave. The sunlight through the fabric was bright enough that his eyes watered.

He realized with a sickening, horrified shock that they

were leading him off the ship. Seized with terror, he stopped on the deck.

His cabin, his sailor—even Taba, when she came—these were his. He knew them. Off the ship, what did he know?

"Where are we going?" he whispered.

"Hush, now," his sailor replied from close by. "Na, na—no questions. You'll be…" the man seemed unsure how to finish. "Got to be better than this life, ya?"

Then the sailor took his arm. Hesitating but compliant, Innel let himself be led down the ramp of the ship. Step by unsteady step, he felt a tearing loss that he could not name.

Once on land, men shouted, horns blared. A clock tower chimed.

A large city, then, the sensible part of his mind told him. The air warm and windy. They were, he concluded, in the port city of Kelerre.

Stairs led up from the docks. "Up, up," the sailor urged. Solid ground, yet Innel's feet trembled with each step.

They walked along a stone road, and Innel caught the sound of Taba's voice behind, brought on the breeze. He tried to turn toward her, but was held tight and pressed forward.

His breath and heart labored as he walked. He remembered when he could run around the garrison track. Another life.

Finally they entered a shaded area—a canopy to block the sun.

"Sera, good today, and good tomorrow, to you." A man's voice, a Perripin accent.

"Ichati. I have the usual for you, unloaded and ready to go." Taba, from Innel's side. At the sound of her voice, he felt his spirits soar.

"A pleasure to be with your trade, sera."

"One more thing," said Taba.

"For you, anything under the sun or moon, sera," said Ichati.

The sound of coins onto an open palm. An appreciative vocalization, then a curious one.

"You will take this one," Taba said, and Innel knew that she referred to him.

"How interesting, sera. Usually I pay you for such ones."

Another clinking of a coin.

"No questions," said Taba.

"In certainty. In certainty."

"This for him, daily. To keep him calm. I don't want him talking."

"I could take his tongue. Much simpler, sera, surely."

"No. Leave him intact. When he gets there, I want him to be able to say my name, and to beg and curse as he suffers and dies."

"What artistry you possess, sera."

"Feed him well."

"With that destination? A waste, surely?"

"Shall I take my coins back?"

"No, no, sera. Forgive. Ha. My weak Perripin humor."

"Keep it to your Perripin self."

"In certainty."

Another clink of a coin. "The destination," Taba said. "Not just any mine. It must be Correaesee."

A sharp inhale from Ichati. "Correaesee?" Then, placatingly: "As you say, sera. A longer journey, you understand? I have other stops to make before that one."

"He is in no rush."

Innel felt himself regarded.

"No, he does not seem to be."

Taba took him by the shoulders, and with surprising gentleness turned him to face her. At the sight of her dim outline through the hood's fabric, so many emotions crashed through Innel that he could barely breathe.

"I sentence you to die, brother," she said, very softly, "inside the earth that you offended by spilling upon it the blood of the finest man I will ever know. I pray that you will suffer a very, very long time before your last breath. Daily I will entreat the Fates to make it so."

He understood then, with full force, that she was sending him away from her. A wrenching ache went through him, and a wordless sound of pain came from his throat as she turned and left.

~

Innel felt heavy, his mind in a deep fog that suited the simple tasks put before him: Walk. Obey. Lift his hood only to eat and drink.

He was rope-tied—neck and wrists—to a chain—a long chain, of some fifty or more men similarly bound, silent but for their footfalls and breathing. When they stopped to eat, they chewed quickly, furtively, as if there might not be more.

They marched a wide road, past houses, farms, the voices of barter, children's laughter. The sun warmed Innel's head, the sea breeze snuck under the fabric of the hood. For a moment, he almost felt his brother walking at his side.

They slowed at another harbor, the air thick with the shouts of dock workers, the cries of gulls. Innel's hopes rose, like foolish birds, singing to him that maybe Taba had changed her mind and would take him back.

Up a ship's ramp, the line of men, then through dank corridors. Down below, into gloom. He was unlatched from the chain.

A room, black on black. A door slammed shut, a bolt dropped. Utter darkness.

Innel, still tied and hooded, stepped slowly backward to find a wall, then let himself down to sticky floorboards.

His thoughts were sluggish. For a moment he considered turning them to his confused feelings for Taba, then decided against it. Better to let the sludge of his mind untroubled.

He worked his tied hands halfheartedly, but the ropes did not yield easily, and he gave up the effort. Even the hood seemed too much work. He gave a long exhale.

"Greetings to you, ser." Innel started at the voice, only a few strides away. A lightly accented Arunkin. "May I have the pleasure of knowing who you are, you who have come to share my very small room?"

Flashes of opulent hallways, bedrooms, meals. A woman who meant everything to him, and a child who meant even more.

"I am no one," he said hoarsely.

"Well, No One," replied the voice with some amusement, "there is a bunk for you, to your right." A pause, to allow Innel to reply, which he did not. "If you wish my help in liberating you from your knots, I will provide. But first I must tell you that not long ago, when I gave such help in similar circumstances, the recipient attacked me as if I were his captor, rather to my detriment. If I release you, ser, may I rely on you to refrain from such impolite behavior?"

A good question. It seemed to him that he knew himself rather poorly. "What do you think, brother?" he whispered. "Can I be trusted?"

"What's that, ser? I didn't hear you."

You seem docile enough to me, brother.

"I believe I can agree to that," Innel answered, "in the event that you see fit to help me."

A moment passed in silence, and Innel found himself worrying that he had said the wrong thing.

All his life, Innel had trusted in his voice and what it could do, only to find—

His mind lurched toward, then veered from, his last conversation with Cern, in which everything that had come from his mouth had turned to shit.

The sound of fabric rustling brought Innel back. A gentle touch was laid upon his arm. It moved down to his hands, and the knots between the wrists. In moments Innel was free.

"Your hood I leave to you, ser." The man retreated to the other side of the small room.

Innel drew off the fabric bag that he had lived in for days and inhaled. Mold, brine, and a whiff of human excrement. None of it worse than his own stink, really. Just different.

"Thank you," Innel said. Then, before he could stop himself: "Where are you from? Arunkel, obviously, but I don't place your accent."

"I am from the Labari province, ser, east of a town called Rott, and a day from the oceanside."

"Truly? I know the place. Not far from where I was born and raised." Half-raised. Before the Cohort. "Who is your family? What is your name?"

A pause. "I am called Pava."

Innel was surprised. That was an animal name.

No, it was a slave name.

"You're Emendi?"

"I am, ser. In a manner of speaking. That is to say, I do not come from the continent of Emendi in the north sea, but was, rather, born in captivity and bred to the work of service. I have been branded a slave since I was a young child."

"But your language is excellent."

The man chuckled. "Kind of you to say so. I was well-educated so that I might provide a better return for my owner. Gifted with good looks, I was told, and clever. My breeders thought me worth the investment, so that they might sell me for a better price."

Innel realized that he had never heard so many words, so well spoken, from any of the slaves he had known in the palace.

"Where are you destined?" Innel asked.

"I do not know that, ser. Do you?"

Now that Innel's eyes were adjusting, a tiny crack in the ceiling offered a pinpoint of light. It was barely enough to see the shape of the blond-headed man.

Innel slowly raised himself up from the floor and drew himself onto the hard bunk to his right. It felt like a luxury.

"Not where you're going, no. For myself, I am enroute to the mines of Correaesee."

A surprised guttural sound. "You must be very important, ser, to warrant such a hard death."

Innel exhaled a bitter half-laugh.

"Not any more."

⁓

"We are special, you and I," Pava said, taking a bowl slid through a floor-slot in the door, "to have our own room. Many share by the tens. This bowl, says the gentleman outside, is for you." Pava tilted his head toward the bowl. "I smell intoxicants. You need not consume it. I will share mine with you."

Innel was surprised at this unexpected generosity. "No, it's all right. I'll eat it. I want it."

Pava nodded, and handed him the bowl. The two of them ate.

Innel finished his greasy porridge with the familiar taste of kanna and twunta, then licked the bowl clean. "Like a dog," he mouthed, wondering what his brother Pohut would say.

At least you have food, brother.

Innel nodded agreement.

In the dim light, across from him, Innel looked at Pava. His mind churned very slowly.

"Do you know how much you're worth, Pava?"

"I do not, ser."

"I do. I used to—" Purchase slaves? "—approve purchasing for…" He blinked. "For a wealthy villa. You would be just the sort of slave that they would have bought to serve the…" Who? "the Eparch-heir."

"What a great privilege that would be, ser."

To Innel's ears, Pava's warm words had the sound of a rote answer.

They returned their bowls to the floor, where the slot would be opened some time in the next hours, and they would need to push them out if they ever wanted more.

Innel's muddy thoughts turned to Taba.

"I'm going to Correaesee to die," he said.

"It would seem so," Pava answered softly.

Suddenly Innel found himself gripped with dread. Not of death. Of something more personal.

"I don't want to die nameless," Innel whispered. "The name I was born with is long gone." It had been stripped from him the moment he had been exiled. Or perhaps it had fled his body as he fell from the high cliffs, gagged and tied, plunging into the frigid Sennant River, washing away all that he had been.

"Pava, will you give me a name?"

"Me?" Pava said in surprise. "It's an honor to name another. I don't think I am of sufficient status to be able to bestow upon you—"

"Why do you speak to me as though I'm any more free than you are? Do I look free to you?"

Pava fell silent. Even through Innel's intoxicated, dampened state, the long pause that followed seemed weighted.

Perhaps he had said the wrong thing. Who was he to demand anything, let alone a name? He assembled some words, then dismissed them as inadequate. He did it again, mouth working, but failing to emit a single sound.

Long minutes passed. When Pava finally spoke, his tone was subtly different. Innel found himself hanging on every word, like a man dying of thirst being splashed in the face with water.

"Here is the thing of it, Arunkin man who calls himself No One," Pava said slowly. "You could be free again. You aren't branded. Your hair is dark. But my hair is pale and I bear the mark that says, no matter where I go, I will never be free."

Innel remembered the palace slaves. For the most part, they'd been very well-treated. They had plenty of food and soft places to sleep.

"Is it really as bad as all that?" he asked softly.

A soft chuckle. "Consider: I cannot walk freely in the sunlight. Outside of an owner's hands, I cannot travel without fear of capture, punishment, and death." Pava's tone was not bitter, but more like a man speaking his true thoughts after a lifetime of caution. Innel held his breath lest he miss a single word. "What you take as given, No One, is simply not permitted to me: to choose where I go, what I eat, who I lie with…" A pause. "Who shares my room."

He means you, brother.

Innel nodded. "But I never saw this hunger for more, that you speak of, in the faces of the Emendi who I passed daily, in the house where I grew up. Never even a hint of it."

"Of course not, No One. It is a beating or worse for us to reveal such thoughts. We learn young to seem as our masters imagine we are. You ask me, is it really so bad?" Pava was silent a moment. "If all people were similarly bound—you, me, the captain—all of us branded captives, never to walk free, it might simply seem a cruel world. But for you to complain about your fortune, Arunkin—your loves lost, your coins spent—and for me to be required to pretend every single moment that it does not matter to me that I can never have these things to lose them—that pretense governs every word I speak, for as long as I breathe, until I am freed by death."

Innel rethought various encounters with Emendi, who he had known were clever. How much more did they know than he had given them credit for?

"I understand, at least I think I do. Since I was a child, I've needed to choose my words carefully, though the cost was not so high as my life. Not until the last."

"Ah. Do you go to your death for poorly spoken words, No One?"

"Yes, and poorly chosen actions."

"At least you had the freedom to choose," Pava said gently. "Do you still wish me to name you, No One?"

Innel took a ragged breath. "I would count it a great favor, Pava."

Pava nodded, a dim shape with a pale head. A moment went by, then another.

"I name you Adra, which in the Emendi language of my ancestors means that which lives in shadow."

Innel swallowed a lump in his throat. "A fitting name. I will live—and die—in shadow. But with a name, and for that I thank you, Pava."

"You are most welcome, Adra."

"May I also…" Innel struggled with the awkward

thoughts and words. "May I also call you a friend?" How foolish the words sounded once he'd said them.

Pava made a thoughtful sound, and was silent a long moment. At last he spoke.

"I have to confess, Adra, that I am not sure that I know much about friendship, or how it is properly conducted."

"I'm not sure I do, either."

"Well, then." Innel heard the smile in Pava's voice. "Perhaps we shall both be better educated as we attempt the matter between us."

ays later the ship docked. Hooded, tied, and chained, Pava and Innel and other slaves stood together on the deck.

Through the fabric of the hood, Innel watched Ichati speak to a short woman, their conversation a hybrid of Perripin and Arunkin.

"All these, then," the short woman said, holding out her closed hand within which was doubtless a token coin, to seal the contract. "Our deal is made."

"Not that one, Jaseps." Ichati gestured to Innel, rather than reaching out to consummate the contract. "He goes with me."

Through the hood Innel saw Jaseps come close to inspect him.

"Did you not hear me? That one is—"

"I heard you, Ichati. I heard you."

"—not for sale."

"Everything is for sale," Jaseps said. She reached high to snatch off Innel's hood. He blinked in the sun, squinting. Jaseps wrapped a fist in the long tangle that was Innel's beard, turning his head one way and then the other.

"Do I speak to myself?" Ichati asked, waving his hands. "I said no. He is destined for the mines."

"The mines? A pretty one, under the hair and dirt. Cleaned up, I may have a use for him."

"Are your ears plugged, Jaseps? Have you become simple? I said—"

"Three na-sorins."

"What? I was paid that much to see him to his destination."

"Then you'll double your purse."

Ichati crossed his arms. "No. It is simply not possible."

"A cho-sorin for the filthy creature."

Ichati made a rasping laugh. "Got a taste for Arunkin flesh, Jaseps?"

"Not for me, Ichati. A cho-sorin and two na-sorins."

"To break my word, Jaseps…" Ichati's held his hands high. "What damage to my spirit! My honor, mortally wounded. Why, my ancestors—"

"Two cho-sorins, two na-sorins. A pair of pairs. How lucky. Your ancestors would be proud. My last offer."

Ichati held out his hand, palm up, to receive the token and seal the contract.

"I accept, Jaseps. Take them. Take them all."

∼

"Again?" Jaseps demanded. "What is it with you?" Innel was bent double, heaving onto the ground. Since leaving the ship, there had been no intoxicants to swaddle him from the hard edges and settle his stomach. He had not known how much good the drugs were doing until he was without them.

"A waste of food to feed you at all. Did that shit Ichati sell me a sick horse?"

Innel had been marching at the end of the line of chained men so that when he threw up he would foul only himself and the ground.

"Kanna," he managed. "Duca. Twunta."

"By the Dragon and Serpent, you're an addict? How did I miss this?" She gave a long hiss and stormed off.

But later that day, at a rest stop, she came back, every gesture angry.

"Open," she commanded, giving a sharp, light slap to the side of his jaw.

In case he didn't understand Perripin? More likely to make sure that he knew that she was in charge. He complied and she pushed into his mouth a wad of twunta. Dry and crumbly, it was nearly revolting enough to make his stomach rebel.

"No, no, boy—you swallow that. Here, you," she snapped at someone. "Water. Now."

With effort, Innel choked down what she'd given him, drinking eagerly from the cup pressed to his lips.

The twunta was nowhere near the quality of what he'd been given on Taba's ship. That night he woke to an annoying keening, surprised to find that it was he making the sound.

Asleep? Awake? He could not tell. Was the Perripin sky above, stars shining down like the points of hung daggers, real or imaginary?

He whimpered.

"Adra," came a soft voice.

"Pava?" he clutched at the other man's offered hand. "Pava."

Through what cleverness Pava had managed to place himself at the end of the chain line so that when night came, he would be close, he could not imagine, but he wept with joy.

Or was he still dreaming?

"Pava, Pava, the things I have done. Awful things. I must tell you. My brother, I—"

"Hush, now, Adra. Hush," Pava said firmly. "You frighten the others, children among them. Some of them are already very afraid. It is up to you and me—strong men of bearing and education—to keep the rest calm, for the journey ahead. Do you understand this?"

"Pava."

"Adra? Now what? Why all this weeping?"

Innel's heart was speeding, even as his eyes blurred. He took gulping breaths of the warm night, his head swimming as he lay back on the ground, Pava kneeling at his side.

"I don't know."

"Then quiet yourself. You walk now no longer in the direction of the horrors of Correaesee and certain death. How fortunate you are to walk with us. Do you understand this? Stop your weeping."

Innel looked up at the sharp points overhead. "Some things are worse than death."

A soft exhale from Pava. "We are friends, you and me, Adra, so I beg you to rely upon my judgment, and hear my advice. What you see and feel now, you must hold within. As slaves, silence is survival. You are a slave now, and you must learn this. And soon."

Pava's words made sense. Or did for a moment, then the meaning slid away. Innel grabbed at it, struggling to put his thoughts into a line, like the line of men and women and children who marched forward daily, but they scattered like flies.

He tried to put them into his pocket, one at a time, to keep them secure.

But he had no pockets. Gone, along with his fine clothes and fine blades and a life that he had thought he owned.

Gone, gone, gone.

He lay back again, utterly exhausted, and stared at the star-filled sky, praying that knife-points would fall true, and soon, and pierce his misery, bleed it into the ground.

"Sleep now, Adra. Sleep and dream of nothing."

The lines of slaves marched. No longer hooded, Innel attracted looks. He was one of only a handful of non-Emendi, with dark hair, with dark skin. With Pava by his side, no one troubled him.

At meal time, the slaves were let off the chain to eat, in sections, but their wrists remained bound in front, and tied around them, to the loops around their necks, like handles.

At a rest stop, one man brought his knotted wrists to his mouth. Moments later, he was grabbed by the neck-loop, slammed to the ground, and beaten nearly senseless by the slavers who watched them.

"Learn quickly," Pava whispered, as the man groaned in the dirt. Minutes went by before the others were given a nod of permission to tend to the man on the ground.

One day, standing in a meal line that led to a huge pot of mash, a dark-haired Arunkin man with one good eye, and one that looked as if it had been torn out some time ago, cut in front of Innel.

Rage filled him instantly. Innel lifted his bound hands, ready to kill, and knowing exactly how. Pava bumped against him.

"Gentle, now, Adra," Pava hissed. "Gentle. You know nothing of this man's pain."

"I don't care. He—"

"Let him be first, Adra. He lost a child at Carpuna. Grief drives him mad. As it does you."

"Carpuna?" Innel knew that name. Knew it from somewhere.

"They call it The Horror," Pava whispered. "The village's children were nailed up as signposts and left to die."

"Carpuna," Innel repeated, shaking his head.

The word was a key to a distant land, a past life. He didn't want to know, he realized, but too late—memory began to tear a ragged wound through him, through which he remembered.

The one-eyed man turned from the pot, a bowl of mash in his tied hands, his one eye hard on Innel. Their gazes caught.

Innel wiped tears from his eyes. What was wrong with him?

Seeing this, the one-eyed man handed his gruel to another, then stepped close. "You, too?" the one-eyed man's anger turned to anguish. "You lost someone at Carpuna, too? I can see it in your face. I watched my girl die, howling, nailed to a post."

"Carpuna," Innel said hoarsely, shaking his head and nodding at the same time.

The man lunged for Innel. All Innel's years of combat training told him what he should do, but he simply stood there, weeping.

Close in, the man pressed himself on Innel, chest to chest, an armless hug, his head by Innel's ear. "I know your pain, my friend. I know it."

Innel made a wordless sound into the other man's shoulder as the one-eyed man sobbed into his own.

In the next weeks, the chained lines of Emendi were broken apart, again and again, women and children and men from Innel's line sold off and dispatched in singles and sets to other destinations. Each time, Innel grabbed Pava's bound hands with his own, to keep him close. As if that would make any difference.

One day the lines were paused at a stream. Innel was grabbed by a handful of slavers, his bonds cut from his wrists, clothes stripped, and he was forcibly dunked in the water, scrubbed, and squeezed into clothes too small for him, his wrists retied behind his back.

"No!" He shouted, struggling, realizing that they were preparing to take from the line.

"Silence, Adra," Pava called softly from the line. "Remember how important."

"No!" Innel cried again. The slavers gripped him tight by arms and neck.

"Each breath means another," Pava called to him as his line was led forward. "Be well, my friend."

For a time—days, it seemed—panic and grief clouded Innel's mind.

Now he stood in a clean, expensive hallway in too-tight clothes, waiting. For what, he did not know. He looked around, dully curious, at ornately decorated walls of lavender and violet. Delicate brushstrokes of green vines stretched up and up, tangling together at the center of the arched ceiling, meeting in sprays of painted lilac flowers. Curved windows inset with amethysts let in triangles of bright Perripin sun.

The hallway was thick with stacks of boxes and barrels, bolts of plum-shaded fabric, and bottles of mauve wine. In a cage, a large fuchsia-colored bird moved about on a perch, agitated, fluffing its wings.

Liveried guards in violet and white stood by a double door, where Jaseps spoke urgently to her assistant.

She gave Innel a hard look. "You," she snapped. "No slouching. No keening. No throwing up. You understand me?"

Silence, Adra.

Innel nodded.

"You had best not be wasted coin," Jaseps hissed.

A head poked out from the room beyond, gesturing to Jaseps. She put on a wide smile and strode forward as the doors opened before her, her arms coming up in a gesture of greeting. Laughter punctuated her entrance.

The doors shut again, muting but not entirely silencing the discussion beyond. It sounded like a negotiation.

From the doorway, another gesture. "Bring him."

Innel was grabbed, pressed forward.

The room was large, ringed with high, wide windows, and crowded with brightly dressed Perripin people, lounging or sitting on multiple platforms. Above them all, three risers high, was a huge purple satin settee, trimmed in a black-and-white checked pattern, upon which reclined a very fat Perripin woman. She was draped in shimmering cloths of violet and mauve and strands of sparkling gemstones.

Jaseps put her arms wide again, bowed, then nodded at Innel, who was pressed further into the room.

"Domina, I have procured a very special gift for you. I hope he amuses. I selected him for you at great expense, with your refined tastes in mind. It is my honor to offer him to you."

"My tastes? What do you know of my tastes?" the Domina replied, rather loudly. "You've never been in my bed. Or have you?" She looked around the room and gave a conspiratorial smile. "I don't recall!"

Raucous laughter exploded from the crowd, along with

finger-snaps of appreciation. Jaseps joined in the amusement, though it was clearly forced. Louder mirth rippled through the room at Jaseps' expression.

The Domina regarded Innel with an undecided expression.

"Skinny," she said at last. "Feed him, wash him, shave him. We'll see if he's a gift or a curse."

Chapter Ten

AS THEY HIKED the roads and trails, Amarta realized that they were not retracing their path from the Xanmelkie valley and the Tree of Revelation, but taking an entirely different route through the mountains, west toward the Nelar Ocean.

Was Tayre trying to protect her from seeing the remains of the farmhouse? She glanced at him. He looked back.

No, she decided, that would be entirely unlike him. Nor would it be necessary; imagination easily served up to her what memory could not: a burnt-out husk of a house, torn bodies strewn across the ground.

Learn to live in the world. Just how much more world could she bear to learn to live in?

Again her mind returned to the hundreds from all across Perripur and beyond, who had witnessed her declaring herself at the Tree. They would return home, those people. Would they talk about what she had done there? What she looked like?

Of course they would, she realized.

As they made their way through the mountains and onto

the flat lands of Atudaka, they encountered no one. This, Amarta realized, was why Tayre had chosen this route.

From Atudaka they would cross into Ulawesan. From there into Dulu, and the port city of Isdren, where they would look for passage to the Spine of the World's northmost island, Turia, where the Island Road formed.

When they could, they walked at night, with moon and stars lighting the way. At daylight they sought isolated spots, camping in thick strands of trees, or in high brush near trickling streams, or deep in rock gullies. Anywhere that could not be seen from the road.

On this day they woke in an abandoned barn. Sunset came through gaping cracks between the boards, touching aglow ragged mounds of heaped hay, making them seem piles of spun gold.

Tayre squatted before Amarta where she sat, his tins and charcoal sticks laid across a cloth on the hard-packed dirt.

"More people, soon, and harder to avoid being seen. Let's make you seem less Arunkin." He took a sharpened stick of charcoal, and began to draw on her face.

Amarta wanted to draw away from his touch or to press forward—she couldn't decide. She tensed. If he noticed, he didn't say.

Overhead, Tadesh was exploring the loft. She peered over the edge at Olessio.

"Jump, darling. I'll catch you." Olessio held out his arms. Tadesh chittered back in clear disagreement with the plan, then made her slow way backward down the ladder.

As he watched, Olessio's lips pressed together, his eyebrows drawing down. He exhaled. "Pah. Let me do that, Guard-dog."

Tayre froze, mid-stroke, his gaze going distant. He slowly stood and turned to face Olessio. The smaller man's smile turned uncertain, his eyes widening. Amarta's stomach knotted.

After a moment, Tayre held out the charcoal stick to Olessio, who hesitantly took it. He knelt in front of Amarta, studied her, and began. His touch on her face was light, fast, and gentle.

Emotion caught in her throat. She swallowed it.

A bit later, he sat back. "There," he said, waving the stick. "No offense, I hope, mercenary? But isn't this better?"

Tayre nodded. "Yes, it is."

Olessio smudged one last line and stood, brushing his hands. "Farliosan have a knack for such things."

After that, Amarta's face became a collaboration between the two men. Each time they showed her their work in the mirror, she looked stranger to herself.

"Very fine, this day," Olessio said, turning and turning. "Very fine indeed."

Game trails had led them to a stretch of rocks and brush. Downslope was a wide lake, ringed in high rushes.

On the way, Tayre had pointed overhead to a circling hawk, drawn his sling—a simple flat of leather and cord—picked up a handful of rocks, and followed the hawk into the brush, trailed by a curious Tadesh.

The result was a rabbit cooking over a small fire. Birdsong and the sizzling of meat were the only sounds in this quiet day.

Olessio's voice cut the silence. He threw his arms high. "The gods say, if you seek bliss, dance under the sun and copulate under the moon."

"The gods say this, do they?" Tayre asked, turning the meat on the spit.

"They do." Olessio looked at Amarta. His smile faded, replaced by a look of concern. "We must search for joy. Wring it from every moment." He cupped the air, as if holding large fruit, and brought his hands to his face, making a sucking sound. "Like this!"

"There are no gods," Amarta said. Then, to Tayre: "Are there?"

Tayre shrugged. "You tell me, after you've laid hands on one. Until then, believe what pleases you."

"Pah." Olessio drew items out of the food pack and began to slice cheese against a rock. "They don't come near if you don't believe in them."

"Hardly a force to be reckoned with, then," Tayre said.

Amarta frowned. "Someone must know if gods exist."

"The mages might," Tayre said.

Olessio snorted derisively, offering Tayre a slice of cheese speared at the tip of a knife. Tayre shook his head. Olessio ate it himself off the blade, speaking around his chewing. "Ask a mage to get five answers."

"Ask a Farliosan to get ten," replied Tayre.

"There is that," allowed Olessio. "But my people's answers are practical." He gave Tayre a look. "Spoken to mages much, have you, Guard-dog?"

Tayre nodded. "A few. I believe in them, so they exist."

Olessio barked a laugh that seemed entirely unfeigned. He companionably clapped Tayre on the shoulder.

Amarta was shocked at this—she would never do such a thing. But somehow Olessio made it seem right, and Tayre didn't object.

"Anyone can make a god," Olessio said, crouching to offer Tadesh the remaining bit of cheese. Tadesh paused her grooming and stretched her long neck toward his hand and the morsel, but just short of meeting him. Olessio snorted, took a waddle forward to deliver it. She took it in her paws, sniffing cautiously, then downed it. "But only a mage can make a mage. Or so they say."

"Wait, anyone can make a god?" Amarta asked.

Olessio's head wobbled back and forth, as if considering nuances. "Maybe only a small god. A flea god, perhaps."

"I don't know that I believe you," Amarta told him.

"I don't know that I believe me either," Olessio said, waggling his eyebrows humorously. "But then, belief isn't necessarily the best test of truth, is it? The Perripin people say that when God broke Herself into a thousand thousand pieces—little godbits spreading across the world like dandelion seeds, or the wet of a sneeze—they sought fertile ground in the spirit of humankind, most failing to germinate."

Tayre removed the cooked rabbit from the spit, setting it on a rock to cool. "The Perripin people don't say it quite like that."

"No. They use too many words. My people use exactly the right number of words."

"And you pray to the gods?" Amarta asked.

"We are a practical people—we pray to everything. Let me make us something beautiful with that meat." He began to carve the cheese. "Here, Guard-dog—you're good with knives, aren't you?" A grin flew across Olessio's face. "Slice up this jicama, long and thin for us, would you?

"Are there gods here, too?" Amarta asked.

Olessio paused. "That distant hill—" he gestured with his knife toward the upside of the rise. "Something used to live there. Gone now." He took a baked yam and began to peel the darkened skin.

"How do you know that?" Amarta asked.

Olessio's shoulders twitched in a shrug. "In the days before the Rift was made, my people saved a godling from near-certain death. In gratitude, the half-god gave the

Farliosan the gift of knowing such things. It's a small thing." He sliced the yam into circles, took a nibble. "Needs salt."

Tayre tossed him a tiny sack. Olessio caught it deftly from the air.

Amarta found herself oddly annoyed. "Your people tell a lot of stories. That doesn't make them true."

"Well said! Amarta, might I impose? Pull off some strands from this ginger? I'll sing you a Farliosan work-song my mother taught me." Olessio began to trill a fast, light tune. Despite the words being strange, Amarta found that the song caught her mind as she drew pungent threads of ginger, laying them in a row.

When Olessio stopped, the song still wound through her mind. He caught her disappointed expression.

"We like our work songs short, and our play songs long. But I'll sing it again." As he did, he stripped pieces of rabbit, laying them across each other, then wove the ginger through the yam at the center. Whatever tiny bits did not fit his plan, he tossed to Tadesh, who stood on her hind legs, catching each one.

"Oh," Amarta breathed as his designs became clear. They were like woven mats from the Accord festival. "That's lovely."

"Thank you."

"It seems a lot of trouble, though."

"Sometimes it is not enough to simply eat."

"You've never been truly hungry, then," she said.

Olessio laughed, smiling into her deepening frown. "You are mistaken, my dear, and very much so. When I was hungry, the beauty of food was even more important. It made me greater than my hunger." He handed Tayre one of his creations, then another to her, and settled his own on his lap.

"How about a story with this fine meal, Farliosan?" Tayre asked.

"Happily! In exchange for a later viewing of all your pretty knives, mercenary."

"Agreed."

Amarta looked at Tayre incredulously. She had always thought his knives were secrets. It had never occurred to her to ask to see them.

"I want to see them, too," she said. "And the story, too. I want it all."

Olessio chuckled, patted her shoulder affectionately. "You shall have it, my dear. All of it."

"I t'll be worth it, I promise," Olessio said.

They had hiked all night. After the convolutions required to sneak Amarta into this room, she was exhausted and stumbled toward the bed.

The early morning was bright through the window, the room already hot. Olessio looked out the shutters, then turned back.

"Come on now, Guard-dog. You saw what I did with a bit of charcoal. Don't you want to see what I can do with quality ingredients?"

"Expensive ones, you mean. How much?" Tayre asked.

Amarta lay down on the bed, grateful to not be moving.

Olessio raised three fingers, squinted thoughtfully, and unfurled a fourth. "Depending on the town's apothecary, of course." When Tayre didn't immediately respond, he gave a deeply dramatic scowl, "It's not enough to run off with, if that's what you're thinking. And I would miss you too much, Guard-dog."

Tayre snorted softly, then turned a questioning look at Amarta.

"Do what you like. I just want to sleep," Amarta said, regretting having opened her eyes to watch them.

"You see? She trusts me entirely," Olessio said primly, then gave a charming grin and held out an open palm.

Tayre dug into a purse, placed five coins into Olessio's hand. Very slowly. "This had better be good, Vagras."

Olessio chuckled, then clicked at Tadesh, who ignored Olessio's offered arm, instead taking an impressive running leap onto his shoulders.

"Ow," he said through gritted teeth, and they left.

When they returned, it was sunset, and Amarta woke, not only to his entrance, but to the stink of spoiled meat. He had a sack in one hand, and in the other, at arms' length, a red fist-sized globular lattice.

Tadesh, tight on Olessio's heels, rose up on her hind legs again and again toward the red globe, snuffling eagerly.

Olessio smiled and waved the red thing in the air. "Stinkbasket! Right there in the brush. Can you believe it? I'll need hot water and two bowls. Would you?" This to Tayre, who made no move to leave.

"It will smell better," Olessio added.

Tayre returned shortly with bowls and water.

Olessio tapped into one bowl a pale yellow powder, then also the white, mixing with hot water. Amarta breathed through her mouth, trying not to gag.

"Mundaran arrowroot," Olessio said happily. "Zaneke guggul powder. And Seuan seafoam! Powdered, of course—alas!—but it will do."

"Do what?" Amarta asked. "And that thing—what is it?"

"Ah, this: the prize." With a small knife Olessio meticulously skinned the red rind, slicing the white flesh into the second bowl, and mashing it with gray powder.

The stench began to ease.

"My people use this to make ourselves seem—hmm, how to say it?—roughed up a bit, as if life has been unkind. Keep the barbarians at a polite distance. Nothing says 'leave me alone' like a wretched, disease-ravaged face." He grinned at Amarta. "On such a lovely young woman."

Amarta blinked. Olessio was a performer, as full of pretense as Tayre, in his way. But did he mean it? Her gaze flickered between the two men, looking for clues, finding none.

Olessio combined the ingredients, creating a pale brown viscous substance.

"Why," Olessio continued, "I could make you look as if your face had been burned half off!" His expression took on a manic glee, then his eyes narrowed with dramatic intensity. "A terrible accident. Barely survived! Why, they won't see your face at all, only your aberration."

"A light touch, Vagras," Tayre said. "We're trying to avoid attention, remember? Let's make her seem to have come through it some time ago, rather than to be bringing plague."

Olessio's smile snagged as if on some memory. He gave a sober nod, then stepped close to Amarta, taking her chin, turning her head one way and then the other.

It would itch, Amarta was suddenly sure. "It shouldn't only be me," she said. "If we're all traveling together."

"Yes! Even better," Olessio cried, giving Tayre a new scrutiny.

"How is it," Tayre asked, returning the look, "that you've never been to these lands before, but you know this native fruit and its uses so well?"

"So suspicious! The same way you know about the roads, I expect: my people wander, and talk to everyone." Olessio dipped his fingers into the gooey substance and held it toward Amarta, pausing thoughtfully. Then: "Hoi! Don't touch that, Guard-dog! It's poisonous."

Tayre drew his hand back from the remains of the stink-basket.

Amarta twitched back from Olessio's fingers. He gave her a hurt look. "Only the meat of the fruit is poisonous, and only a little. This is perfectly safe. When mixed with the guggul powder it becomes impotent."

"I'm not concerned," Tayre said when Amarta gave him an alarmed look. "Those who poison rarely warn their victims in advance. Only in stories."

"I know that one," Olessio said, brightening. "A young king falls in love with his former wetnurse's daughter. One day he—" At Amarta's expression, he stopped. "Quite safe." All trace of humor gone, he waggled his gooey fingers. "Can you not foresee it?"

"Yes," Amarta answered, annoyed at having been so caught up that she hadn't even looked. *Her cheeks would itch for an hour.* But beyond that?

She sighed. Wearily, she began to sort through the minutes and hours that followed.

"Never mind," Olessio said. "Watch." He smeared the gooey substance across his face, leaving brown streaks, then put his fingers into his mouth, sucking them clean.

"You didn't need to do that," Amarta said.

Olessio smiled gently. "Some things can be made simple."

"You've a lot of faith in your people's talk, Vagras," Tayre said.

"Faith in Amarta," Olessio replied. Then to her: "You would have stopped me, if it had been truly dangerous, surely?"

"Of course." If she had been looking, which she had not. "Go on," she said. "Paint me."

Olessio took more onto his fingers and stroked onto her face. It began to itch almost immediately.

She watched him as he worked, his oddly mismatched eyes, his affectionate smile. Did he really think that she was lovely?

Tayre dipped a single finger into the bowl that held the pale brown concoction.

"Hoi, stop that," Olessio said in mild annoyance. "Who knows what's on your fingertips?"

Tayre brought the translucent, brownish paste to his nose to sniff. "I know."

Olessio snorted, then paused in his painting to focus on Amarta's eyes. "I do hope you trust me, my dear. I wouldn't harm you. Not for anything."

His smile was so sweet that she felt herself melt. Then Olessio hummed a playful tune and went back to making Amarta look wretched.

Now Amarta understood Tayre's warning: people stared at the three of them with looks of revulsion and shock, then looked away the moment they came near. As the trio passed, Tadesh well-hidden in the backpack, they looked back, pointing and whispering.

"We're attracting attention," she said softly.

"Keep the disguise for now," Tayre replied. "Descriptions of us will travel east, where they will meet word from the Xanmelkie valley of the seer who broke the pendulum. Those tales will need to find the hunters, who must decide if we are the same people or not. That will slow them down a bit."

Olessio gave Amarta a look. "Could we be three *men* traveling together?"

Tayre shook his head. "She wouldn't fool them for a moment."

Amarta felt self-conscious and stubborn. "I could learn how."

"Yes, with a month to train you. But to anyone who knows what to look for, it'll be obvious that you're attempting a disguise, and then you'll really stand out."

Olessio turned an eye on Tayre. "Obvious to those who see as you do, Guard-dog. But you're rather uncommon. How many of your type are we likely to meet?"

Tayre looked at the road ahead. "It only takes one."

They camped in a forested rise, edged by a wide meadow of tangling yellow flowers. There they slept through the heat of the day.

Amarta dozed uneasily, waking late afternoon to the craving that never left, the hunger that gnawed and pulsed, seeming to start and end in her groin. She watched Tayre pack, realized she was staring, then forced her attention to Olessio, who was pouring water into a small wooden cup. Tadesh poked her nose into the stream of water, lapping as it went by.

Why couldn't all relationships be so simple?

Tayre called them both over. He squatted over some cleared dirt where he had sketched a map.

"After the city of Lisonren," he said, "we'll travel Slow Creek to western Ulawesan. No more ravaged faces. We'll need to dress well and have a solid story to back it." He glanced at each of them. "Again, Amarta and I are a married couple, Olessio, you're the servant. We are headed to—"

"You can pretend to be married to me, but you can't pretend to have sex with me?"

Into the silence that followed, Amarta felt her face go hot. How was it that she could look into hundreds of futures to know what to say, but at other times blurt out something that she damned well knew was a terrible idea, even without foresight?

"Ahh," Olessio said, drawing it out with the satisfied tone of someone who had finally solved a puzzle. He sat back, watching them both.

"Is that what you want, pretense?" Tayre asked her.

"Better that than the nothing you offer me now," she said. "Two years, since…" She trailed off. "Maybe," she hissed, "it's not me who's not ready."

"Maybe it's not," Tayre replied, but it was clear to her that he didn't mean it.

Olessio was grinning. "I knew there was something more between you two."

"A contract," Amarta said tightly, "Nothing else." She stood from the dirt, brushed off her trousers, looking downslope at the meadow and the road beyond. She wanted to leave. This place. This conversation.

"You know what I think?" Olessio asked, getting to his feet. "I think you two don't yell enough."

"We attract sufficient attention already," Tayre said, still crouched on the ground.

Olessio shook his head. "No, no. All this polite, careful talk between you…"

Amarta glared at Tayre, ignoring Olessio. "You mean me, don't you? Attracting attention?"

"Your decision, Seer," Tayre said quietly. "I told you. I follow—"

"Follow? That's what you call this?"

"You see?" Olessio gesturing. "Like that, only louder." He waved at the overcast sky, the trees, the meadow of grasses and flowers. "There's no one, anywhere around. Why don't you two just—get it all out? That's what my people would do."

Amarta tore her furious gaze away from Tayre and laid it on Olessio. "What are you saying, Vagras?"

His grin was unflagging. "Here, I'll show you."

Olessio spread his arms wide, threw back his head, and made a deep growl in his throat that got louder and louder, easily carrying across the tall grasses of the meadow. By the time he finally ran out of air, it had become a full-on howl.

The sound echoed across the valley.

Tayre stood, slowly—resignedly, Amarta thought—his gaze ranging in a long sweep of the meadow and the trees overhead to see what Olessio's cry might have woken.

"That's what you do?" Amarta asked Olessio, incredulously. "You yell?"

He frowned. "We engage. We don't keep it all inside."

"How do you know when to stop?" Tayre asked, still searching the horizon.

"When there is agreement," Olessio said, frowning as if this were obvious.

"Or someone is killed?" Tayre asked.

"No, no." Olessio's waved this away. "If you fight properly, no one is hurt, and everyone achieves a measure of clarity about the other's point of view."

Amarta's mouth dropped open. "Are you insane? You want me to fight him?"

"With words! With gestures! Jump! Yell!" He held up the small wooden cup. "Throw things!" He made as if to throw this at Tayre, who surely noticed, but didn't look at him. "Like any married couple. You two are terrible at this."

"We are nothing like married," she snapped furiously.

"That's not what I—" Olessio made a frustrated sound.

Amarta hefted her pack and strode away, into the meadows, her legs brushing through the yellow flowers.

In moments, she heard the soft sounds of Olessio trailing through the grass, and Tadesh's chittering close behind.

Tayre would be following, too, but his steps she didn't hear.

~

The three of them sat silently on a small stone bench, facing a roadside temple. No one had said much since the morning's argument. Wordlessly they passed around the water bag.

Tadesh began to circle the small, carved stone temple, then took a jump into the grass. She had recently developed an appetite for grasshoppers, and moments later they heard a small snap and crunching sound.

Olessio touched the stone altar with a pebble and put it alongside another on the shelf. A prayer?

Olessio faced them both. "An excellent idea has occurred, here in my fine mind." He tapped his head, then turned to Amarta, and bowed smartly. "Allow me the honor of standing in for this—" He tilted his head fractionally at Tayre. "Lout. With your kind permission, sera, I believe I can fashion of myself a suitable pretend-husband. And you, Guard-dog—" Olessio looked sideways at Tayre with that charming grin of his, "you can play the servant."

Tayre stood, slowly, his unblinking gaze on the smaller man, then he turned the expressionless look on Amarta.

She felt a chill, and opened her mouth, feeling that she must say something. She was just peering into vision for a clue as to what, when Tayre spoke. "Her skin will need to be a bit darker to match yours." He began to dig into his pack.

"Amarta? Will you permit?" Olessio asked.

"What?" Amarta blinked. "Yes."

They walked again. At the next town, Tayre negotiated a ride east with a wagoner.

In the back of the half-covered wagon, full of sacks of turnips, Olessio proved himself right: he was a doting, talkative husband when they were watched, grabbing her hand in his own and patting it affectionately, especially when she went to rub her itching face.

Tayre, playing the servant, helped Amarta and Olessio into the shaded portion of the wagon, and took the full sun of the day for himself, a ragged felted hat shading his eyes.

Tadesh made a study of all the corners of the wagon, of burlap sacks and boxes into which she could squeeze, curl, or stretch, when the day was hot, cooling her pale underbelly.

They passed town after town. Sacks of turnips left, replaced by carrots. Depending on who was watching them, Olessio would point and chatter, half in Perripin, half in Arunkin, sometimes in other languages that she was nearly certain he was making up.

As they rode out of another town, she watched Tayre give an astonishingly convincing performance of being dull. Somehow it riveted her attention. He seemed to be dozing, but probably wasn't. What was he thinking about?

Once, on a deserted stretch of road, she grabbed Olessio's arm. He seemed startled, but smiled gamely, patting her arm reassuringly. Then he glanced at Tayre and gently returned her arm.

Chapter Eleven

AMARTA AWOKE. Overhead, a tarp strung between trees kept off most of the night and morning's rain.

As she sat up, a multi-colored bird landed on a nearby boulder, then fluttered to a branch in one of the pale-barked trees surrounding their camp, cawing loudly. It shook wet, spindly leaves, then launched into a cloud-white sky. The air was heavy, sticky, the grass wet.

"Ah, you're awake." Olessio sat by her side, handing her a bag of water.

In the tree-ringed clearing before them, Tayre moved through his daily practice. He used whatever was handy. Floor, chairs, tables, when they stayed a night at an inn. Here, the ground, trees, and rocks were his tools.

He crouched. A roll, a strike. A jump straight up, and he drew himself over a branch in one motion, easily dropping to the ground on the other side.

Then a fast spin. A sprint. He sprang, launching onto a boulder in what seemed a fall that somehow turned into a handspring. A backflip that shouldn't have been possible. He scrambled up the tree as if it were a ladder.

"Extraordinary, isn't he?" Olessio asked softly.

Amarta nodded, awestruck.

It was not merely what he did—impressive enough—but how: every strike and grab was so precise that he might have been plucking a flower or brushing back a strand of someone's hair.

Memory served up an image of his face as he looked on the Domina Zeted with a smile so warm that Amarta's innards twisted.

Tayre stopped, looked at the sky, then at Amarta.

"Rain?" he asked.

"Yes," Amarta answered. "But when, I'm not sure."

He nodded and dropped to the ground, spinning out a circular kick as he did.

Without taking his eyes from Tayre, Olessio handed her half of his seed-crusted roll.

"Weather is hard," she said. In nearly every future, she could hear the sound of rain pattering on the tarp overhead, but when was impossible to know. "Could be an hour from now, after noon, or—"

She blinked.

"Now," Amarta barked.

Another blink and the sky opened in a drenching downpour, loud slaps against the oilskin tarp.

Tadesh, who had been out prowling, bolted under the tarp, rubbing her wet head against Olessio's thigh.

Tayre did not even pause. A side-strike to a dripping tree, then a roll across what was fast becoming muddy grass. In moments he was soaked to the skin, his clothes clinging, outlining his body all too clearly as Amarta watched.

Body hunger, Maris had called it.

"Stubborn," Olessio said out of the side of his mouth.

"Showing off," Amarta replied.

Tayre came to a stop, glistening as warm water flowed

down over him. Amarta would have sworn that he couldn't have heard their soft voices from this distance over the downpour, but his amused expression said otherwise.

"Practicing, while you two sit under cover," Tayre said.

His gaze still on them, he drew from the sides of his drenched shirt two slender, amardide-handled knives. He tossed one into the air, end-over-end, and caught it by the wet handle. A snap and the knife flashed wetly in the air, and he caught it.

A knife in both hands, a simultaneous double flip in the air, and caught again.

"Must you?" Olessio muttered, then stood with a sigh, digging into his pack. He took out two handfuls of ocher-colored balls and stepped out into the rain. Thunder rumbled distantly.

With a fast, smooth motion, Tayre sheathed his knives and gestured to the center of the clearing, stepping back to give Olessio space. Olessio grinned, shook the rain from his face, and began to juggle.

First three balls, then four, then five, all in the air, caught and tossed. Somehow, while not missing a single catch, Olessio sent a sixth ball to Amarta, who barely caught it in time as Olessio continued juggling.

"Simply toss it back, my dear," Olessio shouted over the rain, "any time you wish."

Amarta watched him keep five balls in the air, moving so fast, and tried to reason out when it would be easiest for him to catch a sixth. She had no idea, and finally threw it back toward him.

Olessio snatched it out of the air. In a flurry, he kept all six balls in motion, breathing hard and swearing.

All at once he stopped, hands out, palms open to the sky, and the balls dropped into his fingers, three in each hand.

Amarta applauded enthusiastically. Olessio bowed deeply to her, and then to Tayre, who bowed back.

Both men were soaked to the skin, but Amarta thought she had never seen them look so pleased with themselves. And with each other.

Deservedly so, she decided. Such impressive, astonishing skills, both of them.

And herself? What skill could she show?

Well.

She stood under the tarp, waiting a moment for the rain to ease. She stepped out.

Light, warm drops splattered onto her head as she walked to the boulder at the edge of the clearing. Carefully—clumsily, she felt, by comparison to either of them—she climbed it to stand on the flat top. She squinted at the horizon, now fuzzed with silvering rain.

There.

She raised a hand. A moment later, a flash of lightning cut the sky in two, right where she pointed. She lowered her hand.

Now.

She raised her arms above her head. Thunder broke—a booming crack—a deafening, rolling clatter that echoed across the sky.

Again she pointed, as if drawing in the clouds. A line of brilliant white flashed, following her finger.

Next she clapped her hands in a percussive pattern. The deep thunder that followed echoed it perfectly.

Olessio gave a delighted grin and Tayre a nod of respect. Elation filled her as, overhead, clouds gathered.

"Sunshine soon," she said, making her way down off the boulder.

Moments later, blue sky had shredded the clouds and sun washed over the campsite, warming and drying.

The show was over.

Olessio coaxed Tadesh out from under the bedrolls where she was hiding. Tayre turned his hands in a deliberate, practiced motion. Amarta tried to imagine what it was. Breaking a hold? Blocking a strike? Crushing someone's throat?

She was suddenly fascinated. "Teach me to do what you do."

He gave a small smile. "Which part?"

She gestured around the clearing, at the course of his earlier practice. "How to fight as you do. As you did with the men outside the Sun and Moon."

He shook his head. "My training was constant from childhood. What I know can't be taught in an afternoon. Or a year. It has to be lived."

"What if you're not around to protect me?"

His look was sudden, piercing. "You foresee something?"

She shook her head. "To understand myself and the world. I need more than my vision. Teach me. Something. Anything."

He raised his hand, palm facing her. "This. This is the fight. Match me."

She stepped close, bringing her palm up in the air to face his.

"I am here," he said, bringing his hand slowly to hers. "You are there." Their palms touched. He pressed. She matched his pressure. "Why do you do this?" he asked.

"What do you mean? You told me to."

"All conflict grows from some seed. Never out of nothing. If you understand its origin, you know better how to resolve it."

With that, he yanked his hand back. Amarta stumbled forward, annoyed.

"You changed the rules."

"Conflict is all about changing the rules." He raised his hand again. When she did not respond, his eyebrows. Then: "Do you want to learn or not?"

She reluctantly brought her palm to face his again. This time, though, she wouldn't press.

He clapped his palm to hers, a soft sound, then stepped back. "There. It's over. That was the fight. Who won?"

She blinked. "You?"

"You're asking me. Tell me."

"Well, you hit my hand, so it must be you."

"But your hand remains in the air, while mine is gone. What have you lost that I have won?"

Self-consciously, she dropped her hand to her side. "This is confusing."

"Fights often are. Who won?"

"Who decides?" she countered.

"Good question. What does it mean to you, to win?"

To have you, good and truly, she thought, but didn't say.

She thought of the Emendi children in Senta, of the slaver ship with cabins full of people who had the misfortune to be born with hair the color of straw.

"You told me," she said, "that sometimes victory is being able to walk away. But I want more than that. I want to be able to protect people."

"That's harder." He looked at Olessio. "Vagras?"

Olessio nodded sadly. "Protecting oneself is hard enough, and you're useless to others if you're oozing life."

"So teach me something," she said to Tayre. "Something real."

"Real?"

In a blink he gripped her arms, bruisingly tight. "By the time it comes to this—" he shook her a little, released her with a gentle push. "The problem is harder. Amarta, your foresight is more useful than anything I can teach you. Practice what you already know."

Her heart was pounding at this fast, rough touch and the near-shocking release that followed.

She shook her head adamantly. "I've been a prisoner too many times. I never want to be helpless again."

"Ah, but he's right, my dear," said Olessio to her. "With your ability, you can avoid conflict entirely. Isn't that more sensible?"

She turned on Olessio. "You don't understand. My visions aren't smart—they scream when things get bad. What if the future isn't clear—only a mist of maybes? What if I have to do something, anything, before I can be sure of what might happen next? What if…" She turned back to Tayre, who, she realized all at once, had by now probably saved her life as many times as he'd threatened it. "What if I only have one chance, and you aren't there?" She felt a tingling from some future. "Teach me," she repeated fiercely.

He gave her a long, unreadable look. Then he pointed to the edge of the clearing. "Get past me to touch that tree."

She dropped back, hoping to surprise him, but he was ready. As she ran, he grabbed her hand, almost lazily, swinging her back to where she'd started.

"Again."

She bolted, trying a direct sprint and passed him. But somehow he was close, his leg tangled with hers, and she was falling. He had her hand again, pulling her up to standing before she even touched the ground.

"Why aren't you using foresight, Amarta?" he asked.

"It might not be enough."

"Nothing is enough. Use everything."

Then, before she began again, he lunged. She blinked, startled, tensing to look into the future. But he knew how to obscure intention, and the gray fog vision offered left her motionless.

Again, her feet flew out from under her. Again, he held her upright by her hand, pulling her to standing.

"You're not even breathing hard." She stepped away, shaking her head. "You're too good. I can't."

"Truly? In no future do you pass me by?" His smile was challenging. "That seems improbable."

She scouted the future again. Was there a future in which she gained the tree? She'd give up and they'd pack to leave, and just before they did, she'd slap the tree, giving him a triumphant look. He'd shrug.

No victory there.

"This is not a good idea," he said.

"What? Why not?"

"You've escaped hunters many times. That day in the forest. Remember?"

Of course she did. It was the day they had met.

"You knew the threat was real," he said. "Now you know it's not. How important is this to you?"

She heard the warning in his voice.

Did it matter? Would it ever? She felt into the future for an illusive trail.

A group of men surrounded her. Each held a short stick that ended in a curved blade. Sharp, she knew, because beyond them someone gasped, dripping blood from a shoulder cut. A fast demonstration, cutting their own man, just to demonstrate their sincerity. They wore oddly styled, rough-hewn clothes. Their faces covered with expressionless masks the color of skin. Each stepped forward, tightening the circle around her. "It is time," came a man's ponderous voice from behind, "that you stopped interfering."

She blinked back to the present, trembling, rethinking every plan she had. Maybe she should go back into hiding.

Become unknown again. Wear disguises all the time. They could go east. East of the Rift, even. Was it possible?

The future said it was. Her life would change, of course. Her days and nights would be about staying hidden and nothing else.

A dark life, full of fear. No protecting anyone but herself.

What would become of the horses? Of Dirina and Pas? The Emendi in Kusan? The many, many more who suffered at the hands of those who had money and influence?

Could she abandon them all? Swallow every injustice?

She looked at Tayre and at the clearing, and in her mind's eye, the world beyond.

"Very," she answered.

He scrutinized her for a moment, then nodded. "Try again."

She tensed to run. In the next breath, he would be on her. But this time, no soft landing. His weight slammed her to the ground, her arm twisted hard behind. He pressed her face into the mud, laughed. "This is how I was taught," he said into her ear. Pain shot through her arm and shoulder and thought fled. She wept. He twisted harder.

A future in which she was again terrified of him. A sickening feeling came over her.

It had not happened yet. She pushed it away, clung tight to vision.

Vision said to drop into a crouch, to kick at him. She did. Useless, from all appearance, and he ignored it almost entirely, but it slowed him. She was on her feet again. He darted forward to grab her, but missed by a hair width.

He lunged. She leaned back. For a moment she thought she'd lost, but no: his fingers brushed her skin as she twitched backward just out of reach.

Then she turned and sprinted. He was right behind her as she slapped the tree, bending double, gasping for air.

Olessio was on his feet, his expression stunned. "How did she do that?" he breathed.

Tayre's response was grim. "She believed me."

Heart pounding in her chest, for a moment she could only nod, watching him warily.

In some future, he had hurt her. She still felt the pain that had never happened.

But also, he had been right: she wouldn't have known what she was capable of, if she hadn't believed he would go that far.

"What if…" she asked breathlessly. "What if it's more than one?"

"How many more?" Tayre asked.

"Maybe…ten?"

"How soon?" Olessio asked, alarmed, looking around, clicking at Tadesh to come.

"No, no—not now," Amarta said. "Not even soon. Just…what if?"

Olessio exhaled, gave Tadesh the all-clear whistle. Tadesh looked at him, annoyed.

"Ten is a large number," Tayre said. "Remember how in playing Rochi you learned the flow of the game? A handful of players, but they only act one at a time. There are three keys to surviving a group attack." He gave Olessio a challenging half-smile. "Care to guess, Vagras?"

Olessio slowly shook his head. "Ten on one? I don't show up for that game."

"The first key," Tayre said, looking at her again, "is to be somewhere else. Avoid it entirely. That you can do."

"What if I can't?" Amarta asked.

"Remember outside the Sun and Moon? Six men. What did I do? I arranged to take them on as singles and pairs. Never all at once."

Olessio grinned. "You kept putting them in each other's way. Lovely work."

Tayre gave an acknowledging nod. "The second key: make the attackers work harder than you do. And the last key, Vagras?"

Olessio's face lost its smile. "Don't miss."

"Yes. Whatever you do—a strike, a shove, a spray of sand, or even words—look to disable. Waste nothing."

"I understand," Amarta said. "Or at least, I think I do. How do I practice? There are only two of you."

"Oh, no, no," Olessio said, waving his hands. "I'm only an observer."

He was wrong, Amarta decided. There was a future in which he would help. She just had to find it.

In the dark, something hit her leg.

"A blindfold," she said to Tayre. Then to Olessio: "Those balls you juggled. May we use them?"

Olessio looked distinctly uncomfortable. "Really rather you didn't."

Amarta pinned him with a look. "You said to me, 'you shall have it, my dear, all of it.' I want this."

He looked away, but Amarta kept staring at him, in mind of how Tayre could influence someone with persistent silence.

At last, Olessio exhaled in a long stream, took the balls from his pockets, and reluctantly handed them to her.

D espite being blindfolded, Amarta could tell who threw which ball. Easily.

"Olessio, you must throw harder," she said. "How else am I to learn?"

"I don't want to throw things at you! And in this grass?

We'll never find them again. Made them myself, you know. With rather expensive tree-sap and flower extract."

"You can make more," Tayre said from a direction she didn't expect. "Amarta, where is the tree?"

She pointed.

"Close enough. Go."

She sank into vision, heading toward the tree.

Vision said slow. Stop.

She did, lifting a foot, just so. A ball landed near it. She turned, abruptly twisting sideways. A slight breeze across her face as another ball flew by.

It was easy, as long as she—no, wait. She lost focus, momentarily uncertain.

That was all it took; a ball hit her leg bruisingly hard. She whimpered.

Well, she knew who threw that one, anyway.

"Are you sure you want this?" Tayre's voice, from another direction. Closer.

"Yes."

The voice kept moving. "In the forest, just before you misstepped and turned your ankle, you were uncatchable. What changed?"

In memory, the sound of an arrow sinking into a tree.

"You're breathing hard." His voice was in her ear. She startled. "Slow your exhale. Slower yet. That's right. Again."

His voice circled her. "Your attention was on the arrow. Your focus narrowed and stopped. There is always a path to failure, is there not? Pain and death? Don't look there. Look instead for what goes forward. Seek doorways, not dead-end alleys. You understand?"

"I think so."

Silence followed.

A ball was coming. A torso hit. She dropped to her knees in agony.

She would learn only if the attack were meaningful; he was doing what she'd asked him to do. Gratitude bloomed atop her thickening fear.

"Don't look for the ball," he said from somewhere else entirely. "Look for where it isn't. Look for the open spaces."

She turned this over in her mind, fed it to her body, and pressed it forward into the future.

A hit to her head. Her mind went blank with pain.

She shook her head sharply to dismiss this and looked again. Where were the incoming balls? No—where were they not? Where was the open space?

There. And there. Amarta stepped into it, reminded in a flash of what she'd felt in Otevan as she walked past guards at the exact moment that their attention was elsewhere.

She stepped again. Then lunged, as if about to step, but instead pulled back.

A ball hit a boulder just beyond, hard enough to bounce.

Open space. No ball. There, and there, and—

There.

She dashed, first one way, then the other. She turned, dropped suddenly. Balls flew over her head. She lurched again to her feet, one more step, and she slapped the trunk of the tree, pulling off the blindfold.

Olessio was blinking at Amarta, his mouth hanging open. "How. How?"

Tayre smiled at her. "Well done."

Was that pride in his voice? She thought so. Elation filled her.

Olessio picked up a ball.

"I'll help you find the rest," Amarta said.

"I'm betting he knows where every one of them are," Tayre said.

Olessio walked the clearing, bending down to pick up

another one of the ocher balls. He snorted softly at Tayre's comment, but he didn't disagree.

By the time they reached the city of Lisonren, disguise was a daily ritual for all of them. They reprovisioned and were back on the road by nightfall.

The next town was small. They slept the day in a room, and Amarta woke and arose to Tayre returning with flatbreads and spiced bean mash.

"Coin being offered for word of a young stranger woman," Tayre said to them both.

"Here but not in Lisonren?" asked Olessio, eagerly folding a flatbread to capture the mash, and breaking off a small part to offer to the dozing Tadesh, who yawned, shook out one of her legs behind in a shuddering stretch, then took the food.

"Small towns pay closer attention to strangers than big cities," Tayre said. "A woman of any appearance. Borderland, Arunkin, even Perripin. From here to Isdren, we'll take only back roads, and stop putting effort into disguise. Put it into speed."

"Who is it after me this time?" Amarta asked.

"The trail of coins points north. Arunkel Houses, I would guess." Tayre sat himself across from her at the table. "Amarta."

At his tone, she looked up from her food.

"I have other news for you. Innel sev Cern esse Arunkel has been executed for treason."

Amarta felt a shock go through her. "Treason? What?"

"Famous fellow. Friend of yours?" asked Olessio.

Amarta slowly shook her head. Innel had been her captor. She had sat by his side in Otevan as he lay dying.

Your empire and queen need you, she had told him, then somehow persuaded Marisel to save his life.

Not a friend. Not in any way. But they had been, in some sense, close.

"Why?" she asked Tayre. "What did he do?"

"That I do not know."

"At least we know he's not one coming after me now," she said, feeling oddly shaken.

"But others will try to finish the hunt that he began."

"No surprise," Olessio said. "Inevitable, even, given what you can do."

"And now that everyone knows what I look like." In Amarta's mind, the sound echoed: the sundering at the Tree of Revelation, as the pendulum, chain, and great branch all fell onto the crowd.

"They don't know where you are," Tayre said. "And that makes all the difference."

Amarta looked at Olessio. Would the Farliosan be willing to sell her for a fortune?

With surprise, she realized that her mistrust of him was gone. He would not betray her. She looked at Tayre. If he were going to give her up, he would have done so long ago.

"I will do whatever it takes to stay free," she told them both.

"Absolutely," Olessio said, agreeing soberly. "Tadesh and I are at your service."

"Do you still want to cross the Nelar ocean to the Spine of the World?" Tayre asked. "Now might be a good time to get some more water between us and your hunters."

The Island Road. The Heart of Seuan. A chance to find others like herself.

"Yes, I do."

"Sooner or later, they'll follow," Tayre said evenly.

"They always do," Amarta replied.

She studied Olessio and his mismatched eyes, then Tayre, who watched her now just as closely as he always had.

"With the two of you at my side—" just then, Tadesh jumped into her lap, leaning back against Amarta's torso, the animal's contented thrumming making Amarta smile, "—the three of you…let them try to take me again. I don't think they can."

Amarta woke to the sound of Tayre sharpening his knives, and sat up in a glen of trees.

She rose, knowing that Tayre saw her go, and walked into the brush. She found a tree, squatted, and considered Tayre's advice to her.

Practice what you know.

She stood, wondering how.

Through the tangles of vine-clad trees, she caught a distant flash. Olessio, talking faintly to Tadesh. She took a small step toward them, then another, feeling forward into the future. Where could she step that Olessio wasn't looking and wasn't listening?

As she picked her way toward him, she tried to think as she imagined Tayre must think, about angles of sight, about layers of sounds. A future in which she stood at that tree, there, just beyond Olessio, but without him seeing her.

Unlikely. Was it possible?

A tricky business, to be behind one tree when Olessio looked in her direction, but stepping again when his attention was elsewhere, when the soft sound of her step might also be obscured by the cry of a hawk.

One step. Another. She paused and turned so she would be side on to him. She waited behind another tree. Not this moment, but maybe this one.

Then she was there, at the tree that was her goal, mere feet from him, and he hadn't seen her.

She grinned with triumph. In a moment, something would change—perhaps the wind would shift—Tadesh would scent her, and come toward her, giving her away.

"Ah, there it is," Olessio breathed. With a quiet rustling above, something small and white dropped and landed in his open hand with a soft plop.

She must have made a sound, because he turned to look at her, a momentarily stunned look on his face.

"Where I come from," he said, "it's considered rude to sneak up on a person."

"I'm sorry," Amarta said quickly. "I didn't…" She felt herself redden. "I mean—"

He fluttered the fingers of his other hand. "I forgive," he said, turning away from her, whatever it was in his hand now out of sight.

He walked toward the camp, and she followed, feeling unsettled. Olessio began to gather things to prepare food, thinly slicing vegetables and bits of dried meat into a pan, heating it with water over a cookfire.

When he scraped the hash into plates for the three of them, Tayre made an appreciative sound. "Where did you find an egg?"

Ah. That's what the white object had been.

Olessio took a bite, chewed, then swallowed. "A sinz-nest. Rare native bird. Sloppy nesters. Caught a glimpse of the egg from below, so I tossed one of my soft rubber balls, just so, just a little tap—" he mimed an upward motion with his free hand. "Nest opened right up, the egg dropped, and with my juggler's gentle catch—" he gestured at the food.

"I don't remember a ball," Amarta said, frowning.

Olessio's smile vanished. "You missed it."

"But they're bright ocher," Amarta said.

A slow blink. "My dear, I trust you're not calling me a liar."

"What? No," Amarta said. "Of course not. You're right: I missed it, that's all."

"I'll call you one," Tayre said pleasantly. "There was no ball. Tell us about this nest-egg trick, Vagras. I'm eager to learn."

"I'm sure you are," Olessio said, waggling his eyebrows. "But secrets of the trade, Guard-dog. You understand."

Tayre's eyes narrowed fractionally. "No. This is a dull story. Want to try a different one?"

Olessio's expression went from outrage to something closed so fast that Amarta had only a hint of the fear in between.

Then he looked away, breathing shallowly, his mouth turned down at the edges, clearly unhappy.

Amarta opened her mouth to speak, but Tayre flashed her a sign: *Wait.*

At last the Farliosan took a breath, exhaled long, turned back.

"Forgive my rudeness, my friends," he said. "It's a trick, a small thing, so simple I am ashamed to confess to you how it's done. Allow me this little mystery, won't you?" His tone was almost pleading.

Tayre made a casual, dismissive gesture. "I'll clean up, Vagras. See if you can small-trick us another couple of eggs for the road, would you?"

Olessio got to his feet with a wide smile, then clicked his tongue, hastily strolling into the brush, Tadesh alongside.

When he was gone, Tayre said, "I wonder what story he'll tell us next."

Chapter Twelve

AS THEY WALKED the road a half-moon rose, crawling up the sky.

How unlike Tayre's silence was Olessio's. Olessio offered no stories, no songs, no jokes. By the time the sky brightened with the hint of dawn and they made camp by a stream, Amarta was drawn and exhausted.

Who knew that silence could be so tiring?

They ate sausage and waterfruit. In the quiet of the meal, Amarta found the stream's hush a half-musical balm.

At last Olessio began to speak. His tone was soft and weighty.

"My people are travelers," he said. "Long before Arunkel was an empire, before the warring states of Perripur made an Accord, the Council of Mages claimed control of the magi.

Olessio's gaze was distant. "In those times, Farliosan children born with…" He put out a hand, his fingers gripping as if he might pull the words from the air, "…a knowing of the elements—what is called magic—were free to do as their natures dictated. Then came Marlefon and the

Council. Do you know, the magi still call him Marlefon the Peacemaker?" He snorted.

"Long ago, a child was born. Even at four, we knew he had the touch. A caring child who would rescue insects and small animals from the heavy tread of our wagon wheels. When he reached his seventh year, a stranger came. He confused us, charmed us, and took the boy away.

"Years passed and the boy's mother went to the sky. Another year and his father lay down, ready to join her.

"The boy, now grown, came to his father's side. 'I will heal you,' he said. His father refused, but asked a deathbead grant. "Scrub the magic from our people, so that never again is a Farliosan parent's heart broken over a stolen child.' His son-the-mage did this great magic. Since that day, my people have been free of the curse that is the magi."

"Until you," Tayre said.

Olessio shook his head. "No. We are free of it, I said."

"I don't believe you, Vagras," said Tayre.

Tadesh nudged Olessio's hand. He stroked her enthusiastically.

"You said that you knew I wasn't a mage," Amarta said. "How?"

Olessio gave a soft grunt. "Some things are obvious."

"To someone like you," Tayre said.

"I told you," Olessio replied. "Don't you listen? None of us—"

"You are *udardae*," Tayre said.

Amarta had heard the word before, but she couldn't remember where, or what it meant.

Olessio's frozen expression told her that he did. He stood abruptly, his lips pressed together, looking around as if something else, anything, were more urgent than this.

"What is udardae?" Amarta asked Tayre.

"Another word for mage," Tayre said, watching Olessio.

"It is not," Olessio replied, turning back. "It means 'suitable' in the tongue of the wretched magi, which I most assuredly am not, not in any way." He glared at Tayre, then his expression changed to anger, replaced by a wounded look. "You knew that. Damn you, you tricked me."

Tayre nodded. To Amarta, he said: "A literal translation of uslata is 'potential'. It was what Samnt was, before Maris took him into contract. Then he became her *taslata*, or apprentice."

"No," Olessio said, waving his hands. "I feel things, yes. Occasionally. Strong magic, certainly, but who doesn't? The occasional living god, possibly. At times an ensorcelled creature from its more ordinary brethren. But none of these things are unusual, I assure you. I am not…not…I assure you…"

"*Udardae*," Tayre said slowly, as he rose to his feet and Amarta followed. "But you don't know that you aren't. You think you might be."

For many minutes, Olessio stood unmoving, shoulders hunched. His mouth worked, but he made no sound. His expression pinched and twisted, as if he were arguing with himself.

"This is why you left your people." Tayre said. "There is no curse. Your people are no more free of magic or the magi than any other."

Olessio shook his head helplessly, as Tayre's words seemed to land like blows. Then he took a gulping breath, exhaled a sob.

When at last he spoke, he seemed to be struggling to do more than whisper.

"You're right. There is no magic to take away magic. But we learn to hide."

"And the egg trick?" Tayre asked.

"I shouldn't have done. I…" His eyes were bright. He

blinked, still whispering. "I loosened the nest a bit. It fell through. A small thing, really."

Tayre made a thoughtful sound, then chuckled.

The sound was so odd—so unexpected—that both Olessio and Amarta turned to stare at him.

Tayre's smile fled completely. "To the list of those in likely pursuit, we can now add the magi."

Olessio no longer hid what he continued to insist was only small tricks. He brought to their meals eggs in mottled blues and spotted pinks, along with edible mosses and tasty, tender seedpods that grew high on the trees. They no longer discussed what Olessio was or was not, but the tension had eased between them.

They picked up the pace, passing villages, and even Tayre did not stop to talk or seek out messages, as they pushed for speed over disguise. Amarta was relieved to forgo the heavy hats and scarves and face paints that itched.

Walking a green, rising slope in Ulawesan, they saw distant glimmers of the blue Temani Gulf to the north, short of which was a pale white expanse with rectangular shapes.

"The Salt City," Olessio breathed. "If only we had the time."

By the time they reached the border of Ulawesan and Dulu, the road was flat and in good repair. They rode when they could, pushed forward when they could not.

Even this increasing pace did not distract her entirely from wanting him, or from ruminating on what, exactly, was between the two of them.

A coin. A single coin. A cheap nals coin, at that, scored with a cross through its center so that it could be broken into four pieces. Those quarter-nals were used by the very,

very poor of Arunkel. Poor, as Amarta had been born and raised.

Did he still have that coin, the one that she had used to seal the contract with him?

To learn to live in the world. To understand yourself.

One night they lay out bedrolls in a stony ravine, a star-studded sky above. Olessio made his bed some distance away, with Tadesh.

She watched Tayre's face in the dim starlight as his eyes closed.

He'd been her first time, and her second. She exhaled softly.

His eyes opened.

"Are you ready yet?" she whispered. He let a small puff of air out through his nose. A half-laugh? She forged on anyway. "Because I am." She felt herself flush, grateful for the dark.

His gaze flickered to her. Evaluating? He shook his head slightly, and Amarta felt the sharp pain of rejection.

"It's my contract," she said, sitting up, annoyed to hear her tone waiver.

"Yes, it is."

"I suppose a single dirty nals isn't that much, after all."

He sat up to join her, his look on her. "A contract is only as binding as the honor of those who have forged it. Are you questioning my honor or your own?"

"Neither," she said, abashed enough to look away, but not enough to stop what she knew was a foolish attempt to sway him. "How do you know you're not ready? Maybe you should try, just to be sure."

Tayre made a thoughtful sound. "Isdren is a large city, with top-notch anknapas. We can spare a half-day for you to—"

"No," she snapped. "I don't want..." What didn't she want? She looked around at the dark stones, a tightness in her throat, a demanding hunger coursing through the rest of her. "Maybe I should ask Olessio."

"I would not recommend that."

"Oh?" She seized on this, struggling to keep her voice low. "You won't say yes, but when I suggest someone else, you tell me no? How dare you?"

He moved closer and put a hand on her shoulder, rubbed gently. A friendly touch, and nothing more. Her eyes stung.

"He is not a good choice for you."

"He likes me."

"He does. And he is knowledgeable. But…"

"Did you say something to him? About me? What did you say?"

He drew his hand back from her shoulder. "I said nothing. He'll say no, Amarta."

"You can't know that."

"I can guess with reasonable certainty. He's not interested in bedding women."

"Who does he fuck, then? Not Tadesh, surely." It was a horrible thing to say, but she felt horrible.

"Men, Amarta."

"What? How can you know that?"

"Because I see how he looks at people—you, me, others. I notice how his pupils widen, how long his gaze lingers. His people are freer with their affections than most, so he's cautious, but there are reactions that can't easily be trained away, and he has them."

If true, this cast a number of things in a new light.

"I don't believe you."

"Isdren. We can afford an anknapa, Amarta. Two, even."

Two? She looked away, angry at him, disgusted with herself. "We don't have time."

"It needn't take long."

"No." Then the words just slipped out. "You. I want you."

"I know."

The gentleness and sorrow in his voice hit her like a gut punch. She swallowed, fighting tears. Of course he knew. He always knew. Nothing had changed.

She wiped her eyes. "You're wrong." Vision offered a tantalizing flash of Olessio, close, his hand on her cheek. She got to her feet. "All your talk about how I decide our course—how sacred the contract is—yet the thing I want to learn most, you won't teach me. And you talk about honor?"

She waited for him to say something, to be offended, to tell her that she was wrong. Anything but this silent, unbearable concern.

Why did she do this, even knowing how it would go?

It wasn't her fault: she didn't want to want him. It was cruel of her body and spirit to ache for him.

She shook her head. There was no reason to look at him now. As usual, his face would tell her nothing.

Nothing. He was nothing. Between them was nothing.

She turned and strode across the campsite, picking her way around a high boulder to where Olessio was sleeping, Tadesh curled tight by his side, under the starry sky.

Olessio breathed deeply in his sleep as Amarta stared. It must be the work of a lunatic, what she was about to do. Or a child.

Surely, she was better than this. She should go back to her own bed. She turned.

"Amarta?" Olessio asked.

She turned back. He sat up. At his side, Tadesh slept on,

chittering softly. "What is it? Come over. Come. Sit." He patted his bedroll, inviting her.

Amarta joined him, embarrassment coursing through her. She would need to ask him before she lost her nerve, and only now did she realize that she had no idea how it was done.

Tayre could at least have taught her that.

He took her hand. "You look upset. What is it?"

"He told me no again." She clamped down on a sob. "But you—you could say yes."

"Yes to what? Oh. *Oh*. I'm a fool. I'm worse than that, I…" He gave a long exhale through his pursed lips. "I have been unkind. Unintentionally, I assure you. I beg your forgiveness."

"No," she objected, meeting his eyes, shaking her head. "What do you mean?"

"My thoughtless, flirtatious words. You've been through so much, and yet you thought to ask me. Me! I am beyond honored, sera, truly I am."

In the pause that followed, in both vision and reason, Amarta heard with painful clarity the *but* that would follow.

"Yes, I could." His voice dropped. "But it would not be from the flame of passion, of which you are most worthy." At her expression, he squeezed her hand. "I would, though, because it is you and you are special. As a…a gift?"

"You find me so unattractive?" Amarta tried to pull her hand away, but he gripped tighter, holding her to stay, and shook his head adamantly.

"It is not that. You are lovely. Anyone can see. It is, rather, how I am made. I don't desire women, not that way. If I did, well. I would want you. It is that simple."

Tayre had been right. "Damn and damn again," she muttered, half crying.

Unbidden, another thought arose, as she remembered the

nights she had wakened to find Tayre gone, returning hours later, in the predawn. She had thought he had gone to scout, to reconnoiter, to check his messages. To see who might be following them.

What if, instead, he had been with Olessio?

"You and he…" she breathed.

"What? Oh, no. No, no." Olessio laughed in amusement, then wriggled around to face Amarta, firmly taking both her hands in his own. "Entirely aside from not wanting to be in the middle of whatever it is you two are not doing, he's….how to say? He's…" Olessio had such an expressive face that she almost knew what he was trying to convey, even as he struggled for the right words.

"Yes," she replied, smiling a little in spite of herself.

"A lot of trouble," Olessio finished, smiling back.

She heaved a sigh, and again moved to rise, but still Olessio would not release her hands.

"Don't go," he said. "It's true that I don't have hunger in my gut and groin for women. But for you, Amarta, I do have something. The desire of spirit, let us say. Will you stay with me?"

She swallowed a painful lump. "What is this, if not hunger? Charity?"

He shook his head. "A different kind of passion." He rubbed her hands with his thumbs. "There are many kinds, are there not? Spirit-food, is what my people call it. Not charity, Amarta, I assure you."

"Then what are you suggesting?"

"We sleep here, tangled up together. Give each other the warmth of body and self." He glanced at his side, where Tadesh, half-asleep, was wriggling backward to press her curled backside against his thigh. "Tadesh would be happy of your company, too."

For a moment Amarta wanted nothing more than to

push him away, to go and hide in a blanket, by the familiar chill of Tayre, and cry herself to sleep in the bitterness of one more rejection.

But Olessio's hands held hers snug, and his warm smile seemed to slowly melt something inside her. Silently, she let him draw her to the cot, as he set himself behind her, wrapped his arms around her, stroked her cheek and hair, his nose nuzzling her neck.

Inside her, something cracked open. It came on her irresistibly, and in moments she was quietly sobbing in his arms, the tears more like a healing wash than a leaking wound.

After a time, she stopped shuddering, and he sang into her hair, a soft, sweet Farliosan tune that seemed to speak of easy times, of kind words and bright smiles, and Amarta felt a calm that she had not known since the years gone by when she had slept alongside Dirina and Pas, before everything had begun.

Then Amarta slept, Olessio and Tadesh curled against her.

The next morning, as the three of them packed for another day's long hike, Tayre watched her. It seemed clear to her that he knew something had happened the previous night. But he did not ask what, and she did not offer to explain.

Olessio, as he walked her to get something, gave her a quick, affectionate touch as he passed, making her smile.

Olessio did care for her. Not in the way she had hoped for, perhaps, but in a true way that fed something inside her that she hadn't even realized was hungry.

Spirit-food, indeed.

Chapter Thirteen

GETTING into the port city of Isdren turned out to be nothing like simple. Even in their best disguises, they circled the city, trying one approach after another, retreating when Tayre scouted trouble, or Olessio saw someone watching, or Amarta foresaw their way to the harbor blocked.

They stood in an overgrown field outside the city, far from view.

"Too many people are looking for you," Tayre said.

"You're famous," Olessio added, with a forced smile.

She met his look. He wanted this, and she wanted it for him. There was not much time to get to the Island Road before it assembled.

"What do we do?" she asked Tayre.

"South," he replied, "to a town called Kergwae with a small harbor."

Olessio frowned. "That won't get us a seabound vessel."

"It won't," Tayre agreed, "but there'll be a way to get to one from there. I've never seen a deep-sea port that isn't surrounded by alternative means into blue water, if you know the right people and you have enough coin."

They waited until dusk and skirted the edge of farms, coming to Kergwae at night, and making their way through the town to a dockside tavern, where they sat at a table and ate.

"I won't need either of you for this," Tayre said as they finished. "Stay in the shadows." He left, and came back in, his walk changed, his shoulders seeming to belong to a different man just by how he held them. At the bar, he took a stool.

"I know: let's go see the ocean," Olessio said to her.

Tayre began to chat amiably to the man sitting next to him. About ships, perhaps, or working up to it. The man laughed at something Tayre said.

"Tadesh. Restless. Wants to come out of the pack. You wouldn't want us two going out there alone, without the benefit of your guidance, would you?"

Just then, a curvy, aproned barmaid emerged from the kitchen, her thick hair brushed back from a high forehead, her dark Perripin skin smooth and beautiful. She leaned over, put her elbows on the bar, and asked Tayre what he wanted.

"A good night for stargazing," Olessio said, his tone warm. "Farliosan constellations. Quite popular. I think you'll find them fascinating."

Amarta spared him a glance, realizing that Olessio wanted them to leave. Why?

She looked. Tayre put his hand atop the barmaid's, looking at her with a smile that promised everything.

Amarta stood, took a step forward.

"Oh, no. No, no." Olessio was quick to stand beside her. "Come on, wife," he said with mock joviality, "let's take a stroll in the lovely night, hmm?"

The barmaid laughed a little at Tayre's words. The two of them leaned in toward each other.

Olessio whispered in her ear. "Passage to the islands. He's working, Amarta. That's all."

And yet, Amarta could not seem to drag her eyes away from what she saw. Now the barmaid tilted her head to the side, showing off a long neck. Tayre brushed something from her shoulder, his expression one of complete infatuation.

Olessio moved to stand in front of Amarta, blocking her view of this unfolding seduction. As Amarta tried to swerve to see, Olessio took her arm, and while still obscuring the drama, drew her toward the door. She resisted a moment, then sense took over, and she allowed it.

Once outside, Olessio's arm threaded through hers to make sure she didn't turn back. With his other hand, he released Tadesh from the pack, the creature climbing up to ride on his shoulder.

"You know it's only pretend, surely?" he asked.

As they walked toward the sound of crashing waves, her feet landed heavily on the hard-packed street. They crossed a lane, then another, and came to a cobbled walkway, where the sand was gritty underfoot and waves lapped a rocky shore.

He watched her in the starlight as they walked, holding tight to her arm as she tried to shake him off.

"Amarta—"

"Of course I know it's pretend," she snapped. "It always is. The only times he's ever been truthful with me was when he was trying to kill me."

Olessio's grip on her went slack. His mouth fell open. On his shoulder, Tadesh seemed to freeze.

Amarta snatched her arm away and strode forward into the dark sea wind.

∿

The salt wind gusted, whipping Amarta's hair around her head and across her face. It was simply too short to stay behind her ears.

His decision, to cut this way. Yet one more thing that had really been his decision.

"Wait! Wait!" Olessio's anguished voice was made distant by the wind. He ran to catch up with her, struggling to match her strides. "He was the one? The one trying to…to…"

"It doesn't matter."

"Of course it does! All that talk about people trying to take your head? That was *him*? No wonder…" He circled a hand in the air. "In response, you would naturally…Yes! of course!"

Amarta walked on, letting him talk to himself.

The stars were thick and bright overhead. There she saw the constellation of Snakes, swirling in their Cauldron of Lunacy, brewing broths of wisdom. She would, she decided, drink from that chalice, were it ever offered to her. Why not? What had she to lose?

Behind her, Olessio seemed to have finally noticed that she had left, and was calling her name.

She turned toward the ocean, leaving the walkway, scrambling over the boulders that separated the road from beach. She hopped onto a boulder, then another.

Olessio was faster. By the time she stepped down onto the sand, he was again at her side.

"Ama," he said. "May I call you that? I hadn't asked."

"I don't care."

"Ah, well, you've larger things to care about. I understand."

Amarta turned to face the ocean; a great, dark, growling beast, its foam fingers groping across the craggy shoreline.

For a moment, the wind brushed her hair back out of her face completely, and her mind sailed off into a vision of the future.

"What I must," she would say, tears blurring her vision, the wind momentarily whipping the hair from her face.

Olessio spoke again, his words lost in the sound of the ocean, the words from the future.

He stepped in front of her and took her hands, stared into her eyes.

It was too much. Amarta sat. The sand was cool under her. Olessio followed her down and Tadesh leapt off his shoulder to explore the shadowy beach around them.

"I understand, Ama. Or at least, I think I do." She looked past him at the dark waves with their dim foam lines. "I do know what it is to be so different."

She looked back at him. Even in the dim light, she could see the different shades of his mismatched eyes. His expression was sad, almost bleak.

"It seems a gift with too sharp an edge, does it not?" he asked.

She nodded mutely.

He leaned forward and Amarta found herself doing likewise to meet him forehead to forehead.

Soft sobs thrummed in her chest, threatening a greater storm to come. What was it about Olessio's gentleness and insight that made her defenses seem so thin?

"I know you have a tangled history with him," Olessio said as they both sat up again, "And I see how much you adore him. Wait, no, don't turn away. Let me ask you something." Again she met his eyes, blinking tears that the wind dried fast. "Have you ever felt that you don't deserve your visions? Your..." he paused, as if searching for words. "Your gift-curse?"

She had certainly thought of it as a curse many times, but rarely a gift. She nodded.

"What is his gift-curse, do you think?" Olessio asked.

"He's been studying to kill since the moment he tumbled out from between his mother's legs. I can't even imagine his having a mother."

"Just so," Olessio said. "You and me, we have a gift-curse. A thing drives us. That chases us, really."

"You're *udardae*," Amarta said.

He winced, but met her look evenly. "And you see the future. We did not choose these things. They were thrust upon us. What about Tayre?"

She shook her head. "Nothing was given to him. He works hard to be what he is."

Olessio smiled briefly. "That he does. But what drove him to begin? Something was thrust upon him. What is his gift-curse?"

This was all a new way of thinking to her. "I don't know."

"Nor do I." He shook his head. "I have seen more than a few fights, Amarta. Some to blood, some to death. I can tell you this: he is not like others. Even among those who kill as easily as you and I might drink a cup of water. He's turned himself into a weapon, into all the weapons that a man can be. He is astonishing in motion, is he not?"

"Yes."

"Yet once he was a babe in the arms of that mother you can't imagine. No one becomes so deadly without something to push them, hard, like a horse ridden far past its breaking limit. What made him what he is, do you think?"

She shook her head angrily. "I don't care."

His skeptical look melted into care. "Tragedy, I would guess. He must have started so young." Olessio's voice was sad.

"I suppose," she said.

"He's not much older than I am, Amarta, though he acts it well. You don't see that, though, do you. Something aged him young. No one, on a whim, becomes what he is."

"Do you trust him?" she asked suddenly.

"Me?" He drew his head back slightly in surprise. "That should be your question to answer, surely."

"I own his contract, at least that's what he says. But that's all. I can't bring him closer, but I can send him away." She turned her head slightly, letting the dark motion of the waves draw her thoughts. When she looked back at Olessio, he was studying her intently.

"And will you?" he asked.

She exhaled. Vision drew her attention, as the waves had a moment before. She felt the words move through her throat, in some possible future.

They were hard. They were heavy. *I release you.*

Her stomach trembled. She pushed the vision away.

And the subject of all this talk, Tayre, what was he doing now? She imagined him in some back room with the beautiful Perripin woman, both of them naked, and he giving her every touch and breath that Amarta had craved all this time.

"It hurts," she confessed to Olessio.

He touched the back of her hand with two fingers. "I feel the weeping of your spirit when you look at him. But how can he ever change in your sight, if his shape in your eyes is carved in stone?"

She gaped at Olessio, struck by the thought that Tayre's shape in her eyes might ever change. It came to her that she did not know Olessio any better than she knew Tayre. But how she saw Olessio—his shape in her eyes—had certainly changed since they met.

"Your people," she said. "The Farliosan. You are so close. I envy you this. I have no people, not any more."

He shook his head, his smile wide. Tadesh jumped into his lap. As he spoke, he stroked Tadesh's back.

"The stories I've told you about my people all hold a grain of truth. Some grains are tiny, though—I freely admit that. But there is a tale I have not told you, one that is full of truth, and that is this: centuries ago, when my people first called ourselves the Farliosan—the wanderers, the seekers, the vagabonds—some of us were bloodkin, yes, but many more were not. We came together out of need to escape from the lands that were no longer home, but also out of joy and hunger, to see the world in its many shapes and colors." He leaned forward, took her hands in his. "To wonder at the earth and sky in companionship. Across the centuries, we took in the many who need belonging. It is our way."

Amarta looked at him blankly, not understanding. In the silence that followed, Amarta dipped into the future to seek out his next words for a clue.

He shook her hands in his own. "Stay with me, please?"

Was she so obvious? Apparently so.

"Explain what you mean," she said.

"You are already my people, Amarta. Can you not feel this?"

No words could pass the sudden lump in her throat. For long moments she stared into his eyes, hearing his words again and again.

Around them, the ocean's song wove and dove, half-heard voices that seemed to be the very brew of wisdom she had glimpsed in the stars above. If only she could drink in sound.

"What do I do with him?" she asked the air.

Olessio smiled, put a hand on her shoulder, clasped it affectionately. "What if his shape in your eyes changes? What then?"

Vision tried to answer, muddy and distant. She shook her head, dismissing it.

Tadesh darted from his lap to his arm, then across to her shoulder, settling herself firmly around Amarta's neck, sniffing at her ear. Amarta rubbed at the tickling. Tadesh deftly swapped sides, her snout at the other ear.

"Wise advice, I'm sure," Olessio said of this, grinning. "What does she tell you?"

The smell of brine. Whitecaps under bright sun. An endless, sparkling horizon.

"That he has secured us ship's passage to the islands."

"Ah, excellent!"

Amarta stood, feeling Tadesh easily balance on her shoulders. As the strong claws gripped tight, sinking through her jacket and shirt to her skin, Amarta winced a little. It hurt, but not so much. More a sting that seemed a tonic to her focus.

Tadesh's motion, her whiskers tickling Amarta's neck, all felt like life and breath. Amarta inhaled, feeling sand beneath her feet, seeing the glorious starred sky above.

The call of a future that she did not need to foresee to step into.

When at last her thoughts circled back to Tayre and the young barmaid, Amarta felt an odd lightness, and her imaginings of whatever he might have done to get them passage were somehow no longer barbs in her heart. She even felt a touch of embarrassment at her earlier emotions.

Tayre's actions were in service to Amarta's own goals, and at least for this moment, she did not begrudge him his methods.

"You look better now, Ama. Yes?"

Olessio stood on a boulder, offering her a hand up. She took it, stepped up beside him. Together they made their way to the cobbled road, then back along the walkway.

She took Olessio's hand and squeezed it gratefully. "Yes," she said. "I am."

Chapter Fourteen

FOR SOME TIME NOW, Innel had sat on a small bed, in a small room, and stared at a pale blank wall.

Innel had been washed, his hair cut, his face shaved. It had been done perfunctorily, in the manner one might treat a valuable animal.

He'd been fed good food, but it all came up through his trembling body, and ended up on the floor. He stared at it with a dull regret.

Servants came, cleaned it up, left a bucket. And more food.

When they came back, much later, Innel realized that he had forgotten about the bucket entirely, and made another mess.

The next visitor announced himself as Ralafi, the Domina's majordomo.

"Simpler food," Ralafi told his assistants. He looked at Innel a long moment, shaking his head slowly. "You're a gift the way a goat is a gift. If only we could throw you in the stewpot alongside the carrots and lemons." He heaved a sigh. "Clean him up. Again."

"Kanna," Innel said hoarsely, flatly. "Duca."

"Yes, yes," Ralafi replied impatiently, giving his people more orders.

As Innel continued to stare at the wall, time passed. Motion occurred. Duca and kanna were put into his hand.

"See if this settles you, goat," Ralafi said sourly.

It did.

When next the meals came, the food stayed inside. The walls seemed softer, along with the bed.

More days passed. Innel found it surprisingly easy to take Pava's advice, to stay silent. A childhood trained to use them, and a lifetime spent wielding words like sharp knives, to steer, to sway, to carve.

They all seemed like evil creatures now, that bit and clawed as they came up through his throat.

Yes, there was much to say for silence. Perhaps if he had learned this lesson sooner—

He yanked his thoughts back from that particular cliff and put them onto the blank wall in front of him.

Lavender, he realized. Not white, but pale lavender. Everything here, from bedspread to floor tiles to bucket, tended toward some shade of purple.

It should mean something. What?

That seemed like just the sort of question Pohut might have asked him, an impossibly long time ago. He felt sad not to have an answer.

Innel was led down a hallway of stone floors, checked in black and white, the one thing not in a shade of purple.

He passed walls covered with painted lilacs. Escorting him were three purple-liveried guards. Ralafi led the way.

Innel caught glimpses as they passed windows, tall and

narrow and arched. This mansion was situated on—possibly cut right into—high cliffs overlooking a seaport.

The Cohort-forged part of his mind told him that distant whitecaps made it the Nelar Ocean, and likely he was in the port city of Bayfahar, in Northern Perripur, in the state of Taluk. They would be south of the Arunkel border city of Garaya by some hundred and half miles.

Bayfahar, known for trade in seafood. Famous for a mid-spring festival called, simply, Oyster.

An arm stopped him from walking into a closed set of high double doors, which were papered in various mauve designs to resemble jungle brush in purple twilight.

"Listen to me, boy," Ralafi hissed into his ear. "One step out of line with the Domina, just one, and there will be no more duca or kanna for you. Nod if you understand me."

Innel nodded.

The double doors swung open, held open by lavender-liveried servants, and Innel was thrust and led into a large octagonal room, hued in shades of purple and occasional black-and-white checks.

Drapes of violet and plum silk descended from the ceiling. Wide windows offered an expansive view of the ocean. A cooling sea breeze came in through open panes of tinted glass.

Ralafi bowed. "Domina. The slave."

"Does he have a name?"

"Adra, I believe, Domina."

Innel's attention was drawn to the walls, where various weapons were on display on shelving. Odd weapons, ones he did not recognize. As he puzzled over what they were, moments passed. Finally he saw that on a very large bed at the center of the room reclined a huge, naked Perripin woman.

He glanced at her, then quickly averted his eyes.

What was the protocol here? His mind was sluggish, but he felt certain that if there had been something in his Cohort education about such a thing, he would have remembered it.

His gaze sought the safety of the shelves and the odd weapons of stone and wood and leather, with gemstone-encrusted and silver-wrapped handles.

Not weapons, he realized with a dim surprise. Nothing of the sort.

He blinked slowly as his gaze took them in again. Until this moment, Innel had never considered his Cohort anknapa education lacking.

The naked woman sat up. A servant settled a gossamer robe about her shoulders. She stood and tied it closed.

Innel at last met her look.

The Domina blinked once, then again, and made a thoughtful sound.

"Now that I've seen him this way," she said, "I think I like him better the way he was. Take him away, Ralafi. I don't want to see him again until he's got that hairy beard back on his face."

"Domina?" asked Ralafi, surprised. "Are you certain? Usually you prefer your Arunkin slaves as smooth as a baby's—"

She lifted a fat, ringed hand and Ralafi fell silent.

"Not this one. And further, see if my hair-man can set him up a thick wig and beard until he can grow his own back. My tastes are ever-changing, Ralafi. You know this."

She gave a full-throated laugh, and Ralafi, after a moment's hesitation, joined her. Even the guards tittered.

A strange world, this purple land.

"As you say, Domina," Ralafi said, bowing.

Innel was led from the octagonal space, back across the checkered tiles, to his tiny room, where he again sat on the cot, starting at the pale lavender wall.

She knows who you are.

A tightness came to his gut.

"I'm no one," he said.

Who you were.

"Impossible. I've never seen her before."

And yet, she knows.

Innel put a hand on his bare chin, the scabbed-over wounds, the lump on his lip that Taba had given him. Even bathed and shaved, he felt filthy.

"Brother. What should I do?"

Innel felt Pohut shake his head. What can you do? Not much, I think. Not yet.

Innel nodded his agreement.

Tokerae, his eparch-mother, and his sister Ella had discovered that while they needed to have one of them follow Undul Etris Tay dua Mage about the mansion and grounds that were House Etallan, it was wise to refrain from speaking with him until he had been fed.

Which, as the three of them stood watching him, he clearly had, judging by the empty dishes on his table, the bits of food in his beard, and the trail of crumbs down his shirt.

The mage had been wandering. He would open doors, even those supposedly locked with the finest devices the House could manufacture or obtain.

At last his mother had recruited a trusted elder cousin—half deaf—to stay with the mage at all times.

The elder cousin now stood by the mage's side. In one hand, he offered to the mage's questing fingers the ever-present bowl of warm scented water. In his other, a small towel.

They all watched attentively while Undul Etris Tay

cleaned his hands, finger by finger, in the water, and with a towel.

"Was the meal to your satisfaction, High One?" Tokerae's eparch-mother asked.

"Some of much," the mage nodded.

Was that a yes, or a no, Tokerae wondered.

The mage drank no wine, but he did smoke an enormous quantity of twunta. The elder cousin set a silver tin of fine leaves and a smoking bowl on the table, then lit the delicate bramble for the mage.

A thin trail of expensive smoke rose into the air. The mage took a long draw on the bowl, and leaned back, his gaze coming to rest on the three of them.

"And what?" he asked acerbically.

Tokerae's mother bowed, an abbreviated, confused affair, in which she ended up bowing twice.

Tokerae hid some amused satisfaction. Even his mother was confused by this creature.

"We wonder, High One," she said, "if you might be able to provide us with some assistance. We have important matters that would benefit from your particularly keen eyesight."

Keen eyesight. The Arunkel euphemism for magery.

The mage made a wide, slow circle with his hand, encouraging her to say more.

"Our various Houses—and some misguided royals—are famous for testing young monarchs. Sometimes they go far too far. We here at House Etallan are concerned that our young queen may be vulnerable, and we hope you can help us to know the fractures in her monarchy, so that we may apply suitable mortar to fortify any cracks before they turn into fissures."

The mage looked at her then barked a loud laugh. "Do your kind actually believe this talk?"

Often, Tokerae thought, but didn't say.

The mage puffed from the bowl, exhaled a stream of smoke, and shook slowly his head. "We do not make monarchs."

"By which you mean…?" Tokerae's mother asked.

"The magi do not remove Iliban monarchs and we do not make new ones."

His mother cleared her throat, then again. "I see." Tokerae heard the disappointment in her tone. "Then perhaps you would help us to find those attempting such a thing, so that we might prevent it."

"Is true?" the mage asked wryly, but it was not a question.

"There is always a weakest link in a chain," Ella said. "We want your help finding it."

He met Ella's look, saying nothing.

The mage Undul Etris Tay had been difficult to obtain, his presence brought at great expense, just as Tokerae's mother had demanded. Tokerae saw in his mother's face suppressed annoyance and a growing uncertainty about the purchase.

Good. Now you know how I feel.

His mother had tried, Ella had tried; it was clearly Tokerae's turn.

"Well and so," Tokerae said, "what *can* you do for us?"

The mage scowled, put his hands flat on the table, and pressed himself to stand. "I can leave."

"Ah! No!" His mother cried. "High One, we are honored by your presence in our humble House. I beg you, ignore my rude son. He was dropped on his head by the wetnurse one too many times." She gave Tokerae a fast, fierce glare, "Perhaps a few more might do the trick."

"There are other mages, Mother," Tokerae muttered darkly.

"In truth," Undul Etris Tay said to him. "If you can get them to come here at all. You won't like them. They think of you as cattle."

And you don't?

The mage looked up at the ceiling. Through it, for all Tokerae knew.

"In Perripur," the mage said, "we are hired for our wisdom, but here, you outlaw us. I don't like the hot lands south, and I hear you have good food, so I come. I see that you Arunkin are daft, absurdly dressed animals, who mouth words you do not understand. The food is not that good."

At these words, his mother was breathing heavily, her resolve toward graciousness visibly shredding. The mage examined her curiously, as if she might perform an amusing trick.

Steady, Mother.

"We welcome your wisdom, High One," Tokerae said, before his mother could reply. He dipped his head contritely. "Indeed, we crave the benefit of your sagacity, so that we might protect our excellent queen's health and security against the betrayers who threaten her."

The mage turned a curious look on Tokerae, then examined the smoking bowl, brushing minute bits of ash on the rim back into the bowl. "Betrayers may want weapons."

Tokerae's mother frowned at this obvious statement. "By which you mean…?"

"Swords? Bows? Whatever it is you use to kill each other."

"Yes, I imagine that they would," his mother said flatly.

Across the years, Etallan had stockpiled many times the per-House legal limit of arms, deep within secure basements, as well as across the city. Ready at a moment's notice.

"A wall around the palace?" the mage asked.

"Yes…?"

"Maybe a crack is found."

"That a mage has made?" his mother guessed, giving him a hopeful look.

Undul Etris Tay laughed at her. "You Iliban hear what you want to hear." He returned to his seat, sprinkled fresh twunta leaves from the tin into the coals and took another smoke-filled draw. "Bribe to make more betrayers."

"Yes, yes," his mother said, no longer suppressing her irritation. "But there are too many to bribe them all. A huge army is garrisoned within the walls. It would be impossible for—" the smallest of pauses, and Tokerae saw her mouth "us" before she caught herself. "—any House to undercut our beloved queen, with how many fighting men are loyal."

The mage smirked. "Bribe those who command them, then."

This, too, they had done. Every House had palace spies, who pretended loyalty to the crown and reported back. Etallan had also been building a powerful cache of insiders in high positions, since long before Tokerae had been born.

But this was not merely about numbers, nor would a simple siege succeed; the palace could withstand a far greater external force of arms. Yes, Etallan owned fighting men inside the walls, but would they be reliable? Unhesitating? How many of them, placed there years—or decades ago— would remember their Etallan loyalties at the moment when it mattered most?

Tokerae had another thought. Perhaps there was another way.

"High One," he said, "we have reason to believe that the queen is with child. The Anandynars are known for troubled pregnancies. This might be the weakest link. If you could—"

The mage laughed, loudly, but it ended suddenly, and he looked not at all amused.

"There is nothing you could offer me, Iliban. Nothing."

Undul Etris Tay again got to his feet. "But I am intrigued enough now to visit this so-called Jewel of the Arunkel Empire, to see what I might find with my…keen eyesight."

"Ah—ah," his mother stuttered. "That's not a good plan, High One."

It was too easy to imagine this crumb-bearded mage strolling through the palace, talking indiscriminately about his most recent meal at House Etallan, or the quality of the twunta there. Judging by their expressions, his mother and Ella were seeing a similar nightmare vision.

The mage grinned into their uneasy looks. "Yes, I will do this now. The famous library. Private gardens. Magenta walls. Maybe I will examine—how did you say?—your excellent queen's health and security. You have a carriage, yes?"

"Of course," his mother breathed.

"What is chef making tonight, so I know to stay or return?"

Stay or return?

He meant to compare their food to that of the palace's kitchens and the royal chef.

"Tonight's feast is second to none, High One, I assure you." Tokerae could feel his eparch-mother's gaze land on him. Relief washed over him as she turned to Ella.

"We'll find out what it is forthwith, High One." She snapped her fingers at her daughter.

Ella gritted her teeth, and took off at a run.

⁓

The mage left soon after Ella had relayed the menu to him in her seductive voice, insisting on walking to the palace himself, waving away the carriage. He refused to say whether he'd be back tonight or tomorrow. Or ever.

Tokerae followed his eparch-mother into the hallway.

"Mother."

She turned on him, and he instantly regretted picking this moment.

"What?"

"The plan. We are ready."

Her eyes narrowed, lips thinned. "How dare you presume to tell me that. I tell you. Not the other way around. If this useless, gluttonous creature had offered us any material help—"

"We don't need him. I have—"

"You?" She stepped close to him, too close. Tokerae stifled an urge to retreat from the small woman. "Did you know that in Southern Perripur, a woman claiming to be the Seer of Arunkel has caused a riot and destroyed an order of monks? No, you didn't. You are entirely ignorant."

Tokerae opened his mouth and shut it again.

Her look was full of disgust. "Leave off making large plans, boy, until you're capable of fulfilling a small one."

Any response he might have made had died on his lips. He watched, mute, as she strode away.

All at once he realized that his mother had no intention of giving the eparchy to him.

Ella approached from the other direction.

"No?"

"Most ardently no. Father?"

Ella scoffed. "He has no edge." Their father was devoted to their mother, but not Etallan born and bred, and lacked the razor-sharp instincts that defined the family.

"We tried," Tokerae said.

"What do you know of this new Lord Commander?" Ella asked.

Tokerae blinked at this change of subject. "Nalas? I know him. Not well. Why?"

Ella made an amused sound. "He had plans to marry a

commoner woman and adopt her boy as his own, but the wedding was postponed. He quietly sent them both out of town. This before the traitor mutt was arrested and executed. Before."

"Before. Where are they?"

She shook her head. "Shouldn't be too hard to find out. Good to have some leverage, should he prove to be a problem."

Tokerae smiled. "You think like Cohort, Ella."

She dimpled, then her smile faded. "Have you been seeing your shoemaker girl recently?"

Tokerae had become covert in his infrequent visits to see Lilsla. That Ella even had to ask was gratifying.

"No."

"Good. Stay focused. I'm thinking of Citriona, for Assel."

The two of them had recently decided that, somehow, they would bring their brother home.

"Citriona's just a child."

"She's sixteen, Tok. More importantly, she's an Anandynar. We're going to need as many of those as we can get." She sighed. "Any chance the child in Cern's belly is yours?"

Tokerae grimaced, remembered his last somewhat humiliating visit to the queen. "No."

"A pity. All this would be much easier from the inside of the palace."

"I did try."

"You were polite and respectful?"

"Yes!"

"That's the problem. The traitor mutt was shameless," Ella said. "He was willing to drop a bloody, dead body on an elegant palace floor, right there in front of her. Not once, but twice."

Pohut.

Eregin.

"Maybe that's what it was," Ella said.

"What *what* was?"

"That she found so attractive about the treasonous bastard. A man who comports himself as her equal, instead of scraping the ground with his nose."

Tokerae stiffened angrily. "I didn't—" Scrape the ground. "You don't understand. With Cern there is a line that you do not cross."

She put a hand on his shoulder. "Or maybe, brother, there's a line that she had best not cross with you."

In her fond, proud smile, his anger melted.

"I'll send Citriona something lovely in your name," Ella said. "Just in case we need her later. In the meantime, go see your Cohort sister again. The moment she names the father, and it's not you, we're in trouble."

Their spies in the palace had told them who had visited during the timeframe that might have led to Cern's conception. Murice. Helata. Kincel.

"If it's Putar," Tokerae said, shaking his head, "that's not good."

"Fates, I hope it's not House Kincel."

Kincel was one of the most powerful of the eight Houses. They had money, information, and commanded waystations, prostitutes, and quarries. But Kincel was not much inclined toward cooperation with Etallan.

"Pitch her again, brother, before the damned thing gets any bigger. If we can marry her, we'll save ourselves a lot of risk."

"We? I'm the one taking the chances."

Or was that unfair of him? Ella had been doing a great deal to further their goals to restore their House's honor.

She reached up to put both hands on either side of his

head and pulled it down gently, meeting his forehead with her own. "You're right, brother. You are."

She took a breath, and after a moment, he did likewise.

"All right," he said. "I'll try again."

Thus far, Cern's second pregnancy had been treating her very well indeed. At this point in the first, she'd been in agony, bedridden, and terrified.

Now, though, a vitality and confidence coursed through her. In truth, she could not remember having ever felt better.

As she dressed today, she chose to forgo the flowing robes that—as Sachare had put it—simply said that she was getting fat. In this snugger outfit, the shape of her stomach made her state obvious.

As Cern and her retinue progressed through the halls, walking slowly to the Council meeting, denizens lined the walls to clear the way. Bows turned into gaping stares and fast whispers.

Good. That would take care of making sure the news got out. Much faster than announcing it herself, and more effective than having a speaker call the news from the palace guard-towers.

Her seneschal opened the doors and bowed her inside, and Cern entered into the Amardide Room, where ministerial eyes widened. She had their undivided attention.

Her belly did, anyway.

The wan morning light suffused the room from overhead windows. On a side table sat the black-and-gold book of names, like a particularly stiff Minister.

Around the table, looks were traded, sold, pressed, as a silent negotiation took place. Finally the First Minister cleared his throat.

"Your Majesty. You are…pregnant."

"Yes."

The council took a moment to digest this.

"There have been…" The First Minister said, his mouth working, as if he were testing words. "A number. Of men. To your rooms. Your Majesty."

"Yes."

"Ah." He cleared his throat again. "Not to come too hastily to the point, Your Excellent Majesty, but do you know who the father is?"

"I do."

"Is it…it's not…" The First Minister looked around the table for help from the other ministers. Not finding it, he looked back at Cern, his mouth seeming stuck in an open position.

Cern took pity on him. "No, it is not the traitor whom I had executed."

Or, for that matter, the unfortunate fellow who stood in for him.

"You are quite sure of who the father is?"

"I said I was."

It hardly seemed possible, but the Ministers looked even more unsettled at this. Cern was not surprised; each of them had extensive dealings with the Houses. She had no doubt that many of their contacts were eagerly awaiting confirmation of the rumor. And a name.

"How can you be certain?" the Minister of Accounts whispered.

She bit back on a sharp reply at being questioned for the third time and instead gave him her complete attention. His ears pinked as he looked down at his hands in his lap.

"Because it is my business to know such things, Minister," she said, as if speaking to a child. "For that matter, it is my business to choose the father of my child, as my father chose my mother, and his grandmother—the great Niala—selected the many fathers of her many children."

"Yes, of course, but." The First Minister spoke again. "Times are changing."

"I had noticed," Cern said dryly.

"Why not simply name the father to us now, Your Majesty?" asked the Minister of Justice. "The traitor would be forgotten and all confusion settled."

All confusion settled? Cern suppressed a laugh at this assertion that a mere name would restore sense to the court, never mind the Houses.

Are we talking about the same court, Minister?

She took a moment to discard the other witty answers that leapt to mind. *Your name, perhaps, ser? Let's see how long you last.*

But no. Her reign was not strong enough yet for humor, let alone cutting, acerbic Cohort humor.

Alas, it might be some time before she could joke with anyone other than Sachare.

"Because," she replied calmly, "as things stand with the Houses now, Minister, if I put my increasing weight on any one of them, the stability of the others who support the monarchy and our essential work would be imperiled. None of us want that."

"This ambiguity seems risky."

She nodded. "All courses are risky, Minister. I do have every intention of naming the father, at an appropriate time. Perhaps after the next child, or the following." She held up a hand to forestall the eager comments that the Ministers were ready to make. "At an appropriate time. But I will name no father until I have prepared those who are not named for disappointment. Until then, let each believe that it might be them."

Except Etallan. That particular meeting had not gone

well enough for Tokerae to wonder if the child might be his. Was there any point in giving him a chance to be better behaved when she was showing with some other man's child? That would be tricky.

She looked around the room. The Ministers either saw the sense in her plan, or the resolution in her expression.

The First Minister gave a small nod, a bow of acceptance.

"It is time," Cern continued, "to begin preparations in earnest. All the Houses must be similarly courted, lest the father determine, from lack of offered sweets, that he is, indeed, the chosen one." None of the potential fathers were simpletons, after all.

"Your Excellent Majesty, you could tell us," the First Minister said. "In confidence."

"I could. It is not that I mistrust you to keep this essential secret." It was exactly that, actually, but it wasn't only the Houses that needed sweetening. "Rather, it is that I must ask you to be my agents and court the Houses on my behalf. Your negotiations are greatly aided if you truly do not know the identity of the father."

"Your agents, Your Majesty?"

"Yes. The Houses have great respect for the Queen's Ministerial Council." Well, not exactly, but no need to spell out the nuances. "You, or those you delegate—I leave that to you—are to address each of the Houses. Illuminate for them, without promising anything of substance, what each House might desire, that the crown might provide. You will then propose to me a plan of royal attentions, arrangements, and favors, such that each House might feel properly honored and respected. This is no simple matter. I need your help."

She could almost hear their thoughts turning, as each Minister considered what they might broker with the Houses backed by the force of a pregnant queen whose father was yet unknown. What could they fashion, they were no doubt wondering, between the royals, with whom they already had connections, and the Houses with whom they yet might?

Advantageous arrangements for each of them, if they did not dally, and let another minister get there first. It was a rare opportunity. A rich one.

It would keep them busy.

She gave them another moment to digest, plan, and scheme.

"Now, to discuss my unborn child's name. Let's have a look at that book, Ministers."

*D*aughter, the Houses are both bedrock and quicksand for the crown. Do what you must to keep them in line. Gifts. Royal weddings. Slots in the Cohort. But never fight them.

It was sound advice, and Cern resolved to keep it, as Tokerae entered her sitting room. He gave a minimal bow, then sat where she gestured, across the small table.

Metal goblets sat before them both, Etallan in origin, rimmed in copper and silver weave. Older than the Grandmother Queen.

A gesture of respect to his House, though it was not clear to Cern that he even noticed. He was tense, as if nerving himself for something.

What now, Tokerae?

They exchanged polite greetings. Wine was poured, the servants dismissed.

Tokerae had been staring at her stomach rather openly.

"I'm here to make you another offer," he said bluntly, putting his gaze on her face.

What, no flowery language? All that Cohort education, gone to waste?

"Do say."

"With House Etallan by your side, the traitor will be forgotten, all confusion settled."

It sounded rehearsed, and was nearly the same phrasing that the ministers had used. She wondered which of them Tokerae had spoken to before he'd come here.

She considered her reply. Something about being impressed with his passion. Reiterate the close historic connections between her family and his House. *A wedding between one of my cousins and one of your kin, Etallan?* That could be part of the balance. There were still a few young marriageables with the name of Anandynar.

Too soon, she judged.

"I trust that the crown and House Etallan will always stand side by side," she said tactfully.

He snorted softly at the polite words and took a breath. "You must know that there are those who are troubled—royals among them—to see you keep a traitor's child as your heir. But this, too, is a problem that can be repaired with my help."

Cern blinked. "Are you suggesting that my child and heir is somehow broken and needs repair? Is that really what you mean to say?"

Tokerae looked dismayed. For a moment she thought he'd apologize. But then his features settled into an ugly determination.

"You need another child, Your Majesty. By a strong father. Soon. Yes, I realize that I speak bluntly. Consider it a measure of my respect—I speak thus for your benefit. Now is the time."

"What is your urgency, Tok?"

"When I become Eparch, my priorities must change."

"That sounds surprisingly like a threat. I'm certain you don't mean it that way."

Their gazes locked. Cern felt as if she were back in the

Cohort, the object of everyone's ambitions, the subject of constant testing to see where her focus and resolve might flex or crack.

Tokerae looked away first.

"Do you care to explain?" Cern asked softly.

He looked around the room then back. "I am your best choice for Consort. What you've got in you—" his eyes flickered to her belly. "Keep it if you wish, but all the next ones would be mine, and you would agree to name them as heirs in preference."

Anger washed over her. You've got a temper, daughter. Compose your words in your head, not with your tongue.

She stood, letting the moment lengthen, while she took hold of her anger and forced herself to think. Even her father had never so insulted her.

Well, no, that wasn't true. He had and often, which was why this moment felt so familiar. Ironically, that familiarity gave her a sort of ballast now.

For a moment she wondered if her father had treated her roughly, deliberately, to provide her the skills for moments like these.

Tokerae stood as well.

"Only Etallan can protect your crown, Cern. Surely you can see this."

"You cross the line, Tokerae," she said coolly. "My great-grandmother would have you in a tower cell for those words."

He inclined his head, taking the point. "Different times, Your Grace. But I do think that if Niala the Conqueror stood where you stand now, she would see the wisdom of aligning with Etallan. Without delay." He cocked his head slightly. "Don't let circumstances turn on you, Cern. All can be set right, in one very sensible decision. Marry me."

Cern ached to call guards, to have him dragged down the

halls, out the palace doors, and thrown into the mud. Some traitor part of her wished for Innel by her side. His cutting wit, his fast blade. She pictured the room splattered with the blood of another headless Etallan scion.

Cern wondered if Tokerae—threatening and promising —represented his eparch-mother's agenda or not. For a moment she considered summoning her to ask. But no— Etallan was not in the habit of providing clear answers, and there would be a cost to going around Tokerae.

Either way, no body dragging or head-carrying would occur today. They could exchange barbed, cutting words— even insults—but Cern would not act against House Etallan, and he knew it.

"Watch your step, Tokerae dele Etallan. The ice is thin where you walk."

Uncertainly passed across his face briefly and was gone. "We are patriots, House Etallan is, despite the unfair accusations and horrendous acts against us. We are Your Majesty's most loyal House. But only if you treat us with appropriate respect."

Appropriate respect. Capitulation, he meant. Reduce her to a gilded broodmare.

A bitter taste filled her mouth, along with many words that she could not say. Her fingers twitched with actions she could not take.

"My condition unsettles me," she said lowly. "I have a tendency to regurgitate at anything distasteful. I advise your hasty departure, lest you be splattered by my royal vomit."

A soft, amused snort. Then: "Cern—"

"My vomit and my temper. Go."

His smile went wry, then sour as he bowed slightly, and back to the door. He knocked. It opened. He left.

Cern took a breath, and opened the other door. There in the side room, Sachare held Estarna's hands. The child stood, on wobbly feet, grinning widely at Cern, her face smeared with red jam.

Cern considered this tableau, the Houses, Tokerae dele Etallan, and what to do.

There was always risk. All she could do was to weigh one risk against another.

"Sacha. Bring back the dogs."

Chapter Fifteen

"SHE'S THE SEER? THAT ONE?"

"Who else? Dressed like beggars, but given entrance to Overlook? Must be."

"Hoi," Olessio whispered to Amarta, as she turned her gaze from the ocean far below to look at the crowded room behind her. "Famous. I told you."

"Ah! She's turning around—look!" "Such a dull face." "Doesn't seem like a seer to me."

Behind her was a huge, cavernous cave cut into the rock of a mountainside. Tadesh, on Olessio's shoulder, turned her head along with Amarta.

Across the room, Overlook's wealthy patrons looked back. They snickered, pointed, shook their heads, whispered.

On the ship journey here, Tayre had covered a full cabin bunk with sketches of Amarta. Some were very good. *No point in disguise, now,* he'd said. *Everyone knows what you look like.*

"They're not even whispering," she said to Olessio. "Do they think I don't understand Perripin?"

"No. They hope you do," Olessio replied. "Ignore them.

It's all the glitter, poor things. Weighs them down, body and spirit."

Perhaps he was right. Drapes of fine mesh clung over brilliantly colored silks and velvets. Bejeweled pins passed through swirls and waves of hair that rose up and up, putting Senta's festival-goers to shame.

Good thing the ceilings were so high.

Everywhere gemstones glittered, on ears, lips, hands, around eyes. Chains of gold and silver draped, coiled, and wrapped around hands, wrists, forearms.

Weighted down with glitter indeed.

It was true that the three of them looked ragged. There had been no time between the ship's docking at the end of the long sea voyage to do anything but find their way up the steep, circling road to Overlook, if they wanted to see the formation of the Island Road, called The Assembly.

Even so, it would not have mattered; they owned nothing that could match this finery.

Amarta returned her attention to the wide expanse of ocean. Overlook was halfway up the side of the high mountain, on the island of Turia, the northernmost of the chain of islands called The Spine of the World.

The room was packed, people nearly shoulder-to-shoulder, the wealthiest from all across Perripur and beyond, gathered to witness—to wager—on the Assembly. Since Amarta and her companions had arrived, they had been maneuvered forward in the room, to the viewing window.

At first she didn't understand why, but then it became clear: everyone wanted to watch not only the Assembly but Amarta and her companions. Now, at the very front, they were part of the show.

With an excellent view. There was an advantage to being a curiosity.

The mountain dropped away steeply from where she

stood, down to the port and the ocean. A dizzy vertigo claimed her, knotting her stomach. She looked at the floor, gripping Olessio's shoulder, from where Tadesh licked her hand.

The nausea passed, the rough tongue oddly comforting, even if it elicited titters from her observers.

By the time Amarta could peer out again without feeling wretchedly ill, six islands were inching into view moving toward a spit of land—a finger of beach— at the north end of Turia. As the islands slowly came close, their unique shapes and coloring became evident. One even had a mountain of its own.

Moving through the crowd filling Overlook were the hosts, men and women dressed in tunics of softly clattering falls of seashells. They brought drinks, they took wagers. As each island came into view, they called out its name.

"Carugrua! Carugrua!"

Rising above the chatter of the crowd came wild cheers and la-las.

North beyond the expanse of blue that was the canvas for the moving islands, a line of mountains atop a thin pale beach marked the continent of Seute Enta.

Seute Enta, where Amarta would find the Heart of Seuan.

Again, dizziness overtook her. Amarta looked at her feet instead of the vista, at a mermaid shape in a constellation of gemstones laid into the floor. Her arms were outstretched, beads of onyx hair swirling. Her spine was diamonds, one for each of the islands of the Spine of the World. At the top of her head glinted Turia.

"Jalui! Jalui!"

Another island, darkly green, entered the ocean vista from the west.

Calls to the Overlook hosts became urgent. Amounts.

Names and positions. Hosts scrambled, writing on thin flats of polished tree bark, waving them dry, breaking them in two.

At their side, a host bowed, her long seashell vest tinkling.

"Virtuous Ones, might you like to wager on the islands?"

"Sombaa for first!" cried a man, waving large coins at her. He was the servant of a man whom Tayre had pointed out to her earlier, the Perripin duke of Dulu. A king, Tayre told her, before the Perripin Accord made Dulu a state instead of a country.

"Your tic, Most Virtuous One," said another host, handing him half of a flat.

"Jalui will be ultimate," called someone. "I was wrong last Assembly, but now I am quite, quite certain."

"A wager, Virtuous Ones?" the host asked again, looking at Amarta.

Olessio grinned, nudged her gently. "Famous."

"Should I?" she asked.

"How is the health of our purse?" Olessio asked Tayre.

Tayre look was amused. "You're an expensive pet, Vagras."

"Pet me and find out," Olessio quipped, then gave Amarta a conspiratorial wink.

Amarta laughed a little at this, realizing that it was her trust in Olessio that made the joke funny rather than unsettling. He touched her reassuringly.

"We could stand to have more coin," Tayre said. "However: Amarta, make small winnings. Confuse your observers."

"Yes, I will wager," Amarta told the host.

Around her, conversation faded. The quiet rippled outward. Bodies leaned, waiting for her to speak. At the door, late arrivals whispered, pointed.

Unnerved by all this attention, Amarta looked back at the ocean. The blue expanse below seemed to pull away from her, yet she felt she might be swallowed by it. Her stomach lurched.

For a moment she saw no islands, no green-blue water. Thousands watched, waiting for her to speak. Her stomach lurched.

She felt Tayre's touch on her arm. "What are you seeing?"

"I'm fine." She focused on the vista below and the present. "Carugrua," she said to the host, "for first position."

A slab was sketched with the name, broken in half, the tic given to her.

Confuse them, Tayre had said. The host was turning away as Amarta said loudly, "And Sombaa for first position."

A bemused muttering rippled back into the excited chatter.

"Both?" asked the host.

"Yes."

A booming laughter silenced through the crowd. A woman's voice rang out. "I had heard the Seer of Arunkel was here," she said, in Arunkin. "I gather that I was misinformed."

A path cleared between Amarta and the entrance. There stood a woman, her wide aristocratic features framed by loose, brown curls and a high collar of yellow and brown.

"House Elupene," Tayre said softly to her. "Child of the Eparch, at a guess. Say nothing. Let it go."

Elupene, one of the Great Eight Houses. *No reason for disguise, now.*

"You know who I am," Amarta called back. "Who are you?"

"Wouldn't a true seer know that already?" The woman gave a flick of her hand, rings of gold catching the light. "But the world is so full of pretenders, isn't it? Been a lucrative performance for you, *Seer*?"

"It's bait, Amarta," Tayre said. "Don't bite."

The woman strode forward, riding boots falling heavily onto the stone floor. As she came close, Tayre stepped back a pace, his head dropping as if a respectful bow to the House Elupene scion.

But Amarta knew better: he was angling his head to see the scene, preparing to fight if he must.

He wouldn't have to; foresight told her that in the next few minutes violence was unlikely.

"I am the Eparch-heir of House Elupene of Arunkel," The woman said. "The greatest House and empire the world has ever known." The woman stopped short of too close and looked Amarta up and down. "You are a pretender who makes two first-position bets. Why not bet on every island for first place? You're bound to be right once."

Amarta felt herself redden. *Don't bite.* She turned her back on the woman.

Below, nine green shapes were now in view, slowly coming closer to the spit of land. The Assembly was about to begin.

The host broke the Sombaa marker in two and held it out to Amarta to take.

"I rescind the Sombaa wager," Amarta said. "But I will make eight more."

"Eight?" someone asked. "Going to wager on all the islands for first place, like the Arunkin suggested?" "Idiocy! She'd lose so much." "Could she be wagering on each position, then?" "No, no. Wrong count."

Shell-clad hosts gathered around Amarta, hands poised over flats of polished bark.

"Sombaa for position two," Amarta said.

A mark was made, the tic broken in half, offered to

Amarta. She gestured to Olessio, who snatched it from the host.

"Molimba for three," Amarta said. "Chosolua for four."

Another tic to Olessio, then another.

Tayre put a warning hand on Amarta's arm. "Amarta. I said let it go."

"Most Virtuous One. Three islands in a row is quite an investment. Four is even more so. Are you certain?"

"And place five?" asked the Eparch-heir, her voice full of mocking excitement.

"Amarta," Olessio said in a hushed tone. "If we lose—ah. Do we have this much money?"

"We do not," Tayre answered.

The shell-clad host held up a hand to the hosts now waving slabs dry. They froze.

The Eparch-heir's grin was wide, challenging. "Anyone can *guess*, Seer. Anyone."

Amarta matched gazes with the eparch-heir.

"Jalui for fifth place," Amarta said. "Tukimpe for sixth."

The other woman snorted, as if vastly amused. "Seventh?"

"Most Virtuous Ones," said the shell-clad host. "This wager is not recommended. Seven in a row. It is—"

"Cadii," Amarta said. "Haulala for eighth. Punaami, ninth and last."

"What is she doing?" someone asked. "She's got it all wrong. There are ten islands." "Pah. Be a fine story to tell back home, anyway."

The shell-clad woman bowed deeply to Amarta. "We cannot recommend this wager, sera. So much remorse, but we cannot."

"What they mean, Seer," said the Eparch-heir, "is that they can't cover your bet, should you win. Even the fantastic wealth flowing through Turia today wouldn't be enough to pay off a nine-island wager. Should you win. Which you won't."

"I don't care about the money," Amarta snapped at her.

Beside her, Olessio made a choking sound.

"Most Virtuous Ones," said the shell-clad woman severely, "Tulia always pays its debts. It is our virtue. But this—"

"I will take the wager for Turia," the Eparch-heir announced. Gasps from the crowd. Whispers of delighted shock. "I am not afraid to pay your winnings, Seer, if there are any. But when you *lose*…"

Tayre tapped her shoulder. *No.* He tapped it again clearly. Amarta stepped away.

"What do you want, Eparch-heir?" Amarta asked.

The woman gave her a wolfish smile. "Five years of service to House Elupene. In the person of myself. I have many friends in Arunkel who are eager to speak with the Seer of Arunkel. At length."

Tayre grabbed her arm. "Amarta. Say no."

"Five years of servitude?" Olessio asked. "Don't agree, Amarta."

"The Assembly begins!"

"Carugrua is attaching!"

While Amarta and the Eparch-heir faced each other, all other eyes turned to the ocean. The business of wagers became very loud, very urgent.

"Jalui is attaching!" someone cried. "Second place!" "What? But the Seer said…" "Oh, wait, no it's not. It's passing Cadii, is what. Exchanging places."

"What did she say about Cadii?" "Seven." "Impossible! Look at how close it is to Turia."

Onto the first of ten alabaster pedestals at the side of the Overlook room, a host placed a large, flat stone of green marble.

The din surged. People stamped the floor, shouted at the islands. "Move, damn you!" "By the gods, what are you doing?" "Come here! I have a wager!" "What did she say for two? What?" "Sombaa, I think."

More cries, bark tics hastily waved to dry, broken in two, hosts dashing through the crowd.

Amarta glanced at her companions. "What should I ask for?"

"Money," Olessio said.

"Letters of credit," Tayre said. "Safe transport to Seute Enta."

Amarta turned to the Eparch-heir. "Letters of credit redeemable in Seute Enta. Transport for me and my companions, whole and safe, to that continent."

"Easily done," the Eparch-heir said, who clearly didn't think she'd lose.

Curses and jubilations and howls swept across the room at a volume that made no other conversation possible. Tadesh snaked into Olessio's pack, and finding it no quieter, came back out to perch on his shoulder.

One by one, the islands slowly came together, linked like puzzle pieces, forming a line from Turia's coastal spit and stretching north to form a floating peninsula. As each island attached, the hosts laid the appropriate marble marker atop a pedestal and closed the wagers for that island.

One by one, Amarta was right.

Punaami set itself at the northernmost end of the chain. Water rippled out from the edges of the Island Road, the wakes spreading out to the horizon.

The room fell silent.

A host spoke. "The Island Road is Assembled, most Virtuous Ones."

"But there were ten last time!" "Used to be more. Why, a hundred years ago…" "I'd better still be getting my Pearls."

Still staring at the islands, Amarta said: "There will be no tenth island."

Her words were repeated, rippling out across the room, as the eparch-heir cursed, loudly, passionately, and thoroughly. She paused, then did it again.

Amarta smiled a little. She would wager that few among the dominantly Perripin crowd behind her knew what those Arunkin words meant, but everyone knew who had won the wager between the Seer and the Eparch-heir.

Amarta did not turn to see the eparch-heir's expression. She had seen it already, in vision.

When at last Amarta did turn, the woman had left the Overlook room. Perhaps to fulfill the wager, perhaps not. Amarta found that she didn't care. Winning was enough.

Olessio gaped at the vista below, bouncing where he stood, expression full of unrestrained rapture. Tadesh, not liking being jostled, made the jump from Olessio's shoulders to Amarta's, some four paces away, sinking her claws in deep to gain purchase. Amarta clenched her teeth at the sudden pain.

Olessio, transfixed, stared at the peninsula of vibrant green below. He stepped close and took her hand.

This is what he meant, she realized as she squeezed his fingers in return.

To wonder at earth and sky. To see the world in its many shapes and colors.

Olessio whispered to her: "I've always wanted to see this."

～

Half the crowd of Overlook eagerly streamed from the room. The other half turned to Amarta.

A crowd would gather. Questions. Demands. Bribes.

"If we don't leave soon…" Amarta looked to Tayre, seeking direction.

He leaned close to her ear, speaking quietly. "So many deals to be made. So much wealth to be had. A shame if someone else got there first."

She blinked, understanding, and spoke the words Tayre had given her. In moments the Overlook room was empty.

"Where did they all go?" she asked.

"To the harbors of the Island Road, Virtuous Ones," answered a host, "where the islanders await their bids for the Islands' unique produce."

"We have to go," Amarta said, rushing outside, the others following.

They had managed a ride up the mountain on donkeys, faster than hiking the steep ascent, but they must descend even more quickly and get to the port before the opportunity passed.

Outside Overlook, one small wagon remained, rickety and mule-led, that had once had sides. A handful of Tulia islanders stood by.

An eager-looking youth approached. "Most Virtuous Ones. We find you a boat to take you to the Punaami harbor, to buy rare, expensive goods. Yes?"

"No, no," said Olessio, still bouncing slightly. "We are walking the Island Road, from Carugrua to Punaami."

"Oh! I am sad for you!" the youth said to him. "It is not allowed."

"Not allowed? What?" Olessio asked. "What?"

"The Island Road," the youth said. "It is so much and very. It is—how to say?"

Olessio smiled uncertainly. "Tender? Exquisite? Alluring? Astounding? Astonishing? Beyond compare?"

The youth's eyebrows twitched and he nodded vigorously, matching Olessio's enthusiasm. "Yes! Kee! The islands, kept apart so long—" he held his hands wide, then brought them together tightly. "Now they kiss. Share breath."

"Breath? You mean breeze?" Olessio suggested.

"Yes! All mix together." The youth waved his hands in the air. "So many things! Grow so fast!"

Olessio smiled wide and gave Amarta a near-manic look. "To walk the Island Road. Amarta?"

"I find nice boat," the youth said placatingly. "See it from the water? Maybe even Island Pearls? Much money, yes?" He looked at them eagerly, gesturing behind his back to the young woman at the wagon, who, Amarta judged from her features, was a sister.

"Ride with us, great Seer," the sister said, gesturing at the wagon.

"I come with you!" the youth said, grabbing their belongings and loading them into the wagon. They were gestured to load up into the back, and the wagon lurched forward down the road.

"My name is Rhaata," the youth said. "Means very clever. I know much! I study the Island Road all my life. Speak many languages!"

Amarta frowned at this likely exaggeration. Rhaata could not be more than twelve.

"Amarta," Olessio said urgently, his gleeful smile turning sickly. "To come all this way…are we not to walk the Road?"

His pleading look tore at her heart, and she set the question into the future. A man in a feathered headdress of bright green and yellow met them on a rocking walkway.

"Kee! Great Seer! They will not let you. But if they do, take me. I can help!" Rhaata was trembling, his youthful eagerness a bright mirror to Olessio's desperate craving.

"Yes, yes," she said. To the air, to the boy, to Olessio.

Amarta took one look over the side of the road, as the wagon made its way down the steep mountainside, and resolved not to do it again. As they went, Olessio urged Rhaata to say more about the Island Road.

"Gods, they are!" Rhaata said. "So much longing! Like lovers separated, together at last, must make much fast, joyous copulation."

"Yes? Yes?" Olessio prompted.

"Flowers bigger than your head! Crickets like dogs! Petals as wide as ships' sails!"

Amarta exchanged a skeptical but amused look with Tayre while Olessio hung on every word.

"Y ou are the one? She-who-knows-tomorrow?"

The old man spoke in stilted Perripin. He wore a cloak of feathers, brilliant green and yellow and purple, his legs spread wide for balance on the floating ocean walkway that connected Tulia to Carugrua. At each side was a child, a boy and girl.

The walkway spanned some fifty feet of ocean between the sandy spit of north Tulia and the Island Road, rocking as the ocean surf lapped at its sides. Behind them on the beach had gathered a crowd of onlookers.

"I am that one," Amarta said.

It was a bracing freedom to claim it, though alongside that was a dim fore-sense that in many futures she would come to be weary of the question.

"What do you want?" he called.

"To walk the Island Road," Amarta answered.

"Many want. Few receive." He gestured to Tayre and Olessio, on either side of Amarta, with a hand missing fingers. "Are these men yours?"

Amarta blinked, surprised at the question, and not at all sure how to answer.

"Yes," she said.

A soft exhale from one of the men. She couldn't tell which one.

At the old man's side, the children gaped at her, at Olessio, and at Tadesh on his shoulders. The old man put hands on their shoulders.

"If you are She-who-knows-tomorrow, say what I will say next. This, tell me."

Ah, the most common of the tests. Of course, anything she said would change his answer, but it would hardly be proof if she told him that.

"'That thing on your shoulder,'" Amarta answered. "'What is it?'"

The man's mouth opened a little in what might have been surprise. "And the answer?"

Amarta looked at Olessio.

"Tadesh? She's my companion," Olessio said.

"Companion?" asked the old man.

Olessio gave Amarta a fast, affectionate grin. "Let's call her my first wife."

"You are strange," the old man said. "Next what will I say?"

Amarta suppressed a frustrated sigh. He would ask more questions, is what he would do, and anything she predicted, he would alter. That's what people did.

"You will say," Amarta answered firmly, "come walk the Island Road, She-who-knows-tomorrow."

The man stared at her a moment. Then he swept off his feathered headdress, handing it to one of the children, and walked forward. His hair was divided into straight braids, slicked back with oil, stretching down his bare shoulders, white against his tanned skin, and as he came close, she saw that his eyes were the color of green seawater, heavily limned in red.

He spread his lips wide across his teeth. It was almost a smile.

"We are honored, She-who-knows-tomorrow. Welcome to Carugrua."

Olessio gasped in delight. He looked at her, his eyes shining, his elation contagious.

To wonder at earth and sky in companionship.

The old man walked back the way he had come, the children trailing, staring over their shoulders.

Tayre grabbed her arm, held her back from following. "Amarta. Are you certain?"

"Of what?" It was just the sort of annoying reply that he might give.

"Of our successful traverse of the Island Road," he said calmly.

Olessio watched them, vibrating with worry.

"There is always a path to failure, is there not?" Amarta asked, tossing his words back at him.

But it was true; all she needed to do to find futures with dire outcomes was to look for them. So much could go wrong in the shallows of the unlikely. What use was there in foreseeing near-impossibilities of death and devastation, when the real events of her past still burned like hot coals in her mind and spirit?

At the far end of the walkway, the old man called over the ocean wind. "Do you come, She-who-knows, or no?"

"Yes! We come!"

But still Tayre held her arm, bent close to her ear. "Always a path to failure, yes. Do you remember when we boarded the *Debt Incurred* to Tulia, and I asked you if we were likely to disembark safely? Answer that question again."

Hot annoyance washed over her. "Do you think me a fool? A child? I have foreseen us on the final island countless times, from countless viewpoints." The deck of a sailing ship. A bobbing canoe. The high cliffs of Seute Enta.

Olessio stared at Carugrua's beach, trees, his hunger and apprehension palpable.

Amarta felt a similar craving as she looked north, to Seute Enta, a line of blue-gray on the horizon, where the Heart of Seuan and answers awaited her.

It could be another hoax, another charlatan, another swindle, but she would not dwell on that possibility. Her own spirit was fed by Olessio's desire and his joy at this dream fulfilled.

If there was disappointment to come, it could wait a little while longer to find her.

She pulled from Tayre's grip and strode forward, Olessio eagerly at her side, Tayre trailing. From Olessio's shoulder, Tadesh sniffed at the air.

"I come, too!" Rhaata called running to catch up, his grin nearly as wide as Olessio's.

~

Amarta and her party stepped onto a beach of stones, shells, and bleached fish bones, trailing the old man and children through a narrow opening in a high wall of thick-grown trees.

As they entered a clearing, they were fast surrounded by a crowd of islanders in bright, rippling silks and feathers, their spears raised.

Tayre dropped back into a slight crouch.

"They are allowed," shouted the old man, waving reassurances. Spears lowered. To Amarta, he said: "Many try to take. Not with honor. We defend. You understand?"

"We are with honor," Olessio said, chuckling nervously. "Nearly made of the stuff."

"I am Tumaya," the old man said. "It means One-who-makes-best-welcome. And it is so."

Tumaya led them forward along a wide path into the brush, the many islanders following. In another clearing, long-necked birds wandered high grasses, their heads to Amarta's waist, tails long. One gave a piercing cry, fanning his feathers into an arch, revealing stunning colors.

Olessio muttered in Farliosan. Amarta needed no translation to understand his awe.

"Only on Carugrua," Tumaya said proudly.

The islanders parted. An old woman hobbled toward them, ancient, her face deeply lined, a gold mesh covering her white head.

She spoke foreign words. Tumaya translated: "Here is the eldest of our Mothers. She says yes."

He held out to Amarta between his two whole fingers a spiral shell in shades of beige, pink, and cream, hanging on a leather thong. "This signals other islands that you are welcome. They must accept, as we accepted their travelers, when we were more worthy."

Amarta took the offered conch. "It's beautiful. Thank you."

The old woman spoke again. "The Mother says your footsteps honor us," Tumaya said. "Know that our hospitality is not bested. Tonight you feast as you have never feasted before."

"Feast!" Olessio whispered happily.

Tumaya barked an order. At once, everyone was in motion, islanders hefting sacks, bundles, striding or skipping in an inland direction. A toddler ran at the large birds, waving his arms and laughing. A man picked him up and set him atop his shoulders along side a full pack.

As people loped forward, earrings and necklaces of bone and shell jangled, hair swept back with combs and dotted with flowers and abalone fluttering in the breeze. Many passed them, waving. Some sang. All smiled.

"What a friendly people," Olessio said, his grin unsteady.

No, Amarta realized: not unsteady. He was awestruck.

"This is it," he breathed. "The Island Road. We are walking it."

The Island Road was a raised dirt path.

As they walked, the Road rose and fell, continuing unerringly north. Islanders swirled around them, dashing forward.

They passed fragrant forests, sprawling meadows, a lake where bright blue fish darted and jumped. At a thicket of pink flowers, islanders picked berries and seeds, tucking them into waist-bags.

In a glade of high saplings covered with vines, children darted about, poking hands into huge white flowers, coming away with fingers of pale pollen which they scraped into baskets that dangled from their shoulders. A few wore ornately carved bracelets. The children of the island's elite? The Mother's kin?

"Only bloom during the Gathering," Tumaya said. "Tomorrow, petals drop."

At a field with rows of knee-high orange and green seedlings, Tumaya excitedly said: "A day old! In four days, as tall as you are. Winds blow. Wings beat. We harvest."

"Wind?" Amarta asked. "Wings?" She looked questioningly at Tayre.

"I think he means pollen, seeds, spores, insects—whatever breeze and birds can carry."

"That is so," said Tumaya, nodding. He gestured north,

made a jabbing motion. "I will return. Much to do. The Road is…It is…" He spoke a few words.

"Straight and forward," supplied Rhaata proudly.

"That is so."

Tumaya stepped off the raised Island Road, striking out toward the east, leaving them to walk the Island Road without him.

Chapter Sixteen

"WHY DO THE ISLANDERS SPEAK PERRIPIN?" Olessio asked.

"It is must," Rhaata said, shrugging. "Finest merchants, always Perripin. Money makes for best speaking, yes?"

Olessio chuckled.

"Then why did we bring you?" Tayre asked Rhaata.

"Kee!" Rhaata exclaimed. "Much is said, but what is meant?" He thumped his chest. "This I know."

They passed fields where islanders scattered seeds. At a grove of high bushes, another group plucked ripe berries. A smiling woman offered them some, and Olessio fed one to Tadesh. Children squealed, offering more berries to Olessio's shoulder, and before long, Tadesh's muzzle was stained purple.

It was as if three seasons were compressed into one.

As they topped Carugrua's final rise, to the east and west glittered open ocean. They descended into a clearing, bordered by a wall of trees similar to the one they'd passed on the south side.

Long tables were set with bowls and boards, fruits and

breads, pots and carafes, seeds and flower cakes. Seated were the Perripin duke and his wife.

"How did they pass us?" Amarta asked Rhaata as they approached.

"Take boat. Not walk," Rhaata answered.

The duke gave Amarta a cautious nod of greeting, an ebony and silver pipe in his fingers trailing a thin line of spiced smoke into the sea breeze. Behind him and his wife stood a five-count of servants with enough luggage to make Amarta's group's carry-bags seem paltry.

"We must be the shabbiest travelers to ever walk the Island Road," Olessio said, smiling at the duke as they sat across from him. "And yet, walk it we do."

Rhaata began to sit at Olessio's side, then abruptly stood again, to stand behind Amarta's chair, a mirror of the duke's servants. Amarta turned to tell him that he was not a servant, and certainly not hers, but at the sight of Rhaata's proud, lifted chin—and the duke's condescending stare—she stayed silent.

Tumaya strode into the clearing, trailing a hoard of happy island children who flocked to Amarta and her companions, showing off scrimshaw bracelets and necklaces and vying to get close enough to Tadesh to touch her.

Tumaya smiled fondly, then shooed them all away. He addressed Amarta and the duke. "Show the conch at each island. You do not want to be mistaken for trespassers." He gestured north, through an opening in the treeline where the Road continued.

They turned to look. Some thirty feet past the trees, the raised Road transformed from Carugrua's fine, golden sand to a coarse red, as it led into an orange-yellow tangle of bushes.

It took Amarta a moment to understand what she was seeing.

"The next island," Olessio breathed.

There, where the islands merged, small hillocks of broken sand in two colors surrounded the raised Road.

"It is not us, but our god Carugrua, who decides who may walk the Road," Tumaya said, his gaze roaming the table to the Perripin duke, then to Amarta and her companions, pausing a moment in puzzlement at Olessio, who was feeding bits of bread to Tadesh. "The Mothers tell us what Carugrua wishes. During the Gathering, foreigners try to steal from us, not bid for harvests, as is proper. But you—" he gave Amarta a look. "You are different. You hear the god's voice yourself."

"I do?" Amarta asked, confused.

"Did you not speak for all the gods, when you named the aligning of the Gathering?"

The aligning? The order of the Island Road, he meant.

"Well, I…"

Olessio breathed into her ear. "Yes. Say yes."

"Yes," she said, spared the need to say more by the arrival of what seemed to be all the Carugrua islanders arriving at once, setting out yet more platters, bowls, and baskets, then sitting to eat, passing around dishes.

"Always best to agree with the hosts," Olessio said, taking a leg of baked crustacean from a passing platter. His gaze roamed the table hungrily. "I think it is long past time I became quite, quite fat."

"Here, try this." A smiling Tumaya offered Olessio a plate of dripping pastries. Olessio took two, stuffing one into his mouth, the second disappearing under the table. To Tadesh, no doubt.

Tumaya smiled even wider as Olessio made loud sounds of appreciation. "Remember how excellent is our feast, honorable ones, and how perfect our hospitality. The other islands will tell you they are best, but I pray you remember Carugrua. Will you?"

"Yes!" Olessio said around a full mouth. "So good!"

Tayre, standing, had a hand on Amarta's shoulder and leaned in close. "What might be safe for them, or safely intoxicating, might be not be for us. Amarta, be prudent."

"I check everything," she said.

"Everything?"

Amarta tightened at his challenge. She took an offered leaf curled around some thick paste and set it on her plate alongside other mysterious foods, then passed her hand over each piece. Like Olessio's performance. Or a Rochi table host about to deal.

"Safe," she said.

A young woman held out a bowl of white pollen to Amarta, demonstrating how to consume it by dipping a finger and sucking off the powder.

A sense of lightness, a sweet joy. A welcome easing of hard memories, into a gentle present.

And later? A mild headache. No worse than drinking wine.

"Amarta," Tayre said, "I recommend against—"

He trailed off as Amarta put a powder-coated finger into her mouth. A little sticky, a little sweet.

"Well, if you're having some…" Olessio said, likewise dipping in his finger.

Tayre stepped back, declining the offered bowl.

Calm came over her quickly. The feast progressed, the sun setting in a warm red glow, silhouetting trees. Lamps and firepits sparked to life, taking on a cheery glow in the deepening dark. Smiles seemed joyous and kind. Even Tayre's expression seemed softened.

Amarta exchanged a happy look with Olessio.

More and more food. A cup, pressed into her hand, cut of a wide reed. A light, sweet drink.

"Fermented tree-sap," one of Mothers said warmly, sitting nearby, her gold hairnet giving a friendly glint.

Islanders took up a ululating song and began to dance around the fires.

Tumaya gestured to them. "We call to Carugrua, with our gratitude, and promise to be more pious."

Again, the bowl of white powder was held out to Amarta.

"Will it affect your foresight?"

She was surprised at how close he was. She was finding it hard to keep track of people, but also finding that she didn't mind in the least.

"No," she said, but she let the bowl pass her by.

The Mother spoke in her island tongue. A story of some sort, Amarta was nearly sure, from the occasional Perripin word.

More food—sweet, sour, and tastes she'd never known before.

Olessio rubbed his stomach, groaning in a pained delight, then reached forward to a passing plate. "Oh, maybe just one more."

Amarta found herself laughing along with the two Mothers closest to her. Dancing, drumming, singing was all around, and into her hand was pressed another tree-sap brew.

Amarta didn't know what she was laughing at, but she could not seem to stop.

Amarta stood unsteadily, stepping out from under a half-tent that the islanders had set for them on the beach.

Tayre was instantly by her side. "Are you well?"

"Yes." Her head ached, but it could have been worse. She

did not expound; if he wanted more, he could ask. How many times had he forced her to do just that?

Olessio was already up, stretching, toes of his bare feet curling into the sand. He handed them each a length of grilled cane left over from the feast, then looked north to the red sands of the next island.

"How do you suppose they attach?"

"Something underwater," Tayre suggested, taking the offered cane.

"Tentacles?" Olessio asked, dropping a strip of the cane into Tadesh's waiting mouth.

"Magic?" Amarta suggested.

"Not that I can feel," Olessio said, sucking something from his teeth. "Tentacles it is." He bent down as if to lift Tadesh. She didn't wait, scrabbling up his arm. He winced as she settled across his shoulders and nuzzled his neck.

Amarta held out a baked leaf. Tadesh twisted around to take it in both paws, balancing on hindquarter, then munching diligently.

"What are they?" Amarta asked of the islands. "Sea creatures?"

Rhaata stepped close. "Gods," he said. "They are gods."

"No," Olessio said. "Alive, yes, that I could believe. But there are no gods here."

"What? How do you say this?" Rhaata waved his arms, agitated. "Tumaya say Carugrua is a god."

"You believe everything you're told?" Tayre asked mildly.

Rhaata gave each of them a stern look before turning his wondering gaze to the land around them. "How can all this be, otherwise? They come together. Make richest harvests in the world. Must be gods, yes?"

"Ah, to be so young again," Olessio muttered, putting a friendly hand on Rhaata's shoulder. "Let me tell a story about how Farliosan once brokered a deal between the magi, the horse-people, and the great serpent." Just then, Tumaya came toward them, trailed by a group of children. "Perhaps another time."

Tumaya was dressed plainly this time, no cloak, no feathers. The children offered Amarta and the others packages of wrapped food, and offered bits to Tadesh, clearly held out for that very purpose. Standing on Olessio's backpack, Tadesh hissed in reply. Full at last, perhaps.

"To keep you well until the next feast," Tumaya said. "Meager though it will be, compared to last night." He held out to Amarta a spherical, brilliant blue stone. "The Mothers wish you to have this, She-who-knows. Few see one, fewer still hold."

Amarta took the small stone, examining the intricate carving, the face and claws and folded wings, all tight in a ball.

"Oh, it's lovely," she said.

"Worth much to be sold," Tumaya said gravely. "Without price, to be given." He gestured north. "Your footsteps now take you to Sombaa. We see you at the final feast. We will remember you. Remember us."

"We will," Amarta promised.

Tumaya put a hand on the shoulders of the two smiling children to either side of him, their empty sacks and baskets slung and strung across their shoulders, ready for another day of harvest. To his right, a boy child smiled back at Amarta, his expression so like Pas's that the ache rippled through her.

At her expression, Tumaya nodded. "They have never known a day of sorrow. And they never will." His look turned sad. "If you speak to our god," he said to Amarta, "say we will do better."

Before she could answer, he waved farewell with the hand missing fingers, and turned back to his island.

They followed the Road, from Carugrua to Sombaa, passing through an opening in a heavy tangle of high bushes with twisted orange-yellow limbs. The air was pungent with spice.

As before, they were greeted by a crowd of islanders, some at work bundling reeds, others drawing from belts long bamboo spears. Amarta held up the conch shell. Weapons were lowered.

A gray-haired woman cradling an infant stepped toward them. "You are She-who-knows-tomorrow?"

"Yes, I am," Amarta replied.

The woman handed the infant to another. "Welcome to Sombaa. You will find our hospitality and food unmatched by any other island, despite what you may have heard."

"Thank you," Amarta said, hoping that was the right answer.

They were drawn forward along the Road, accompanied as they had been on Carugrua, by adults and children pacing them, passing, singing, waving, scattering seeds, and dashing to and from the Road, toting the produce of their harvest.

In a thickly wooded valley, they paused to watch a cloud of tiny shapes that made ticking sounds as they flitted from tree to tree, leaving pale dots on bright leaves. A blink and they were gone.

Islanders left the Road to pluck the leaves with mottled two-tone yellow spots, laying them carefully into baskets. They loped off to the east.

"Where do they go?" Olessio asked.

"The island harbor," answered Rhaata. "It is must, so islands can send them by canoe to the last island. Too delicate to run."

"And the yellow spots on the leaves?" Olessio asked.

"They are…" Rhaata made a sound, then another, finally shrugged. "Expensive."

"I've seen powder in those two colors," Tayre said, "in heavy glass bottles. In a swordmaker's smithy. Called razor-powder. Hardens blade edges, turns them blue-black. Rare."

Rhaata nodded enthusiastically. "Expensive."

"Ah, that's what that is!" Olessio replied. "I had thought the blue-black edging a mage touch."

"Not everything extraordinary is mage-made, Vagras," said Tayre, tossing his words back to him.

Olessio laughed.

The Road led straight on. They passed fields of brilliant vermilion, trees webbed with vines, and what seemed a boiling puddle until they came close to see blue and green lizards in a frenzy of mating.

When at last they reached the end of Sombaa, the feast was underway. Thick, sweet drinks were thrust into their hands, nuts were offered. Olessio took a handful of large ones and began to juggle, quickly attracting an audience of delighted children, who wanted to show off their newest white bracelets and necklaces, carved with designs of fish and mermaids and starfish.

"They carve as soon as they can speak," a Sombaa mother said, a fine gold mesh around her neck.

"The children?" Amarta asked, surprised.

"Yes. To honor Sombaa, between the Gatherings."

Amarta listened to how they spoke, the words they used. One name was repeated. Amarta asked the Mother about it.

"It means 'beloved'," the Mother answered, reaching out to grab the gown of a small child hurtling past, using his momentum to swing him up into her arms, and laughing, holding him close, murmuring affectionately, as he squirmed to get back down. She set him on the ground and he ran off.

"Truly splendid," Olessio said of the frothy drink.

"Your pleasure honors us," the Mother replied. "It comes from the underside of the highest branches of the *algratha* tree. Nowhere in the world but here. By the grace of our god Sombaa."

"Beyond compare," Olessio said, upending his cup into his mouth, then giving it a sad look. Wordlessly, Tayre passed Olessio his own untouched cup.

"We know that you were given a godstone by the lesser island whose name we will not even voice."

It took Amarta a moment to decipher this. She nodded warily.

"Ours is superior." The Mother opened her hand to reveal an ornately carved sphere that glittered with swirls of pale pink and white, and into which was carved a fierce face.

"Thank you," Amarta said, stunned at the beautiful thing. She slipped it into one of her pockets alongside the other.

"When you go to Molimba, they will say their welcome is finest. Do not be deceived. We are best. The islands remember. Remember us."

"I will," Amarta said, not quite sure what she was promising.

The Mother stared at Amarta intently. "What does our god say, She-who-knows-tomorrow?"

Amarta opened her mouth, uncertain how to reply.

Cheerily, Olessio broke in. "Mother, She-who-knows hesitates to put to plain words the glory of your great Sombaa's intentions. But anyone can see that your hospitality is magnificent. I can scarcely imagine another island could be better. Though, perhaps…"

"Yes?" the Mother asked, concerned.

"Is there more of the algratha?"

The Mother gave him an amused smile, then called out for more.

The island of Molimba was rocky and muddy, though the elevated Road stayed dry.

They passed swamps, high tangles of wet trees. They walked through thick reeds that oozed green into puddles at their base and were then spooned into jugs by children.

Islanders crouched at the edge of ponds, snatching turtles, turned them upside down, scraping their undersides and tossing them back in the water.

Laden islanders with heavy packs hurried past them on the Road, waving, calling greetings, and talking loudly. Though Amarta understood none of the Molimba words, she was coming to recognize a few words. *Quickly. Beloved.*

"Kee!" Rhaata called in delight, pointing to a boulder covered in vines with mauve flowers that seemed to twitch. As Rhaata lurched off the road toward it, Tayre gripped the boy's shirt, holding him on the path, and pulling him forward to continue marching.

The Road led through a forest with tree trunks glistening with moisture, and branches thick with buzzing insects. There children scampered around the leggy roots of the trees, picking fist-sized fruits off branches. They ate a few, then put the rest in sacks and ran off.

Amarta pointed upward at the higher fruits out of reach, and gave Olessio a questioning look.

"What? Oh, no. I don't think…" Olessio looked troubled. Then he gave a tentative smile that slowly spread. "Well, why not?" he asked the air. "Why not, indeed?"

Olessio stepped off the Road, stood under a glistening tree, and looked up with a baffled expression.

A moment passed, then another, and a fruit dropped into his open palm. He held it up triumphantly.

"Safe?" he asked.

"Safe," she replied.

He popped it in his mouth. "Ah," he said, juices dribbling out the sides of his mouth, and turned back to the tree, holding his palm out for another and another.

"I'll pass," Tayre said.

"Come on, Guard-dog—have some joy of life! To eat a fruit this rare? Such chances only come once."

"Even so," Tayre replied.

"Even so," Olessio said, playfully mockingly, then offered one to Amarta.

She gestured to Rhaata first, now vibrating with eagerness. "Kee!"

When at last she bit into one, it reminded her of the cold mountains of her home in Arunkel and the tiny red and blue berries that grew there.

They continued on the Island Road. At the final rise before the dark sands of the Molimba north beach, another lavish feast was set. Amarta and the Perripin duke exchanged familiar nods.

As before, the island's Mothers extolled their virtues and plied them with food and drink. The evening turned to music, song, and dance. An old man, joyous and inebriated, made his way around the tables, speaking and clasping hands. A woman gave him a comb from her hair. A young man offered a thick, carved bracelet.

When the old man came close, the Mother sitting nearby took an ornately carved torque from around her neck and put it around his neck. He danced on.

Amarta noticed that his hands were missing three fingertips.

"Is he special?" Amarta asked the Mother.

She smiled. "He has given much for our place and harvests, so he is beloved and happy." She turned to face

Amarta. "They say you speak to the gods. Does Molimba say why we are lesser this gathering?"

"No, I don't actually—"

Olessio squeezed her hand and leaned forward. "She-who-knows tells me that your god's language is so beautiful that she can hardly speak it. But I am certain that Molimba is proud of this astonishing bark ale that comes from your island. I've tasted nothing like it across the world. I pray to Molimba myself, for even one more drop!"

The Mother laughed, then clapped urgently to have another brought for him.

"Bad luck to argue with people about their gods," Olessio said softly to her.

"But they're wrong. You said—"

"Bad luck."

"Especially while we're on their islands," Tayre added.

Late that night, when the feast was over, they sat together on the long, gently sloped beach, looking up at a night rich with stars. Behind them, Rhaata spun, around and around, arms wide, staring up, in drunken glee.

"What do your people believe?" Amarta asked him.

He flopped down on the soft sand. "The ocean is our god. When I die, I will be reborn as a great sea turtle. My ancestors take me down and down, where all my questions are answered."

It was beautiful. No truer than what the islanders believed, though. She leaned close to Olessio.

"No gods here, either?"

Dim in starlight, his expression was unusually somber. "No."

The Molimba godstone was amber, into which was carved interlocking fishes. Amarta showed her growing collection to her companions.

"So rare," Rhaata breathed.

Without price to be given, Tumaya had said. She returned them to her pocket.

At Chosolua, Amarta again waved the conch, and again they were welcomed by the island's Mothers.

So heavily traveled was the Road now, with islanders coming forward from all the islands, that it was some time before they were alone again.

"Some of the elders are missing fingers," she said. "Is that about their imagined gods? A sacrifice?"

"That would be my guess," said Tayre.

"So they cut off their fingers for nothing?" she asked, aghast.

"Not for nothing!" Rhaata looked at each of them seeking agreement, his expression turning dark when he did not find it. "You think you are so smart. I hear it in every word you say. You need a poor island boy like me to explain this to you?"

"It seems we do," Tayre replied.

Rhaata waved his hands in the air. "So much! Harvests beyond imagine! Gold weave in the Mothers' hair! Gemstones! How do they have this? It is simple: gifts to their gods. In return the gods give them harvests to sell to travelers with too much money." He gave a sharp nod. "It is must. If it did not work, they would not do it."

"There are, perhaps, other conclusions to be drawn," Tayre said mildly.

"They make things to please their gods," Amarta said, following Rhaata's reasoning. "Then their harvests bring them coin. They think one thing causes the other." Into her mind flashed her last look at the Monks of Revelation. The loud crack of the branch. The cries of the crowd. The missing monks. "But we can't tell them, can we."

"Not while we're on their islands," Tayre said.

"Hoi! Let them believe what they like," Olessio said lightly. "Not my gemstones, not my fingers. I have believed a false thing or two in my life, myself. Costs us nothing to let them be."

Amarta worked the fingers of her left hand, the knuckles still aching, and considered her refusal to let Maris heal her. It was nothing like chopping off a finger, but was it any more sensible? Why did she insist on keeping the pain?

A glimpse from some future: she looked at her hand, as she was doing now, with sorrow, as she understood the answer to the question she had just asked.

A future that held sadness, she thought wearily. That, at least, could be relied upon.

They walked the Road for a time in silence. A settled sense came over Amarta. Olessio was right: she could not cure islanders of their beliefs.

And why should she? These were not her people to set right. She had her own future to attend to. She would walk the Island Road with her companions, go to Seute Enta, find the Heart of Seuan, and her own answers.

When at last Rhaata spoke, it was clear from his tone that he had been nursing a grudge. "You think I'm simple," he said. "But you can't even see what's right in front of you."

At the Chosolua feast, a bowl of small seeds was passed around, pinches taken into mouths.

Amarta declined, foreseeing colors, and too many of them.

Olessio tilted his head close. "Should I pass as well?"

"Very potent," Amarta said, trying to focus her answer. "Only three, and you are happy, but not throwing up."

"Ah," he said, grasping her shoulder gratefully.

Later that night, someone—the duke, Amarta suspected from how many seeds he had consumed—was retching onto the beach.

The next morning the Chosolua Mother took Amarta's hand in her own, and pressed into her palm a godstone, deep translucent green, with glints of gold. Into it was carved a smiling face that showed teeth.

"Remember us."

Jalui was rich with color. Clouds of thumbnail-sized moths swirled, shimmering blue and silver. Birds ran by, long-necked, with red feathers and eyes of gold. The trees seemed painted with oil, bark of pink and black, leaves of green and yellow.

At the edge of a lake, islanders pulled from the shallows long fronds, laying them on bamboo racks to dry in the sun.

"We sell to Seuan," said the Jalui Mother, gold mesh circling her head.

"Seuan?" Amarta asked, suddenly attentive.

"To make qualan."

Olessio perked up. "Qualan? From that?" He stared at the drying fronds.

The Jalui Mother took a long leaf from the rack and gave it to Olessio, who took it reverently.

"It does nothing," the Mother said. "A secret, what Seuan does, to make the qualan."

"White or bronze?" Olessio asked.

The Jalui Mother laughed, then laughed again. "We sell

one plant to Seuan. What they do with it? Ask them." To Olessio, who was sniffing the leaf: "Make you sick to eat raw."

"Oh," he said, quickly handing it back.

Again the Mother laughed, motioning the party onward.

At a meadow, a group of islanders surrounded a huge butterfly, wider than a man's shoulders. The fluttering wings were deep blue and purple, spotted with gold, its face ringed in white fur. The black eyes seemed to see everywhere, and a curled tongue flicked out, then back as it tried to escape.

With wide straw mesh panels, islanders directed the creature into a man-sized wicker cage that was decorated with gemstones and bone pendants.

Olessio clicked his tongue, calling Tadesh back, as she started forward curiously.

A cheer went up as the islanders latched the door shut, hefting the cage and butterfly onto their shoulders, marching east along a crossroad.

"To the harbor, to be sold?" Amarta guessed.

"Yes!" Rhaata said, eagerly. "Collectors across the world will bid much for such a creature!"

Amarta could too easily imagine the creature's journey. Below deck, a captive in the dark, stolen away from the only home it knew, to be used for some mysterious purpose, by strange powers. Sorrow came over her for this creature whose only sin was to be born a rare thing.

The island of Tukimpe was thick with fog and the sounds of crickets. Glistening frogs jumped alongside the Road.

When at last the sun broke through, they rested by a

thick, mossy expanse, passing around water and the food the islanders kept giving them.

Amarta lay on her back, staring up at large fronds, high overhead. She slipped into a pleasant doze, then half-woke to a droning, like the sound of grass-bees about their work.

Not quite: it was deeper than that. Then it was louder and louder, until it might have been the call of a thousand people.

Which was strange, she thought sleepily. There were not so many people here.

With that thought, she sat up suddenly, looking around the mossy, shaded glade.

Not here. Or not now, in any case. It was some other time and place.

"What's wrong?" Olessio asked her, sitting up. Tayre, perched on a nearby boulder, watched.

Amarta shook her head, getting to her feet and began to turn. Something had happened, or was about to happen. A future trail went forward. It dissipated, like smoke on the breeze. Here and gone.

She walked to Tayre and put her hand on his arm. "No. It's not you."

It could be, though, in the moment she touched him, distant shallows of unlikely possibilities. There were always ways to die.

Perhaps this strange trail she was sensing was a similar thing—a half-dreamed vision of a far-distant flash. A remote threat. Dismissible.

But it nagged. What was so near to happening?

And where was Rhaata?

There—he crouched, examining something on the ground. At the foot of a sapling tree, a large mushroom of pale brown, with orange and blue-gray dots, that seemed to have grown arms that hugged the thin trunk.

Amarta put a hand on Rhaata's shoulder, and saw it: two or three moments hence: the boy would reach out to the mushroom, his fingers full of imprudent curiosity.

It was not likely. In most futures, Amarta would caution him, and he would pull back.

Where was the future in which crowds cried deafeningly, and beat sticks? How did this moment possibly lead to that one?

Thousands looked at her and howled.

The future was complicated: a path could branch off, yet lay atop another one. Amarta carefully put aside the clearer one in favor of the lesser trail.

Rhaata was part of this, somehow, starting with the soon-to-come but near impossible touch of his finger to the mushroom, followed by the even less likely moment in which he would put his fingers to his lips.

She lost the trail, found it again, grabbed tight.

Rhaata would dart off into the brush. They would follow. Rhaata would come upon an islander, a mother nursing a baby. With intoxicated glee, Rhaata would snatch the child from her arms, and twirl himself and the child around and around, singing as he did.

Amarta would arrive, breathing hard. The child's mother laughing, unoffended. Amarta would take the child from him—an excess of caution, worrying what he might do to the small thing.

Who knew that the mushroom's effects could transfer with such a light touch?

The baby, Amarta, and now the baby's mother, as Amarta returned the child to her, were all fast taken into the intoxication.

Days would go by in a haze. Amarta would find herself in front of the islands' Mothers, all of them. She answered their questions—who could be mated with whom—the extent of the Island Pearl harvest to come. Amarta spoke unrestrainedly, without the hard-earned good sense acquired across the years.

The mushroom, still active in her, would force her to reveal much too much.

How did this all lead to the roars of thousands?

"Amarta?" Olessio asked.

"Foreseeing," Tayre answered.

The many called to her, howling with anger. Overlapping, competing flashes. Different crowds calling different things.

Her head was hurting, but no, she would have this answer. She must. The droning voices from the future dimmed as she followed the more immediate trail, closer and closer to the cries and howls and…

There it was. A fight, between the islands, over her. The islanders joining in a confusing three-way battle. She and her companions would slip through the first skirmish, making their way to the east Tukimpe harbor, seeking a way off the island.

But no. Surrounded by hundreds of armed islanders, a Tukimpe Mother would say: "Our god wishes you to stay. You will help our god become great again."

Tayre could not take on that many, but he would try. When Tadesh was snatched, Olessio, too, would fight. Rhaata would refrain, but it would not save him.

Blood and more blood, and Amarta the prize in the middle. At last, the islands would separate again, going their ways across the world's oceans, and Amarta—

No dark room this time. A cage, like the cage that held the huge butterfly. Tayre was gone. Olessio was gone. Tadesh…

No, no, no.

Amarta broke back into the present with an anguished

cry. She was on her hands and knees, clods of dirt and moss gripped in her fists.

Tayre knelt at her side. "Tell me."

She shook her head, tracing the trail of horrors back to the now, then looked around.

Rhaata, on his knees, at the spotted mushroom, drawing his hand back from having touched it.

"What? No!" Amarta cried, stumbling to her feet, lurching toward him, stopping short. He turned to look at her, eyes wide, mystified.

Slap his hand away? But no, that opened another trail entirely, no better.

Damn him for being a fool. Damn herself for being distracted by the very vision that was warning her.

"Don't," she said sharply, hoarsely. "Don't—"

But even as she spoke, Rhaata, eyes wide in confusion, put his fingers to his lips.

Amarta howled frustration.

Olessio did not understand, but Tayre, thank all the Fates, read her perfectly. He stepped between Olessio and Rhaata, gave sharp orders to both, kept them apart.

The boy touched his lips again and began to smile, very wide.

"I don't understand," he said. "Did I do something wrong?"

Chapter Seventeen

TAYRE KEPT the confused-yet-smiling Rhaata at arm's length with simple, sharp orders, until a Tukimpe Mother could be found and brought.

The Mother looked at Rhaata with disgust. "Every island child knows not to touch."

"He is not an island child," Amarta said, trying not to snap at her. "Can you help him?"

The Mother gestured to her warriors, who had surrounded Rhaata with sharpened sticks, holding him beyond arm's length.

The Mother's gaze went sideways to Amarta. "A bargain, She-who-sees. Tell us what our god Tukimpe needs to put us in the final place at next Gathering, then we fix your foolish servant for you."

Vision offered Amarta no answers to this question, which she took to mean that nothing the Tukimpe islanders did would affect the next order of the Island Road. Either there were no gods, as Olessio claimed, or their gods didn't care.

Rhaata was trembling violently, his smile painfully wide.

Could Amarta lie? How hard would it be, after all, to

convince people who already believed that she spoke to their gods? Surely no more challenging than a Rochi bluff, and she'd gotten good at those.

As Amarta began to search forward, Olessio spoke.

"Cure him first."

Amarta gave a frustrated sigh, and Olessio, understanding, mouthed an apology. Amarta had been about to say something similar, but the result was different now, and the future she had been about to put into play was no more.

"Tukimpe says," Amarta said, "be kind to strangers."

The Mother pressed her lips together, clearly displeased with the answer, but after a moment, she spoke to her people. One of them went running off.

"Did I do something wrong?" asked Rhaata again, his gaze on the sharpened sticks ringing him, his smile still bizarrely wide.

"They will cure you," Amarta assured him.

The islander returned, handing a small earthenware bottle to the Mother. She uncorked it, sniffed, stepped into the circle of sharp sticks, examined Rhaata's eyes, then threw the liquid into his face.

Rhaata blinked and blinked again.

"Oh," he said, looking around as if waking. "That was beautiful." As he took the expressions of those surrounding him, his smile faded. "I think I must have done something wrong."

Amarta and her companions were escorted back to the Road and urged to refrain from touching anything as they went northward across Tukimpe.

Amarta considered what had happened: Rhaata touching

the mushroom, his lips, and what would have followed if Amarta had not interrupted events.

Her own intoxication, islanders slaughtering each other. Tayre and Olessio dead. Amarta finally and irrevocably imprisoned.

The whole trail was unlikely from the start and full of near-impossibilities. None of it should have happened at all.

Was there some quality about Rhaata that made him prone to such things?

When she looked forward again, she saw that despite what should have been a lesson in caution, Rhaata would be drawn to other similarly dangerous temptations, and the islands were full of them.

Maybe the puzzle had a simple answer: Rhaata was young and impulsive and the unlikely swirled thickly around him.

At times, Amarta had needed to bring something nearly impossible into existence. In Kusan, she had been groping for a single path forward to save the city. In those days, she had not understood how one thing might lead to another, how giving her cloak to her friend Nidem could save Kusan, but kill Nidem. Amarta had simply followed the trail to the outcome she needed, and Nidem had paid the price with an arrow through her heart.

The memory still bit hard. Amarta had barely known what she was doing then. Yet, half-knowing, she had done it anyway.

As they walked, Amarta kept her face turned from Tayre, lest he somehow read her thoughts: *Did you kill my friend?*

After she had buried the ache again, she lagged, letting Olessio and Rhaata walk ahead.

"I think we must send him home," she said softly.

"I agree," Tayre answered.

It did not take much to excite Rhaata—and Olessio—to the idea of seeing the eastern harbor, where Tukimpe's extraordinary produce was staged for transit. At the next crossroads, they turned east.

The harbor was littered with stacks of boxes and barrels, crates of jugs and glass bottles, baskets of flowers and long stems. A scattering of mesh cages held small creatures, from dun-colored lizards to pink mice.

All were quiet, the loudest sound that of the footfalls of the Perripin youths from the ships, who served as messengers, running between ships' merchants and the islanders standing by their produce, delivering written bids and returning answers.

As they strolled among the cages and tanks, Tayre wandered off. Amarta paused at a glass tank where a small gold-and-black eel came to her finger. At another cage, crimson birds spread wide, orange wings.

Amarta kept an eye on Tayre, across the market. At last he gave her a nod. She led Rhaata and Olessio to join him.

"That one?" asked a Perripin woman, a ship's first mate, giving Rhaata a tilted head.

"That one," Tayre confirmed.

Rhaata was clever. In a number of futures, he would understand quickly and resist.

"You're going home," Amarta said. Tayre joined in to persuade, and Olessio, catching on, added his own brand of warm encouragement, along with pressing into Rhaata's hand some items that he'd been given along the Road as an inducement, including a small pouch of seeds that was probably worth a small fortune.

Rhaata, downcast, objected, then apologized. Ultimately he complied, letting himself be ushered aboard the ship headed back to Tulia. From the deck, he waved.

"Saving him from himself, I assume?" Olessio asked her.

"And us from him," Amarta replied.

In Tulia, Rhaata could sell Olessio's gifts. Or he could

stay on the ship and become a wanderer. Amarta looked at Olessio. Perhaps not such a bad life for a clever young man.

Whatever Rhaata chose, Amarta had given him a chance at a future, something that she had taken from Nidem. Rhaata, Amarta decided, was one more to the good in her accounting.

Would there ever come a time, she wondered, when she could stop trying to balance the scales between those she had helped and those she had harmed?

Inside her, vision swirled, attempting an answer. Amarta was unsurprised when it failed to provide one.

T he Road led them through the island of Cadii. There, villages of bamboo, open-air roofs, and woven walls were home to spiders, centipedes, snakes, lizards, and the strangest crawling creatures Amarta had ever seen.

The islanders proudly brought many of them to Amarta.

"No thanks," Amarta said quickly, when urged to hold a huge dark purple-and-black spider.

"Safe! safe!" assured the Cadii Mother. "Pretty, yes?"

"Yes," Amarta said, relieved when they all began to move along the road again.

At a rest stop with food and drink, another Cadii Mother held out a handful of tiny, dazzling blue snakes. She spoke to Amarta in her island language, and then, to Amarta's surprise, in formal, if rusty, Arunkin.

"She-who-knows, tell us which of these grow fat in the middle, make babies by morning, so we may feed her more tonight."

An easy enough prediction, that, so Amarta gave it, only to find that this resulted in islanders bringing her more and more creatures, from scorpions to toads, asking similar questions.

The future was clearest if she held the creature, foreseeing eggs or wiggling larvae. Despite islander assurances and echoing ones from foresight, she had to nerve herself each time.

By the north end of the island, the Mothers—clearly pleased with Amarta—presented them all with packs made of a black, silky material.

"Spider silk," the Mother said. "Do not believe Haulala when they say their sea-silk is stronger. It is not."

"How could it be?" Olessio asked effusively. "You are Cadii."

"Just so!" the Mother said, smiling back at Olessio.

At the feast, Olessio hesitated over nothing, not even to pick insect legs out of his teeth. Tadesh was equally enthusiastic, readily crunching one candied bug after another.

Amarta wondered when a dish of something as familiar as fruit or bread might come by, but none did.

"Quite good," Olessio assured her, chewing something. He offered her a fried tidbit that stared back.

"No, thanks."

Overhead, the moon was filling, half-showing through shreds of clouds.

The moon was still with them. As strange as things were here —lands and islands—what people ate, wore, and believed—the moon did what it always did, waxing and waning. The sun, the moon, the pull of the earth—some things did not change.

Tayre put a baked centipede in the center of Amarta's empty plate.

"Learn about the world," he said, "and yourself."

Amarta looked around at the islanders of Cadii as they

laughed and drank and ate, then back at Tayre. In his quiet look, she heard his words again and again.

At last she picked up the baked bug, gathered courage, and took a bite. She chewed, keeping her focus entirely on the flavor.

Somewhat nutty. If she thought about nothing else, Olessio was right: it was quite good.

$\approx$

The Cadii godstone was milky white with a glint of blue, like a star. The carved face had many eyes. Amarta put it in her pocket with the others.

The island of Haulala began with a beach of near-black sand and a border thicket of dark, thorny bushes.

Islanders surged around them, taking them forward, many passing at a near-run, with shouts and calls.

At a hilltop, they paused to rest. Around them, in aromatic trees of large, pale, pungent flowers, a flock of thumb-sized birds hovered at the flowers to suck nectar, then flashed into the air, gathering and swirling in puffs of green, the sun giving a hint of dark rainbow to their exquisitely small wings.

Then they paired up, grabbing each other, and took flight with four wings, making tiny chirping sounds.

They watched the display.

"Are they…mating?" Amarta asked.

"Enthusiastically," Olessio said.

The pairs broke apart and came together again in a midair dance. Gusts of wind buffeted and transported them up and down, and sideways in spirals. Yet none fell.

Then a larger gust moved the whole flock southward. A single feather remained midair, titling and turning, landing a bit off the road, atop thick loam. Amarta crouched down to retrieve the tiny thing, no longer than a thumbnail.

As she began to stand, a distant motion caught her eye through trees. A woman's face, barely visible. Amarta smiled at her. A rustle of leaves, and it was gone.

They resumed their travel, Amarta displayed the feather, iridescent black-green, and shot through with white. Olessio complimented it as only a Farliosan could, his words themselves like flowers.

Tayre smiled.

"What?" she asked him.

"Feather is a name I've used."

Amarta was oddly moved at this revelation. How poorly she knew him, after all. She offered Tayre the feather. He declined.

They were welcomed in usual fashion at Haulala's feast at the north end of the island, where hundreds of islanders from the earlier islands clustered across the wide beach. She saw many whom she recognized. As they spoke to each other, she saw deference in their postures and gestures, a ranking based on island order.

The Haulala Mothers pushed food on them eagerly, describing their island's hospitality in the grand form that Amarta had come to expect. Another precious godstone was pressed into her hand, this one a deep, marbled green, its face surprisingly friendly.

As the sun set, across the sand and campfires, Amarta glimpsed a familiar face. She stood, weaving her way among the camps.

Tayre followed. Of course he did.

It seemed to her that he had been following her for the entirety of her life, for one reason or another, though of course it had not been so long as that. What exactly was between the two of them? Was it really no more than a one-nals contract, made over clasped hands?

She passed a campfire, then another. Hands and voices reached out to her from the sand, all offering food and drink. She smiled and waved and politely declined.

She came to a woman and two young children barely old enough to stand, seated on the sand. The woman rushed to her feet, ducking her head, brushing sand from her dress.

"I saw you in the trees," Amarta said.

"You are She-who-knows-tomorrow," the woman said with awe. "You speak the will of Haulala."

How to answer? "As much as anyone," Amarta said, wanting words not too wide of the truth, but that Olessio, back at the table gorging himself, might approve.

The woman touched her two toddlers affectionately. "Haulala blesses me with two. Which is most beautiful, She-who-knows?"

Amarta laughed a little at this absurd question and lowered herself to the ground with the woman. The girl climbed into her mother's lap. The boy scrunched fists of soft sand, bringing his hands to his eyes, fascinated.

"They are both beautiful."

The boy, seeing his sister getting hugged, clamored into his mother's lap. She put her arms around them both, then turned the girl to Amarta. "She is more, though. Yes?"

Amarta glanced over her shoulder, still hoping that Olessio, with his golden tongue, might advise her.

But no, only Tayre, standing watch, standing silent.

"I suppose so," Amarta answered.

"Then it is so!" The woman cried, holding her giggling daughter in the air for a moment before hugging her again.

Warmed by this display of affection, Amarta stood, leaving the woman to mutter fond words to her offspring, *Beloved* among them.

The boy had gone back to the ground, grabbing handfuls of sand, his expression full of the deep pleasure that only the very young knew. Amarta lingered a moment more, remembering Pas at that age.

With the perspective of time and distance, Amarta now knew that Dirina had been an excellent mother. She had always made time for Pas. No matter how hard things were— on the run, unsure how they would eat next—Pas never went hungry for affection.

Likewise, the Emendi in Kusan were devoted parents. A Kusani toddler could go a whole day in the arms and laps of various adults, her feet never touching the stone tunnel floors.

Amarta made her way back to the Haulala table, Tayre at her side.

"What was that?" he asked.

"It seems to me that it is very easy to suspect the worst of people."

"Especially when you always look for it," he replied, "as you so often must, to use foresight to protect yourself."

She was surprised at this insight. He was right: Amarta was always seeking the dire outcomes that must at all costs be avoided, and rarely looking for anything else.

Amarta glanced back at the woman with her two small children, now dimly silhouetted in the distance. She smiled.

"Sometimes, the good is right there, in front of you."

"Sometimes."

The next morning they crossed the mashed sands that marked the end of Haulala, pressed up tight against Punaami.

As they walked onto the final island, The Road was thick

with people singing and chanting, dashing, running. Some beat sticks together as they went, others blew into reed flutes. The old man from Molimba passed them, his necklaces and bracelets so thick that Amarta was impressed that he could move so fast. His smile at them was brilliant.

At rises, Amarta caught glimpses of the ocean, of long canoes filled with barrels, boxes, and bundles, all going north.

The duke's party passed them from behind, striding remarkably fast, laden servants trailing behind. Suddenly everyone was running forward.

Tayre asked one of the Punaami Mothers what had changed.

"The Pearls come," she replied. "The Gathering is nearly over. Tonight we feast, give thanks to our gods, make marriages. A day more, perhaps two. Then the Sundering." She shook her head sadly, smiling. "It goes so fast."

Tumaya caught up to them, breathing hard. "I am proud to give more!" He raised his other hand, a finger wrapped in bandages of paste and leaves. "Carugrua knows my devotion. When you speak to our god, will you speak well for us, She-who-knows-tomorrow?"

Olessio elbowed her lightly, giving her a warning smile.

Amarta tamped down the anger that rose inside. "I will," she managed.

"I pray that our hospitality has made you happy."

Olessio grinned. "Your feast was most assuredly the finest."

Tumaya looked pleased. Relieved. "Stay with us on Carugrua, She-who-knows, after the Sundering. We take you back from the final feast. Treat you so well. Better than any other."

A chill went through her. *Our god wishes you to stay.* A future that had never happened.

"We go north, to Seute Enta," she said sharply.

Tumaya ducked his head. "But if others ask, you will say the same?"

"Yes," she said.

"If you change your mind—"

"No," she said.

He nodded his understanding. "The islands remember. Remember us. Hurry! Not to miss the Pearls."

Tumaya ran forward, pausing a handful of steps beyond them. "Does it rain tomorrow?" he asked Amarta.

Weather. Always the hard one. "Yes," Amarta answered. Then more softly, "I think."

Tumaya surged forward, joining the river of islanders.

As they walked, Amarta struggled to understand Tumaya and his missing fingers. Well, if she thought that someone could intercede on her behalf with gods that truly existed, would she not also seek to influence them? Of course she should.

But they didn't exist, these island gods.

It didn't matter, she told herself. The islanders lived as they wished and did not need Amarta to mend them.

They picked up their pace, following a road heavy with footprints.

Punaami was large enough that they must break the trip into two days. They slept that night in a sheltering lean-to just off the Road.

All through the night, islanders passed them, striding toward the final north shore.

They rose early, feeling the urgency. No time to gawk at the astonishing foliage, or creatures unlike any they had ever seen. Once, Tadesh ran off, returning to Olessio's call with something tawny twitching in her mouth that she cracked and swallowed before any of them could get a good look at it. Olessio worried. Amarta reassured him.

It was early afternoon when they reached Punaami's north end. There the Island Road on which they had walked for many days ended abruptly against the red-gray sand of Punaami's north beach. As they approached the end, the raised, well-trodden dirt underfoot was framed on both sides by mats of green iceplant that coiled and tangled, purple petals wilting back on themselves like melted spikes.

They stopped at the edge to look at the scene before them.

The wide beach made a long, gradual slope to the ocean, where the red-gray sand met blue water. Huge sea vessels were moored alongside smaller ships, canoes, and barges. The docks, judging by their precariously tipping angles, had been hastily assembled and connected by bamboo walkways. Well-dressed merchants at the edge of the dock were having animated discussions with Mothers from various islands.

Off to the side on the beach, nine long tables were set with food, one for each island.

A sharp inhale from Olessio. "The Island Pearls."

In the middle of it all, where the Road ended, a thick, porridge-like substance stretched toward the docks. It seemed a viscous lake atop the red-gray sand, with lumps all through, like white, rainbow-tinged melons.

Around it islanders swept and shoveled the heavy goo into mounds on large, thin sheets of what Amarta recognized as black spider silk. The corners of the silk snapped in the wind.

"Ah, you are here!" Tumaya called happily. "Do you wish to bid on the Pearls?" He gestured urgently to the docks. "The numbers are high. Hurry."

"What are they used for?" Amarta asked.

"Many uses," Tumaya said. "Cure diseases. Heal wounds. Make poison."

"Worth their weight in gold," Olessio muttered, staring.

"It is so," Tumaya said. "Gold so that we buy what we cannot grow during the long years of the Sundering."

Much of the white sludge had already been packaged for transport, the corners of the huge sheets gathered like drawstring bags, tied off, then dragged to the edge of the docks by a high crane.

Dangling from a crane was a black bundle. A group of islanders cranked the sack up high, then swiveled the crane to swing over the deck of a ship that flew the Perripin flag. A cheer went up from the sailors on the deck. As the sack was lowered, they detached it with great care.

Boxes and trunks came down ships' ramps. Gold, perhaps.

On a swaying dock, the Perripin duke spoke to a Jalui Mother, lighting his pipe.

"When the Sundering comes," Olessio asked Tumaya, "You sail? How do you steer an island?"

Tumaya glowered at him. "You do not understand. Not sail. Not steer." Tumaya gave Tayre a similarly disapproving look, but favored Amarta with a great smile: "But you understand, She-who-knows. The god decides all."

With force of will, Amarta kept her tongue. She thought of the Monks of the Revelation and how powerful a belief could be. They wanted answers. They did not want the truth.

Tumaya looked across the islanders on the red-gray sands, shoveling the white, glistening Island Pearls into mounds, on top of black silk.

The ground.

Amarta braced herself. Beneath her, the ground shuddered sharply, then was still.

The islanders at the Pearls paused, then redoubled their efforts.

"More to come," Tumaya said to them. "Soon the Gathering is over. Tonight we trade young for marriage, take our share of the Pearl payment, give gratitude to our gods, and take a final feast together. After the Sundering, we part for many years."

He looked around at the beach, his expression turning dark. "Our place, this should have been. But we failed Carugrua." His look at Amarta was hungry. Into her mind flashed her cage from vision. "Much to do," he said. "I go. You stay for the feast. All tables welcome you, but Carugrua is best. You know this."

He strode away, not waiting for a response, up the beach, then up slope to a group of islanders who waited at a rocky rise, on the far side of the beach.

"One last, great feast," Olessio said, patting, then addressing his midriff. "You are too small, belly, to hold all the delights I must fit inside you tonight. Best I get started." He went to the nearest table, dancing his fingers across the various bowls. He took a long, yellow thing—baked vegetable, or slug, or what, Amarta could not tell—and put it in his mouth. At his happy sounds, Tadesh nosed out of the pack, climbing his shoulder, curious about his food.

Tayre was gazing out to the harbor. What was he thinking?

How are we getting to Seute Enta?

Amarta pointed. "Any of those four ships can take us to the continent."

Tayre nodded, as if he had asked aloud, rather than in some possible future. Amarta felt a passing disappointment that he was not impressed. But then, he had seen that trick before.

The clouds were thickening, making Amarta's prediction

of rain more likely. A single, white wide-winged bird flew north. She tracked it a moment, wondering if it was heading to Seute Enta. Reason said yes. Vision agreed. An easy question, an easy answer.

Amarta knew that vision could tell her what was likely far more easily than what was not. That was why she continued to puzzle over Rhaata and the mushroom. Nothing about that event, nor what had followed, had been in any way likely to happen.

Whereas the ground shaking again was a near-certainty. Though just as with wind and rain, vision could not say when, only *soon*.

"I'll see what I can arrange." Tayre said, stepping wide of a puddle of Pearls on black silk, heading toward the harbor.

"Wait," Amarta said.

She met Tayre's inquiring look and shook her head slowly, confused.

A drop of rain splatted onto a plate on the nearest table. Something else tickled at the edges of her mind. The usual vague hints of dreadful, unlikely outcomes, she supposed, and nothing more. But…

A bit of fluff sailed overhead, some plant matter carried on the breeze, from one of the other islands. She reached up to grab it, as if it were the insight that she sought, but it slipped through her fingers. Her fist closed on empty air.

She scanned the tables for a hint.

Tayre was at her side. "What is it?"

"Nothing, I suppose."

He followed her gaze as it swept across the tables and remaining puddles of Island Pearls, out to the harbor, and up to the sky.

"This nothing," he asked softly. "Does it have a sound? A scent?"

The wind gusted again, bringing a delicate, familiar hint

of smoke from the dock where the Perripin duke gestured with his pipe at a black sack of Pearls.

It reminded Amarta of something. A distant, burning farmhouse. The incense of the Monks. How those in power were so willing to take advantage of those who were weaker. Whether the monks truly believed in what they did, they did not hesitate to take what they could from those who had faith in them.

The islanders, though…devoted to nonexistent gods, yes, but she had seen how fiercely they loved their children. They did not disregard the welfare of their most vulnerable.

She felt a tickle of a distant, unlikely future. Near impossible, like Rhaata and his mushroom. As thin and far away as pipe smoke. Or the smell of burning hair.

Again, the ground.

She dropped into a wide-legged stance. Olessio and Tayre did likewise. The island gave a quick, sharp shake.

"I'll watch you for direction," Olessio said, after the ground stilled, and began to wander the tables. He took another pastry. Some in his mouth, some for Tadesh. So much food, all waiting for the final feast, for the islanders of the entire Gathering.

Around them, the beach was nearly clean of Pearls, large black bags staged at the docks for the crane.

Olessio took something round from a platter and stuffed it into his mouth. He pulled off a bit for the eagerly chittering Tadesh.

Amarta turned and turned in place, trying to catch hold of the illusive something.

"Where are the rest of the islanders?" she asked.

A distant clatter of sticks, a rhythmic beating, a sound so faint she never would have heard it over the crashing surf and ocean wind, had she not also been hearing it in vision. An echo of some unlikely future? She grabbed the gossamer thread in which the patterned sound was louder, and gently pulled.

Chanting. Water. Drapes of chain. A child's face, slack-jawed, smiling.

A face she knew.

Which is most beautiful, She-who-knows?

The old man. The long, heavy necklaces and bracelets of scrimshaw.

All at once she understood, reason and vision colliding inside her, followed by a sick chill.

The moment Tayre saw her face, he would read her plan. No time to think. She strode toward the rocky rise near the cape cliffs where Tumaya had gone.

Almost immediately, Tayre followed. Almost.

In a now-past possible future, Tayre grabbed her, turned her, demanded to know what she was doing. There would be words between them, and the moment lost.

A tiny change, her walking away without warning, staying just out of his reach. So small, but an outcome shifted.

"Where are you going?" Tayre asked from behind her, his tone calm but intent. "What are you doing?"

"Changing the future," she answered.

"What? What's this?" Olessio called, his voice closing as he followed: "What is it?"

Amarta felt a tearing intensity pulsing through her. The future was turning vibrant, clear, and awful. She barely felt the shifting shale underfoot as she ascended the slope toward the cliff where Tumaya had vanished into the rocks.

"She's foreseeing," Tayre said.

"Do you know what?"

"I have a guess."

The future in which Tayre had tried to stop her was gone. Had never been.

Chapter Eighteen

THE RHYTHMIC SOUND came from beyond a rocky rise. Amarta stepped around a high boulder, then another one, and then through an opening in a stone cliff.

Before her and below, a large, deep tidal lake met the ocean through gaps in another rise. Across the farther rocks sounded the crashing and roar of the ocean that fed the surging pond, water rising and falling with the surf.

Across the rocky shores of the lake were the nine groups of islanders. Each was dressing a handful of elders and children, some naked, adorning them with combs, bracelets, and chains made of bone, abalone, and stone.

At each island group, people struck sticks together in a cadence.

There at the Jalui group was the large, blue-purple butterfly, its wings unable to open fully in the constraints of the cage. Not in a ship's hold on the Nelar. Not enroute to be sold to some foreign collector.

Something else entirely.

Amarta did not need proof, not with foresight so clear, but there in the churning water of the lake, rising and falling with the surf, floated the body of the old man from Molimba, chains and bones and shells wrapped around his arms, wrists, neck, waist, keeping him just under the surface.

At the Haulala group, the woman with her two toddlers knelt by the rocky banks of the lake, arranging lengths of heavy stones around her daughter's neck. The girl's mouth was unnaturally slack, her smile lopsided. Her mother was cutting off locks of her hair to put in a small fire.

The smell of burning hair reached Amarta.

One by one the islanders looked up, noticing Amarta standing above them on the rocky shelf.

The elders and children being adorned were clearly intoxicated. *They have never known a day of sorrow in their lives and they never will.* Tumaya's words now took on a very different meaning.

The beating of sticks faltered and stopped.

Tumaya, with the Carugrua group, walked quickly around the perimeter of the lake toward the slope that led up to where Amarta stood.

The chill Amarta had felt when she put the pieces together was turning into a wave of heat that prickled at her skin, then settled deep inside, hardening alongside memories. Emendi slaves in chains. A mother's voice. *Please don't take my baby.* The smoke of a burning farmhouse.

"Amarta," Tayre said, "What is your intention here?"

Had she not turned away enough? It was past time to even the scales, she decided, and as her resolve hardened, the future shifted.

"They can do what they like to themselves," Amarta said. "But to their elders and children? For a god that does not exist? No. Not even for one that does."

Olessio exhaled, shocked, his eyes flickering around the scene as he took in her meaning.

Amarta gave him a hard look. "Do you still think it costs

us nothing to let them be? This—" Her voice cracked. "This is a wrong thing."

Tadesh chittered from his shoulder, her striped tail thrashing. Olessio hugged her tail to his chest.

"I agree with you, Ama," he replied soberly. A fierce grin came to him and he looked at Tayre. "What do you say, brother? Shall we help Amarta change this wrong thing?"

"No," Tayre said. "There are too many of them."

Tumaya climbed the slope, his hands wide in greeting. "It is good. I told the Mothers that the gods would want you here, and they said if that were so, the gods would bring you. So they have."

The stick-beat rhythm resumed. Islanders again began wrapping their slack-jawed elders, children, toddlers, cutting their hair short. Cords and chains. Stone and bone.

Jalui men hefted the butterfly cage, brought it to the water.

"Tell them to stop," Amarta directed Tumaya. "No more drownings. No more death."

"Ah! You misconceive. They are not drowned. They go to the god. It is a great honor. What remains—" he gestured to the old man's body, bobbing under the water. "Is only flesh. He is with Molimba, now. He is truly Beloved."

Amarta heard the word as she should have before. *Beloved.* It was not a name. It was a death sentence.

In the Chosolua group, an old woman took off her clothes. With a blissful expression, she held out her arms to be draped in iron chains.

"Tell them," Amarta snapped.

Tumaya's smile faltered. "You misunderstand, She-who-knows. The gods make the harvests that bring us wealth, that keep us alive through the Sundered years. We must give them something in return, to show our devotion, to gain their favor in years to come. You know this."

Below, the islanders continued their grisly preparations. The woman took her weighted-down daughter in her arms, and put her by the edge of the tidal lake.

Amarta shouted: "Stop! Stop!"

Some looked at her, but of those who understood the words, none seemed inclined to comply, though the Mothers watched her warily.

Amarta blinked. Not the right words, then. What would be?

I've spoken to your gods, and they tell me…A story—any story—would delay. But then?

After the Sundering, the islanders would resume the drownings.

Your gods do not exist! Listen to me!

She followed this path forward, and watched in horror as more and more islanders walked willingly into the lake, inspired to prove their faith to the doubting She-who-knows.

No, no, no.

She had to change it. How?

"Be certain of what you do here, Amarta," Tayre said.

Certainty was impossible. *Always a path to failure.* Disaster lived at the edges of the probable.

Amarta was searching through hundreds of futures, leaving her no time to tell Tayre what he already knew.

A million paths, and the only ones she could find led to more death. A million paths, but she only needed one.

Tayre put a hand on her shoulder. A firm touch. To upset her focus?

"This is not our fight, Seer."

He was wrong, but she didn't have time to tell him that. If she turned her back on these Beloveds—these children—if she looked away again, who was she?

Someone she loathed.

What if she set them against each other? From previous visions, she knew it could be done. What then?

Foresight crowded against supposition, showing her multiples of futures. Crowds, armed for battle. The sounds of the many, the roars of different futures overlapping. Hundreds and hundreds of futures, thousands and thousands chanting.

A line of armed soldiers and cavalry drew swords and pikes to meet another line, to meet on a great field of battle, certain carnage to come. They were chanting one word, again and again.

What was it?

Her name. It was her name.

No, no—that future had nothing to do with the islands. Too far, too wide. Closer now. Tighter.

There it was. She must go to the core of what the islanders cared about. That, and careful timing.

Amarta shook off Tayre's grip, and took a step forward. She stood wide, her gaze sweeping across the islanders.

Abruptly, she gestured, arms and fingers high, as if flicking water into the air.

Just as she did, the ground convulsed. Once. Twice.

Hissing. Whispering. Those who had seen her gesture were quickly relating it to those who had not. All at once, she had everyone's attention.

"Oh, nicely done," Olessio said.

"Your gods decide all, and you are grateful," Amarta said, pitching her voice to carry across the lake. "But this, what you do now? This does not please them."

Those who could understand translated for those who could not.

"At every island you ask me, what do our gods say? Now I will tell you: they say they are angry that you think to change their minds with fingers, large moths, and Beloveds.

They love you like children, but—" she gestured to the lake and the drowned old man floating there, "Why do you think he floats, rather than being swallowed? The gods spit him back at you. They do not like the taste of the feast you offer."

In their faces she saw outrage. Shock.

Doubt.

The mother of the small girl pulled the laden child away from the water, hugging her tight. The island Mothers pushed through the crowds to meet together, talking urgently among themselves.

"Are you sure?" called one woman. "Did Punaami say this, or one of the other gods?"

"Who are you to say what our gods want?" This from one of the Tukimpe Mothers. "You betray our hospitality."

"Seer," Tayre hissed. "Don't just tell them no. Give them something."

"He's right," Olessio whispered. "Anything. Quickly."

"Like what?"

"How to win," Tayre said.

She thought fast. "I know the will of your gods. I predicted the order of the Gathering. You want their favor. For the Pearls. The harvests. The order. I will tell you how: you must honor the Beloveds in life. Very long lives."

For a moment she thought she'd gone too far. Perhaps not: urgent talk broke out around the lake. Arguments between those who had Beloved children and those who did not.

Some elders wrapped in chains looked around, uncertain. The old woman was pulling hers off. A man came to stop her. She shoved him away. He stood frozen in shock.

As she looked around, Amarta saw that she had planted not only the seeds of doubt, but argument. Futures fanning out from this moment showed her islanders resisting the gruesome pull of their history, and the authority of the Mothers weakening.

The Mothers from all the islands formed a new group and were striding around the lake toward the rise. They trailed men with spears.

"Time to go," Tayre said, turning her around and pushing her the way they'd come.

≈

They walked fast toward the beach, Olessio tucking Tadesh inside his pack.

"Should we run?" asked Olessio, glancing over his shoulder.

Behind them, the Mothers and armed islanders had just come into view, clearing the rocky rise.

"Not yet," Tayre said, scanning the docks. The red-gray sands were clear of white Pearls, and islanders were attaching one of two remaining large black bags to the crane. "If they see us run, they'll wonder if they should stop us. Amarta, which ship takes us off the island? To anywhere?"

This time, Amarta realized, as she thought back on what she'd just accomplished, she had found the middle path, by sowing just enough doubt that going forward, the islanders would remember and hesitate to obey the island Mothers. Her words, *very long lives* would stay with them. Bit by bit, the islands would change.

A step toward balancing the scales, evening the accounting of the lives she had cost.

"Amarta," Tayre said sharply. "Which ship?"

"Yes." Amarta looked at the ships, searching through their near futures.

She blinked in confusion, looked again. Then again.

"Something's wrong. We can't go to the docks. It's the Mothers, they—"

They would call out to the ship captains that any ship that took She-who-knows would never again be allowed to come near the islands. No Pearls. *The Islands remember*, they would say.

Ships would pull up ladders, draw back ramps.

Something had changed, just in the last moments. Had the mothers decided something?

They had. The Mothers wanted Amarta captured. And that meant…if Amarta left the island, the islanders would be able to remember her, to resist their history and the Mothers who kept it in place.

But if she stayed, the mothers would—

She gasped at the pain that vision laid upon her, the agony of having her tongue cut from her mouth. The islanders, seeing her caged and mute—impotent—would return to their lethal traditions.

"Find us a way off the island, Seer," Tayre said.

Again, Amarta scanned the ocean. Most of the ships already had their Pearls and goods, had raised their sails, and were pulling away. The few that were still moored were in various stages of preparation.

At the dock, one final ship waited for one final sack of Island Pearls, which now hung midair, on the crane, as the islanders there tried to decide which was more urgent, finishing the transfer of the Pearls, or obeying the as-yet unclear but distantly heard yells of the Mothers.

"I think…" Amarta breathed, "I think I might have made a mistake."

All the futures she could find were turning violent. The three of them encircled, ushered at spear-point to the lake, where the Mothers would demonstrate that only they could interpret the will of the gods.

Tayre would have been right: there were too many of them.

But he would try. In future after future, she watched him and Olessio fighting, wounded, then bound and sinking, their lifeblood mixing with churning seawater. Tadesh fought, took a spear, gnawed furiously at the shaft, and shuddered as she died.

Amarta's stomach heaved.

Tayre pushed her forward, away from the dock and the Mothers both, hand to her back, toward a far finger of land, where tangles of brilliant green grew.

Behind them, the Mothers had finally reached the docks, and were giving commands.

"Don't look back," Tayre said. "Look forward." Then, to both Amarta and Tayre: "Now we run."

They sprinted, red-gray sand sliding under their feet as they ran. They reached the trees. Olessio in the lead clawed a path through the thick brush.

They broke into a sandy cove. Blue ocean spread wide before them. Escape, if they could only find a way to float. But there was nothing, not even a log.

Amarta's breath turned ragged as panic threatened. Tayre took her by the shoulders, turned her to face him.

"Slow your exhale," he said. "Like that. Do it again. Yes. Is there any future, any at all, in which we stand safely another shore?"

Her voice cracked. "I can't find it. I can't—"

Tayre pulled her to him, holding her in a tight embrace, his head snug against hers. To her utter astonishment, he kissed her neck.

Over his shoulder, Olessio's eyes widened incredulously. "Yes, finally, good, but perhaps later?"

Into her ear, Tayre whispered: "Feel into all directions, Amarta. In what future do we entwine and couple again?"

He brushed her ear with his lips, exhaled softly, the scent of him intoxicating. "What do the next minutes hold, from that future? Find it. Find the path back from there."

His voice, his tone, his body, his scent, all backed the promise of his words. Fury at his manipulation was fast doused as Amarta saw its stunning wisdom. She let the promise—a lie, perhaps, but with him, what wasn't?—drive her to a future, in which…

His skin, his touch, his scent…

There. Now back.

A pitching ocean. Heavily accented voices. A language she didn't know. A woman's voice. "Get her up here."

"Canoe," she managed.

Her body was a traitor, unwilling to pull away, even now, with armed islanders moments away.

He did it for her, pushing her back. "Where?" But he kept her hand tight in his own, caressing it. "Feel the pull, Ama. Feel it."

Flickers, forward and back, forward and back. Terror warred with desire, the future a million mazes.

"I can't see…"

He swung her back, put his lips to hers, and she slid into a melting, numb shock, awash with desire.

"Keep looking," he murmured around his lips.

A room. Heavy shutters. A hot, dry breeze through the cracks. He lay at her side, a hand caressing her stomach.

She tore herself from the kiss, proud, angry, terrified, all at once. "This way." She led them to a game trail through a thicket of trees, to another sandy cove.

The wind whipped her hair, carrying the intermittent cries and shouts of pursuit not far behind.

More brush, trees. A third cove, tiny. There it was: a beached canoe. Olessio and Tayre shoved it into the water.

"Get in," Tayre snapped and she obeyed. Olessio spilled

the chittering Tadesh next to her. The two men gave the craft a hard push into the water.

"Now you," Tayre said to Olessio who splashed through the surf, clamoring in alongside Amarta and Tadesh.

Tayre turned and ran back up the beach.

"What are you doing?" she cried.

"Oars," said Olessio bleakly. "Oars."

And it was so: the canoe held no oars.

Tayre dashed across the beach, fast searching through brush and trees. Four islanders armed with knives stepped out from the other side. Tayre's back was to them. The wind was high. Had he heard? Did he know? Amarta almost yelled a warning.

Another four stepped out. Another three. Eleven on one. Amarta's breath caught.

Tayre's back was still turned as the armed islanders fanned out around him, cautious but unafraid, some glancing at the canoe, as if gauging how far they would need to swim out to get Amarta after they were done with him.

There was a touch of uncertainty in their look at her. Were they conflicted? Whatever the Mothers had told them —capture, injure, or kill—Amarta and her companions had, until recently, been guests. That mattered to the islanders. She was no stranger.

The eleven men turned back to the task at hand and converged on Tayre.

"Tell me it turns out all right," Olessio said to her, holding Tadesh close to his chest.

"Don't blink," Amarta said.

Tayre, his back to the approaching warriors, somehow conveyed perfectly that he had just found the oars. He picked them up, one in each hand, every movement speaking volumes: that he was clumsy, that he knew nothing of the islanders behind him.

Then he turned and everything changed.

Even knowing in broad strokes how this was likely to go, Amarta could not follow the action. How did he manage to move both oars at once, in such brutal efficiency?

Look to disable. Waste nothing.

In a blink, four men were on the ground, one unmoving, one clutching his throat. The other two crawled backward, knives dropped. The remaining men paused, bewildered, defensively crouched.

Tayre charged them, yelling. Unnerved by their fellows on the ground, they pulled back.

With the bit of space he'd made, Tayre turned and took a running leap into the ocean, the oars in the water in front of him. A moment, his head popped out of the water at the edge of the canoe, handing up the oars, and he climbed inside, dripping.

Olessio set the oars to row. Tayre pushed him out of the way and began to pull. The canoe moved.

On the shore, the islanders stood, mouths hanging open.

"Damn good work, that, brother," Olessio said.

Breathless, Tayre didn't answer, pulling in powerful strokes. The canoe retreated from Punaami.

Amarta gaped at him, astonished, yet again, at what he could do. Yet his hard breathing told her that he was not invincible. Somehow, it was easy to forget.

On the shore, the Mothers had arrived, additional armed warriors in tow. The Mothers gestured urgently, at the canoe, at each other—some argument—but it didn't last. Islanders ran off in all directions.

As the island drew away, they saw more trees, more coves. More canoes.

"Amarta," Tayre managed, "Where do we go now?"

She turned her attention to the other direction, looking out to sea. A handful of ships dotted the horizon. Which one would let them on?

She followed one future trail after another. They kept looping to the island, and once back on Punaami, there was blood and death and pain.

An anguished cry ripped from her throat as she looked back to the island.

"Doorways, Seer. Not dead-ends," Tayre said. "Look for the open spaces."

A canoe of armed islanders launched from the dock. A second. A third. Now that they knew what Tayre could do, they would not come close enough to let him do it again. All of them had spears.

The open spaces. Amarta turned back to the ships, clawing through possible futures as fast as she could.

Crumpled in the canoe, Tayre gripped the shaft of a spear sunk through his stomach.

Not that one.

A vantage from a ship. Everything moved, as a huge wake lifted them into the air. On her hind legs, Tadesh looked over the railing.

That one.

Amarta pointed at a huge ship, just now raising Seute Enta sails. To reach it, their canoe would need to move closer to the north harbor. By then the ship would have moved to…there. She pointed again, farther north.

Tayre tracked her finger, nodded sharply, kept rowing.

"I can spell you," Olessio said told him. Tayre shook his

head.

For a moment, no one spoke.

"Hoi," Olessio said heavily. "I hate to be the bearer of bad news, but the islanders are gaining on us."

Tayre did not respond, nor did he slow. He must be tired, but he did not flag. This, Amarta realized, was what his training gave him. This.

They glided north, closer to the harbor. Two more canoes of armed islanders launched from the harbor.

On all the ships, figures lined the railing to watch the chase.

"Amarta," Tayre managed.

He didn't need to say more; she knew: he wanted answers.

She gave a gasping exhale. "It keeps changing. Every moment." Wind, clouds, waves.

They could now hear Mothers yelling from the docks—at each other, at the boats. More islanders poured into canoes.

There were just too many moving parts. A Rochi game was simple by comparison.

Tayre spared a glance behind him.

"Amarta."

"We can make it, I think. If we…"

All at once everything changed. Wind, waves—she did not know what. They would come close to the ship that was their destination, where crewmen watched. The only ship that would take them.

Not close enough, not soon enough. Canoes would intercept, surround them, and then…

She knew that outcome.

At their ship, a crewman began to lower a ladder. Another stopped him. An argument.

Damn, and damn again—was nothing simple?

They were a stone's throw from the ship, but it wasn't

close enough. The many canoes on their trail now began to surround. Islanders put down their oars and took up spears.

A stone's throw. So close.

"Don't suppose you have a crossbow hidden somewhere in those wet clothes, do you, Guard-dog?" asked Olessio.

Tayre stopped rowing, turned to Amarta. "Give me the godstones."

Amarta dug into her pockets, passed all nine spherical stones to him.

An islander called out across the waves to them. "Give us She-who-knows-tomorrow, and we let the rest of you go."

Olessio stood, struggling for balance in the rocking canoe and barked laughter across the water. "You think she's the one? Ha! It's been me all along. Didn't you see me whispering in her ear? You want a Seer, you want me. I'll go with you, but the others go free."

"Olessio, it's a lie. They won't let anyone go," Amarta said.

"Figured," Olessio said softly. "Any other ideas?"

"I make forty," Tayre said, taking out his sling and shaking it open. "I have nine missiles."

"Make them count, brother," said Olessio.

Amarta fought tears. "I should never have…"

"Regret later," Tayre said sharply. "Amarta: fight or surrender?"

Head throbbing, she pushed herself to foresee. Where was the narrow doorway? Anything—however unlikely—that could take the islander's attention, just long enough to give the four of them a chance to reach that ship?

Spears dropped, many into the water. Islanders looked far away, taking up oars, desperately trying to turn their crafts. Shouts, calls, horrified looks.

A thin line. A wisp of a chance.

"The Pearls," she managed.

Chapter Nineteen

AT THE HARBOR, the final black silk bag dangled from the crane, paused midway in transit from shore to ship, hanging over the dock.

"The Pearls?" Olessio asked Amarta, confused.

"Remember the egg in the nest? The fruit you made drop?" Amarta said. "Open a hole in the silk."

Olessio followed her gaze to the hanging sack, suddenly understanding. "From here? Not possible."

"It is."

"No, no. I'm not a mage." His expression was stark.

"You're *udardae*," Amarta said. "You're nearly a mage."

A spear sailed between them, narrowly missing Tayre. Their canoe rocked sharply as Tayre loosed a missile from his sling in return. An islander cried out, blood spurting from an eye as the godstone hit hard.

Amarta and Olessio dropped low in the scant cover of the canoe. Olessio put Tadesh under the seat. She nosed his hand.

"It's our only chance," Amarta said to the hunched Olessio.

"Not a mage," he muttered.

Such a contrast to his courage a moment ago, when he offered himself to the islanders in her place, risking whatever horrors awaited back on the island.

Another spear sailed overhead.

"You can," Amarta said. "You must."

Tayre let fly another godstone. An islander clutched his side and stumbled over the edge into the water, rocking his craft enough to distract the rest. But not for long.

The future was a hash of boats and spears, of churning waters. None of it went well if Olessio did not act now. What was the one thing she could say?

"Tadesh."

His eyes widened as he took in Amarta's meaning and looked down at the face of his small companion. She looked up at him, chittering nervously.

"Tadesh," Olessio echoed. Then his face changed, the fear gone.

No, not gone, but alongside something else: a firm resolve. He met her eyes, nodded. They stood together in the canoe.

In the canoes surrounding them, islanders with spears held high paused. They wanted her alive. Stripped of her companions, judging by vision's dreadful warnings, but alive.

She moved close to Olessio.

"Never done this before," he muttered, half to himself, staring at the crane. "Quite the trick, if I can pull it off. No magery in me, none at all, so I can't say—ah!" A sound of pleased surprise.

Tayre launched more godstones. Islanders ducked into their canoes. Another toppled into the ocean.

"That was the last one," Tayre said, taking up the oars and handing one to Amarta.

Olessio's fingers twitched in the air, then his face fell. "It's too far. Ama, I am so sorry. I can't."

"You can," Amarta said. "I've foreseen it." Not quite true, but close enough. It was there, in the unlikely shallows of the future. A shadow of a maybe.

"Oh," Olessio said. "Well, then."

Amarta held up her oar, flat side facing the closest canoe, like an absurdly narrow shield. Too narrow to cover a person, but wide enough for a spear-point, if one knew exactly where it was going.

"Maybe," Olessio said thoughtfully, "if I…"

Amarta twitched the oar in front of Olessio. A point scraped across the wood. The spear clattered sideways into the choppy water.

At this, the islanders gaped, but the shocked pause didn't last. She needed to buy time for Olessio.

"Give me the other one," she said to Tayre, who did.

Amarta held one oar in each hand, dancing them across Olessio and Tayre. Another spear went sideways. This time, Tayre grabbed it before it hit the water and sent it back at the attackers, one of whom yelped, and sat heavily in his boat, trying to pull the shaft from his arm.

She diverted another spear and another.

Olessio was entirely transfixed, hands held high, fingers splayed and twitching as if he were playing a floating instrument. He was humming.

"Hoi! There you are," he cried with delight. "Come on, now."

Someone at the crane gave a distant, distressed shout.

"Olessio," Amarta said wonderingly. "You're doing it."

He grinned wide, unseeing. "Ah, not much to it. Just turtle and handkerchief trick, really."

The sack of Pearls suspended from the crane began to drip.

"Olessio! Yes! More!" Amarta cried.

Under them, the canoe rocked. Tayre took hold of her arm. Amarta passed the stability to Olessio by gripping his shoulder. His eyes were closed, his face flushed red, but his smile was full of joy.

"Just so. Just so. Who knew."

A grinding, creaking sound came from the boards underfoot. At the same time, the islanders looked down with expressions of confusion.

"Amarta," Tayre said. "What is he doing?"

"That," she replied, pointing to the suspended sack at the harbor, where the impossibly strong spider silk suddenly tore wide open like wet paper, splattering heavy, thick globules of Island Pearls all across the dock. The emptied bag fluttered raggedly in the ocean wind.

Alarmed voices carried over the water from the dock. Mothers and islanders were on hands and knees, desperately and fruitlessly trying to gather the gooey, slick, priceless Pearls.

Their attackers gaped at the harbor, weapons forgotten. Some exchanged spears for oars and began to row toward the dock to help.

"Aha!" Olessio's eyes sprang open, a triumphant smile across his face. "Not so hard after all." He rubbed his nose and frowned at his fingers, which had blood on them.

Their canoe shuddered beneath them. From the prow came a wet, crunching sound.

"Olessio. You've done it." Amarta said. "You can stop now."

Olessio blinked, then blinked again. A pink tear trailed down his face.

Not pink. Red.

"How odd," Olessio said.

Amarta stared at him, stunned. His swarthy skin—face,

neck, arms—were glistening red, as if he were sweating. Her hand on his shoulder was wet with blood.

"Tadesh," he said.

Amarta picked up Tadesh, pressed her into Olessio's arms, feeling a sickening chill.

"She'll be safe?" he asked, his voice odd.

"What? Yes, of course. Olessio, whatever it is you're doing, stop."

"I don't know what I'm doing, Amarta."

Amarta's feet were wet. She looked down. Their canoe was leaking.

Vision was warning.

"The boat is coming apart," Tayre said. "We need to get clear before—"

A loud crack. A timber snapped out from the siding on the canoe.

All their attackers were rowing away, and many of them were sinking.

Tayre gripped her arm. "We need to get clear before this comes apart. We're going in the water one way or another."

At the high railing of the ship that had been their destination, the crew pointed excitedly at the harbor.

Even from this distance, Amarta could see the island of Punaami shaking hard enough that the docks were coming apart.

She looked at the ship, at the island, at Olessio. Nothing made sense. Not now, not in the future. The unlikely trail she'd taken to get here was unclear going forward, tangled and confused. Vision was a din of warnings.

And Olessio was bleeding everywhere.

"I can't see it!" she cried.

"I can," Tayre growled. In one motion, he lifted her over his head and hurled her clear of the disintegrating canoe, toward the ship.

All thought fled. Amarta inhaled, then hit the ocean and went under.

The cold was a numbing shock. She flailed in the churning water, then surfaced, gasping for air, and sank again. Vision warred with panic. It was all she could do to not inhale seawater.

Something grabbed her around the waist and thrust her up and out. She was at the side of the ship's hull, where a rope ladder had been let down.

"Climb!" Tayre shouted, pushing her. From overhead came shouts and cries.

She grabbed and pulled, Tayre right behind. Clear of the water, still gasping, she clung to the rope and looked back.

All that remained of their canoe were two strips of wood. Olessio balanced precariously, Tadesh still in his arms. His clothes were dripping red, his skin sagging, his eyes and mouth wet with blood.

He looked toward Amarta. With a gurgle that might have been her name, he hurled Tadesh across the gap of water.

Leaning from the ladder, Tayre outstretched a forearm. The wide-eyed, hissing creature landed on him, scrabbling up his arm to his shoulder, Olessio's bloody handprints vivid on her pelt.

"Olessio!" Amarta called.

Throwing Tadesh had cost him the last of his balance, and under him, the two remaining boards sank. Arms windmilling, his limbs floppy, like a rag doll, Olessio toppled into the ocean and went under.

"No!" she screamed.

"Amarta, climb!" Tayre shouted, pushing at her legs with his one free hand.

"Olessio!"

"You. Me. Tadesh. Climb!"

Vision was howling. Swells so high an ocean-going ship

would capsize. This very ship, hit broadside, if it did not start turning now.

Amarta looked up into the foreshortened point of an arrow trained on her from the railing. Fast shouts from Tayre below her, fast enough that she made out little beyond numbers. Bribes.

The arrow point did not waver.

"Amarta, get us on board. Find a way."

A figure at the side of the man with the bow pointed urgently at Punaami.

Amarta moaned, as vision howled warning after warning, demanding that she act.

She caught a whiff. Like the mushroom, like the feather. Looking up at the railing, she opened her mouth, yelling the sounds just forming in her head. One syllable, then another. A third and a fourth.

The Seute Enta crewmen gaped down at her. She repeated the sounds. They pulled back.

"What did you say?" Tayre asked.

"I don't know. I don't know."

As they clung to the ladder, the ocean became choppy. The ship to which they clung began to turn.

Over the railing another face appeared. It was the Arunkin eparch-heir.

"Get them up here," she barked.

"Where is he?" Amarta cried, scanning the waters from the railing.

At the Punaami harbor, a final ship was frantically trying to cast off, sailors hacking at the thick ropes binding it to a fast-disintegrating dock. Huge, churning waves rippled out from the shores of the island.

Then the island shuddered and rocked and began to submerge. The ship, not yet freed from the floating remains of the dock, was yanked over into the water, spilling people and boxes and barrels and bags.

The island of Punaami sank into the water. Ocean flooding across the beaches, then the forests, until all but the highest mountain top was under water.

Then the island began to rise. The mountain grew out of the sea, the forests streaming water. As Punaami surfaced, a huge swell of water rippled out from its shores.

Shouts and screams cut the air as every boat and ship went into full-on panic, trying to turn prow toward the huge approaching wakes.

But it was too late: only the smallest, nimblest of canoes could turn in time. The ship on which they stood had begun to turn before she and Tayre had finished her climb and was now facing the largest of the oncoming swells.

The huge wakes hit ocean-going ships broadside, knocking them over, spilling into the water all manner of supplies, howling people, and black sacks of Island Pearls. Two ships, brought close by crossing swells, went over like child's toys, crashing into each other, the sound of shattering timbers almost drowning out the screams of terror.

Amarta gripped the railing as a great cliff of water reached their prow, forcing the ship higher and higher, giving her a horrifyingly good view of the chaos spread before her.

Across hills and valleys of water, a few intact canoes paddled desperately away from the turmoil. The swells carried broken canoes, shattered docks. People floundered, grabbing what they could to stay afloat.

"Where is he?" Amarta cried again, looking for one red figure.

Tayre was at her side. "Amarta," he said softly. "He's gone."

Olessio.

From Tadesh came a growling moan, as she ran back and forth, rising up on her hind legs, paws on the railing, looking out at the chaos of ocean, then dropping to all fours to run to the other side, to rise up and look again.

Amarta followed her, from one side of the ship to the other. He was not there. He was not anywhere.

Amarta felt as if she were expanding, while at the same time contracting, as if all the breath had been stripped from her lungs. Yet somehow in the next moment she was inflated to near bursting. Nothing in the world was the right size. Her limbs seemed made of string, of jelly, of air.

Bodies floated lifelessly. At the railing, she scanned the ocean again and again. People clung to debris, some swimming desperately from ships still capsizing and sinking. Some called out, begging for help, and went silent, as sudden vortexes sucked them down.

None of them was Olessio.

He could not be gone. He could not. She would find him. She pushed herself into vision.

The sea chopped white and frothing. Something huge rose out of the water, like a great pale finger, up and up and up. It was a giant tentacle, just as Olessio had once speculated.

The Eparch-heir and the ship's captain were at Amarta's side, asking questions, demanding answers. How did she know to turn the ship? What would happen next?

In minutes, the Island Road would begin its Sundering. The islands of the Gathering would move faster than they had before, submerging to follow down the sinking Pearls, then rising again to shake off centuries of forests and mountains, sinking and shaking, dousing the devoted and doubting alike, sacrifices and carvings and buildings and dreams washed away. The islands would dive, again and again, for the one thing the islanders had for generations denied them: the Pearls, their eggs, at last released into the nursery of the ocean.

But nowhere, in no future, could Amarta find one small Farliosan man.

Her legs gave way, her limbs becoming impossibly heavy. She crumpled to the deck.

A sound came from somewhere, a horrible keening howl, a wailing that seemed to encompass sea and sky. It filled her ears, her eyes, her chest, and her throat.

It wasn't loud enough. Not nearly loud enough.

Read More!

Be sure to read all the books in The Stranger trilogy!

Unmoored
Maelstrom
Landfall

Available at your favorite retailers!

It's True. Reviews Help.

IF YOU LIKED THIS BOOK, please consider giving a rating and a review. Even a short "Can't wait for the next one!" will do nicely, and help the author to make more books for you.

About the Author

Sonia Orin Lyris's stories have appeared in various publications, including *Asimov's SF magazine*, *Wizards of the Coast* anthologies, and *Uncle John's Bathroom Reader*. She is the author of *The Seer*, an epic fantasy novel from Baen Books. Her writing has been called "immersive," "ruthless," and "unsparing."

Her passions include martial arts, partner dance, fine chocolate, and the occasional human critter.

She asks questions and gives answers, but not necessarily in that order. She speaks fluent cat.

A note from Sonia

Thank you for being part of my creative process. I have regular chats for subscribers, on my Patreon account, here:

https://www.patreon.com/lyris

Never miss a release!

I announce new projects on my Facebook feed:

https://www.facebook.com/authorlyris

You can also sign up for my newsletter:

https://lyris.org/subscribe/

Connect with Sonia

Web: https://lyris.org

facebook.com/authorlyris

goodreads.com/Sonia_Orin_Lyris

twitter.com/slyris